Pra[...]

Pra[...]

"Maggie's not really [...]st groundbreaking fea[...] ca-nine-cozy genre. . . . T[...] canine heroine might ruffle some fur in this genre, the resulting conflicts allow Orgain to put a new spin on some of its conventions. The true winner in this tale, however, is Yolanda, the over-bearing friend who chooses you."—*Kirkus Reviews*

"Charming . . . Multiple suspects, a little romance, and a good dose of humor make this cozy a winner."

—*Publishers Weekly*

"It may be a dog-eat-dog world, but Orgain will have you laughing out loud, even as you puzzle over whodunit and race to the finish in time for the Tails and Tiaras fundrais-er. Pull up a chair, put your martini glass on ice, and enjoy *Yappy Hour*, the first in a hilarious new series."

—Kate Carlisle, *New York Times* bestselling author of *The Old Homicide*

WITHDRAWN FROM COLLECTION

"With its entertaining mystery, touches of romance, and quirky human and canine characters, *Yappy Hour* is the perfect cocktail to quench your thirst for a good story. More fun than a basket of puppies!"

—Diane Kelly, author of *Laying Down the Paw*

"A toast to Diana Orgain, who has written a charming-ly fun mystery with an out-of-her-comfort-zone amateur sleuth who rises to the occasion. A delightful whodunit with plenty of twists and turns, quirky characters, and quirkier cocktails."

—Avery Aames, Agatha-Award winning author of *As Gouda as Dead*

Also by Diana Orgain

YAPPY HOUR

Diana Orgain

St. Martin's Paperbacks

NOTE: If you purchased this book without a cover you should be aware that this book is stolen property. It was reported as "unsold and destroyed" to the publisher, and neither the author nor the publisher has received any payment for this "stripped book."

This is a work of fiction. All of the characters, organizations, and events portrayed in this novel are either products of the author's imagination or are used fictitiously.

YAPPY HOUR

Copyright © 2015 by Diana Orgain.

All rights reserved.

For information address St. Martin's Press, 175 Fifth Avenue, New York, NY 10010.

ISBN: 978-1-250-09669-2

Our books may be purchased in bulk for promotional, educational, or business use. Please contact your local bookseller or the Macmillan Corporate and Premium Sales Department at 1-800-221-7945, ext. 5442, or by e-mail at MacmillanSpecialMarkets@macmillan.com.

Printed in the United States of America

Minotaur hardcover edition / November 2015
St. Martin's Paperbacks edition / October 2016

St. Martin's Paperbacks are published by St. Martin's Press, 175 Fifth Avenue, New York, NY 10010.

10 9 8 7 6 5 4 3 2 1

For Tom Orgain

Chapter One

"What do you mean, you fired her?" I said into my cell phone as I brushed sand from the beach towel.

It was at least the fourth time I'd had the same conversation with my great-uncle Ernest. Grunkly-E we called him, which morphed into Grunkly, but on occasion turned into Grouchy or Grumpy. He was one of the reasons I'd recently relocated to Pacific Cove. He and my sister, Rachel, not to mention the fact that my stint as a financial advisor in New York had come to an abrupt end after the market had crashed.

It was time to hit the reset button on my life. What I needed most was some fresh seaside air, and when I'd learned that the Soleado Mexican Riviera Cruise Line had opened a new port in town, the position of bookkeeper/purser practically shouted out my name.

"Well, Maggie, she was real mean. She wanted me to walk around and stuff," Grunkly said.

A few months back, Grunkly suffered a mild heart attack. He'd been hospitalized and on the verge of "the great beyond" as he called it, but he'd battled back from the heart attack and the case of pneumonia he'd contracted. Actually, at his age of eighty-four, the doctors all considered it a miraculous recovery. Now our biggest obstacle was finding him a day nurse that he liked, or rather, wouldn't fire at the drop of a hat.

"You're supposed to walk around! Breathe some fresh air. That's how you're going to get better."

"I'm already better. Plus, she didn't like Benny. Actually told him I wasn't home, when I was."

I laughed. Benny was Grunkly's longtime bookie. If anyone got in the way of Grunkly's gambling they were sure to get the ax.

"I wanted to place a bet on Winged Arrow. The odds are seven to two. Is he there now?" Grunkly asked.

"Here? I'm at the beach," I said.

"I know the trainer, Aaron, was going to take Winged Arrow out there, to walk in the salt water. It's good for the hooves. I thought maybe Benny might be with them."

I glanced up and down the beach. There was a couple near me perched on a plaid blanket, a platinum blonde who looked like an escapee from *America's Next Top Model* with her Ken-doll boyfriend. Then in the distance was a group of people walking their small dogs.

I figured the group had to be the Roundup Crew, or at least part of them. I knew from my sister, Rachel, that this group met every Friday on the beach for a walk that ultimately ended up at her bar, The Wine and Bark, for Yappy Hour. My sister was as happy-go-lucky as they came, and I was glad she found her calling running a bar; it seemed the perfect fit for her personality.

"No, Grunkly. I don't see Benny or Aaron and Winged Arrow."

"That's too bad." He paused. There was a small sound as if he was lighting a cigarette.

"You're not smoking, are you?"

Grunkly had smoked for over sixty years.

"No," he said, almost too fast. "I'm not supposed to be smoking, Magpie!"

"I know you're not *supposed* to be smoking! But it kind of sounded like you just lit a cigarette."

"No," he said again.

"So, what I'm figuring is that the nurse who came over today wasn't letting you smoke and—"

"Sweetheart," he said quickly. "I'm wondering if I could bother you to run an errand for me."

I smiled to myself. He'd do anything to get me off the topic of his smoking.

"What errand? I'm not buying you a carton of Lucky Strikes," I said.

A seagull landed on my towel and thrust its beak out at me, accusingly. No doubt looking for crumbs. I pulled a roll of Ritz Crackers out of my bag, the motion scaring the bird away.

"I was thinking you could pick me up a nice cut of steak. Go to the Meat and Greet. They always have some nice filet mignons on hand."

The Meat and Greet was a locally owned shop that sold quality cuts of meat and hand-painted greeting cards. The downturn in the economy had hit Pacific Cove so hard that it seemed almost every shop or storefront did double billing just to stay in business. There was Bradford and Blahnik—which was a law firm selling designer shoes in order to keep their practice open. Dreamery Creamery, the ice cream shop that sold kids' clothes, and Magic Read, which was part magic shop and part bookstore/café.

Even Rachel was running a semi-double business with a wine bar that catered to dog owners and their beloved beasts.

"Sure, there's nothing I wouldn't do for my Grunkly," I said, breaking up a cracker and dropping the bits on the sand next to my towel. The seagull returned followed by a flock of its friends. I crumbed the rest of the package and stood. It was getting too hot to sit at the beach, anyway. Sweat was dripping down my face. I needed some shade. "I'll pick up a couple of steaks and be over later."

◇◇◇

After dropping my beach bag at my apartment and taking a quick shower, I frantically checked messages. There was no update from the Soleado Cruise Line. Well, after all, it was late Friday afternoon. I couldn't be too disappointed.

Didn't most hiring managers reach out early in the week?

Yes, Monday I would surely get a call to schedule an interview. I just had to stay optimistic, and there was nothing like shopping to keep one's spirits up. I slipped my credit card into my jeans pocket and headed downtown.

It was a short walk on a small cobblestone path. The town should have been called Pacific Charm, because that's exactly what it exuded. There was a fountain in the center of the town square with a marble statue of a man on a horse. It was rumored that the statue was of the town's founder, yet the placard had mysteriously disappeared ages ago, and nobody I talked to could remember the founder's name. The statue looked remarkably like John Wayne. The only way I could reconcile this in my mind was that either the Duke had founded Pacific Cove or the artist who had created the statue had been a fan.

The town square was flanked by restaurants and little shops. In one corner of the square was a sundial and opposite that was Rachel's bar. I glanced at my watch. It was early, still only 4:00 P.M., but Rachel might already be there prepping for Yappy Hour. I decided to pop in on her after picking up the steaks for Grunkly. From another corner, the smell of homemade waffle cones wafted through the air.

Ah, the Dreamery Creamery!

First the steaks, then I'll splurge on a cone before dropping in on Rachel.

I stopped in front of the window of Designer Duds. There was a handbag in the shape of a chicken prominently displayed. I stifled a giggle. The jacket on the mannequin next to the chicken bag, however, was what caught my eye. It was navy blue with little white anchors embroidered on it. I imagined showing up to an interview with Soleado Cruise Line wearing the jacket.

Too overzealous?

Probably.

I walked on toward the Meat and Greet and entered the small butcher shop, a bell going off as I stepped on the welcome mat.

A voice called out from the back. "I'll be right with you."

"No problem," I called back, marveling at the selection on display. There was a large butcher counter filled with prime cuts, and in front of the counter was a delectable-looking collection of gourmet cheeses and chutneys.

I noticed a small rack of greeting cards and picked one up. It was a hand-painted watercolor rendition of the beach. Another was a watercolor version of the town square. The sundial was depicted in various cards. Some cards were of parts of the cove itself that I had yet to visit, but most were studies of sea creatures. My favorites were a close-up of a starfish, and another of a jellyfish, its luminescent colors splashed across the card. They were all done by the same artist, someone named Coral.

Something stirred inside me. Years ago, when life was simple, I'd loved to paint. I probably was never as gifted or dedicated as Coral—whoever she was—but maybe it would be a nice pastime again. Life had been so busy in New York that I'd felt I'd almost lost myself; maybe painting would help me put some pieces back together.

"Thanks for waiting." A middle-aged woman in a butcher coat appeared from the back of the shop and hustled to her place behind the counter. She had unruly dark hair and dimples when she smiled, making me smile back at her.

"No worries," I said. "I just came in for a cut of meat for my uncle."

The woman studied me a moment. "Your uncle? Who's that? I know everyone in town and I don't think we've met yet."

"My great-uncle Ernest—"

"Oh! Are you Maggie? Ernest has told me so much about you! His little Magpie. He is so proud of you, and of Rachel, too. Well, the whole town is proud of Rachel. What a doll, an absolute doll. How do you like Pacific Cove?"

"Just getting settled in—"

"Yes, it takes some time. Are you staying at the Casa Ensenada Apartments? *Ensenada* means *cove* in Spanish, did you know? Those little apartments are so charming. Do you have one with a little patio and ocean view?"

I laughed. After living in New York City for a stint, it seemed unreal that a perfect stranger would not only know where I was living, but actually know the layout of my apartment. "I do have an ocean view."

The woman smiled. "Lovely. Lovely. You'll have to have a housewarming! We could do something fun," the woman continued. "Like a stock-the-bar party." She wiggled her eyebrows at me.

"If I manage to get hired at Soleado, I'll schedule a party immediately," I said.

"Oh! Have you applied to the new cruise line?" she asked.

"Yeah. Bookkeeper, but I guess in ship lingo it's called purser."

"Right. I hear you're a financial whiz!" she said.

"I don't know about that—"

The woman laughed, a low deep satisfied rumble that would make anyone in earshot vibrate. "You're just being modest! Rachel raves about you. You should have her put in a word for you. They need someone sharp. You have to deal with foreign currency and whatnot. Now what can I get for you? Is Ernest feeling any better? We had such a scare a few weeks ago. Is his appetite back?"

"He's requesting a filet, so I think we can safely say he's on the road to recovery."

The woman took a tray of meat from behind the counter and placed a few cuts onto butcher paper. "I know he likes the marbled ones. How many filets?"

"Two," I said.

I hadn't officially been invited to dinner, but I suspected Grunkly would want me to stay. Besides, I didn't have any other plans except to hover over my phone waiting for a call from the cruise line. It'd be good to get my mind off it for a while.

The woman wrapped up the meat and placed it into a pink plastic bag. I paid and headed out into the bright sunlight, a cool ocean breeze sweeping over my face. Thankfully the heat of the day was finally relenting a bit.

My phone buzzed.
Soleado!
I pulled my phone from my pocket and glanced at the
screen. It was a text from Rachel.

> Maggie, I'm going out of town unexpectedly. I know it's
> short notice, but can you tend to The Wine and Bark until
> I get back? Yappy hour is at 5pm. You have a key, don't
> you? If not, ask Dan, the manager at DelVecchio's. xoxox

How strange. This wasn't like Rachel at all.
She was going out of town? Where?
Why hadn't she said anything about it to me earlier?
While I had no problem helping out my sister, I hesitated
over dealing with the dogs, as they never seemed particularly friendly to me.
I checked my watch; it was almost four thirty now. I
fumbled with my phone and dialed her number. I did have
a key for the bar on me, but something in my gut began to
buzz with worry.
Her voice mail clicked on.
I left a quick message, "Hey Rach, what's going on? I'm
on my way to the bar now. Hope you're okay. Call me." I
made my way across the cobblestone walkway toward The
Wine and Bark. I dialed Grunkly next. He picked up on
the first ring.
"Hi, Grunkly, I got a message from Rachel. She needs
me to cover for her at the bar."
"Oh, uh huh."
It was his distracted voice. "Grunkly, are you watching
a race?"
"No, it's ten minutes to post," he said.
That explained it.

"Have you seen Benny?" he asked.

I laughed. "Well, I didn't run into him at the Meat and Greet."

"Uh huh," Grunkly said.

"I got your steak, though."

"Great," he said.

"But I have to go to The Wine and Bark—"

"No problem, honey. I'll have a can of Dinty Moore stew."

"All right. Should I save the steaks for tomorrow?"

"That'd be really nice," Grunkly said with such a flat tone that I knew he wasn't listening to a word I said.

Nevertheless, I insisted on asking, "Do you know where Rachel is?"

"Oh, Magpie, I got a call beeping in. I have to get it. It could be Benny."

Before I could say anything else, Grunkly hung up on me.

I sighed as I stood in front of the antique wooden door of The Wine and Bark. It was painted blue and orange and had "happy vibe" practically pulsing right through it. I had to give Rachel credit, she'd built the place from the ground up with limited funds and now the business was thriving.

I laced the pink plastic bag around my wrist, then dug for the key in my pocket. When I shoved the key into the lock, the first thing that struck me was that I hadn't needed the key after all. The door wasn't even locked.

Now that really isn't like Rachel.

The hair on the back of my neck stood up. I pushed open the door and stepped into the darkened bar. My eyes adjusted slowly, the outline of the great L-shaped mahogany bar coming into view, then a few tables with stools perched on top to facilitate mopping the floors, and then near the back of the bar, right in front of the small corridor that led to HIS and HERS, the silhouette of a woman standing over a body slumped on the floor.

Rachel, what have you got me into?

Chapter Two

Every neuron in my brain fired off at once, urging me to turn tail immediately and run out the front door. But the neurons didn't seem to connect to any of my limbs, because I remained frozen like a statue, hoping the woman wouldn't notice me.

She was slim, wearing a short skirt and stilettos. And, of course, she spotted me immediately. A small dog appeared from behind her and began to bark, running toward me, its tiny nails scratching along the terra-cotta floor.

The woman let out a shriek and waved her arms around in a panic. "Rachel! Oh my God, oh my God, Rachel. It's Dan! I think he's dead!" She stepped over the body and came rushing at me in the dark. She grabbed my hands, the pink Meat and Greet bag swinging between us.

"Thank God, you're here," she said. Then suddenly, she shrieked even louder and released my hands as if stung. "You're not Rachel!"

"I'm Maggie. Her sister."

It was a common mistake. Rachel and I had the same

athletic build, were the same height, and had the same heart-shaped face. Physically we were very similar, but the resemblance ended there.

"Oh! Oh." The woman shook her head trying to make sense of what I'd just said, but it seemed too great a task, because she started shrieking again in hysterics. "It's Dan Walters. He's dead. I'm sure of it. I think he's dead."

Dan? The manager at DelVecchio's?

Something tickled at the back of my brain.

Rachel and Dan had had a fling last summer and she had been complaining about him recently.

"I came early to meet Rachel. About the fund-raiser," the woman said, reaching for my hand again and pulling me toward the man slumped on the floor. "It's awful. Come see."

"Let's call the police," I said.

The woman watched me, but didn't seem to register what I'd said. "I came in through the back door. I brought the box of flyers." She pointed to a box near the body. "Then I saw him."

I flipped on the bar lights, and suddenly the man on the floor came into full color—at least the dark-red blood that had pooled around his head did. He was large, had probably been very tall. He was wearing a suit and had dark hair that was now matted against his forehead.

The woman and I both recoiled. She began to shriek again. "Oh my God! Oh my God."

I echoed her chorus, and pretty soon the both of us were in a state of panic. I pressed my hands into my forehead, took a deep breath, then chanted to myself, "Calm down, calm down, calm down."

The woman noticed I'd stopped shrieking and nodded to the rhythm of my chanting. "Yes, let's calm down," she said.

My mind reeled. What had happened? A freak accident or a burglary gone wrong? Or something else entirely?

"Is there anyone else in here?" I asked.

The woman's eyes grew wide. "Anyone else? I didn't think . . . you mean . . ." She stared toward the corridor where the restrooms were. "The killer could still be here?" she asked in a dramatic stage whisper.

I stared at her, suddenly nervously aware that she'd been standing over Dan when I'd arrived.

Indeed. I could be looking at the killer.

A humming sound filled the room, causing us both to jump, and the dog, a Yorkshire terrier, to bark.

It was the refrigerator coolant system kicking on.

Something warm and wet hit my ankle. I gasped at the sensation and looked down. The small dog barked excitedly at me.

"Ewwww!" I yelped.

The woman laughed nervously and bent to scoop him up. "Beepo! Naughty, naughty." She turned to me. "I'm so sorry. Beepo's never done anything like that before in his life!"

Beepo eyed me with his big, brown, watery eyes, in that way that dogs have that made me feel like he could read my mind. He'd known that for a split second I'd suspected his owner of something heinous.

The woman pressed the small dog to her chest. "We must call the police," she said, continuing on with her theatrical whisper.

I figured if no one had rushed out of the restrooms at us, then we were probably alone with the body. I moved around to the back of the bar and released the Meat and Greet bag onto the floor. I grabbed the phone and punched in 9-1-1, then snatched a bar towel and wiped my ankle.

The 9-1-1 operator answered. "What is the nature of your emergency?"

"We need the police over at The Wine and Bark immediately," I said, tossing the soiled rag on the floor.

"Oh? Rachel? This is Jen. What's happened? A robbery?" the operator asked.

Even though Pacific Cove was a small town, I'd barely met anyone in my few weeks here. Rachel, on the other hand, probably knew everyone in town, even the 9-1-1 operator, it seemed.

"Not Rachel. This is her sister, Maggie. We have a dead body here."

The operator gasped. "A dead body? Are you sure? Did you check for a pulse?"

I looked up at the woman who was hovering by the door of the bar. "Did you check for a pulse?" I asked.

She shook her head.

"No," I admitted into the phone.

"Check for a pulse. I'll hold," the operator said.

"Can you check for a pulse?" I called to the woman.

She gasped. "Oh no! I'm not touching him."

"All right, you come talk to 9-1-1," I said.

She reluctantly came around the bar, still clutching the dog, who growled at me as they approached. "Hush now, Beepo." She took the phone from me. "Jen? It's Yolanda. Maggie's going to check for a pulse. It's Dan, you know? I came over early to meet with Rachel . . . no, I don't know where she is. . . ."

I approached the man on the floor. Next to his bloody bashed head was an oversized bottle of wine.

Dear God!

Someone had clobbered him in the head and the blow had killed him. What kind of person would do something like that?

I knelt beside him and closed his eyes with my fingers, sighing at the loss of life. He was definitely dead, there was no need to take a pulse, but I grabbed his wrist anyway. When I lifted his arm slightly I saw a paper on the floor, trapped under the man's coat.

What was this?

I grabbed the slip of paper and saw Rachel's name on it. It was probably nothing and yet my stomach seemed to fill with dread.

I glanced toward Yolanda; she was still chatting with the operator. Almost without thinking, I shoved the paper into my pocket.

Yolanda looked up. "Anything?" she asked, sounding almost hopeful.

I shook my head.

"Just the police then, Jen. We don't need an ambulance," Yolanda said. "Oh, you send one anyway?" She was silent for a moment, then said, "Right, right. No sirens."

Yolanda hung up and stared at me grimly. "I'm so sorry about this, Maggie. I wish we could have met under more pleasant circumstances."

"Yeah, I know," I said. "This is awful."

"Where *is* Rachel?" Yolanda asked.

I wished I knew. Why had Rachel suddenly decided, mysteriously, to leave town?

I glanced toward the restrooms, the paper burning a hole in my pocket. I stood. "Um. She's out of town. I'm going to check the restroom."

Yolanda's free hand thumped against her chest. Beepo's legs cycled rapidly, alarm coursing through his tiny body. "Oh God! I forgot about that. Should you? I mean what if someone's hiding . . ."

I waved a hand at her, hoping she would take it as a sign to calm down and, more importantly, shut up. For God's sake, it was bad enough to find a dead body, did I have to be assaulted by a chatterbox, too?

Now that was mean. I just need a minute of quiet to think.

"I'm sure there's no one in there, Yolanda. I'm gonna check the window and stuff."

Yolanda came around the bar, squaring her shoulders. "I should go with you. Safety in numbers and all that."

I shook my head. "No, no. I . . ." What could I say to this woman?

I have to be alone to read this note and see if my sister is involved in a murder?

"Uh . . ." I faltered. "I think I'm going to be sick."

Yolanda's face softened. "Oh, honey." She marched toward me, Beepo yelping and snarling as she got closer. She linked her free arm through mine. "I'll hold your hair."

I released her arm from mine. "I can manage."

"I don't blame you one bit. It is an awful, gruesome sight."

"I'll be okay. I need a minute." I took a step away from her and toward the corridor that led to the restrooms. She still seemed to want to follow me. "Why don't you pour yourself a brandy?" I suggested.

Yolanda looked at me thoughtfully, then glanced back at the bar. "Yes, you know, I think you have the right idea. A brandy. I'll pour two. We've had quite a shock."

I nodded, keeping an eye on her as I pressed against the restroom door with my hip. When she seemed suitably distracted, I ducked into the bathroom and yanked the piece of paper out of my pocket.

Oh crap!

It was a letter from Dan to Rachel. I scanned it. Due to customer complaints, as the manager of DelVecchio's, he was threatening to file charges against The Wine and Bark for serving alcohol to minors, serving alcohol after hours, and becoming a "disorderly house." Next to each charge was a reference code to the Department of Alcoholic Beverage Control regulations along with a possible penalty of a fine or imprisonment.

In addition, there was a reference to a violation of the Environmental Health Statute 114030 regarding the harboring of animals inside a food facility.

I shoved the note back into my pocket, suddenly feeling hot, nauseous, and claustrophobic all at the same time.

Oh God, I was going to be sick, after all.

I tugged at my shirt trying to fan my face. It gave me no relief, so I opened the bathroom window, then ran the water in the sink.

I stuck my head under the faucet and let the water run down the back of my neck.

Breathe, Maggie. Everything is going to be fine.

Surely Rachel didn't kill this guy.

Even if their fling ended badly and she didn't like him anymore.

Even if he was . . . threatening her. . . .

Okay, so she had a motive, but . . .

I turned my head toward the water, letting it pour directly into my ear, hoping it would drown out the memory of the sound of Rachel's voice as I recalled her famous joke, *"Good friends will help you move, but a sister will help you move a body."*

Chapter Three

A commotion was building outside in the bar area. Beepo was yapping relentlessly, Yolanda was alternating between calm, soothing tones that I guessed were directed at Beepo and a high-pitched, nervous tone that I figured was directed at the baritone voice that was cutting in and out. Obviously, the police had arrived.

I cringed. I had to get myself together.

Why had I called the police before figuring out Rachel's involvement?

I turned my face into the stream of water and drank unabashedly from the faucet. The water did nothing to relieve my nausea.

And what the hell was I going to do about the letter?

How many copies were out there? Fortunately, the guy hadn't cc'd anyone on the letter, but he had to have a copy on his computer. If he'd threatened closing down Rachel's bar, I could only imagine how angry she'd be.

But even still . . . she would have challenged him . . . or hired a lawyer . . . or something, but she wouldn't have bashed him in the head with her best bottle of merlot!

I ran the water through my hair, then turned off the faucet and straightened. I evaluated myself in the mirror. Not only did I look like a drowned rat, but the color had completely drained from my face. Worse still, I looked like I had something to hide.

Prying open the door, I peeked out into the corridor.

The body was still sprawled across the sienna-colored terra-cotta. Disappointment wracked my body.

What? Had I been hoping the dead guy had been a figment of my imagination?

Yolanda was chatting with a tall uniformed officer with his back toward me.

He had broad shoulders and a narrow waist, and when he turned toward the sound of the creaking door, I froze.

In his hand was a sheet of paper.

Could it be a copy of the letter?

How?

I cleared my throat nervously.

Yolanda smiled at me. "Maggie, come meet Officer Brooks."

Officer Brooks leveled his gaze on me. My legs turned to Jell-O as I stared back at his electric-blue eyes and square jaw.

Crap! Crap!

This was no time to be thinking of igniting my nonexistent love life. This was the time to focus! Focus on getting that damn paper out of his hand. Focus on getting Rachel out of hot water. Even if she had dumped the bar on me, I still owed her that much at the very least.

I opened my mouth to speak but no sound came out.

Officer Brooks stepped toward me, shoving the paper into his back pocket.

Shoot!

"Maggie?" he asked. "I understand you found the body

here, along with Yolanda. You have a key to the front door?"

Wait a minute. That was wasn't right. I found the body with Yolanda? No, she was here first. She found the body. I found her straddling the body.

He was close to me, maybe only a few feet away, yet his voice sounded distant. I shook my head, thinking it would help my hearing, but now there seemed to be something wrong with my eyes, too, as if suddenly I had no peripheral vision . . . as if suddenly things were closing in on me.

My hand shot out to the wall, knocking into the row of famous dog portraits. The framed photos banged against each other, sending the 8 by 10 of Gidget, the Taco Bell Chihuahua, crashing to the floor. The autographed portrait of Rin Tin Tin was safe, luckily.

I steadied myself against the space vacated by Gidget and pressed my cheek into cool stucco. I pulled at my shirt collar again, trying to breathe deeply.

No, no, no.

Not a panic attack. I hadn't had one of those since . . . since . . .

Oh no, don't think of that! Think of the letter. Think of Rachel.

Focus!

My knees began to buckle and rational thought abandoned me. The pressing issue became getting air. I pulled at my shirt again, trying to fan my face. I was burning up.

I had to get my shirt off.

The restroom suddenly looked miles away.

I groaned.

Officer Brooks was at my side, his hand on my elbow. "Hey, are you all right there?"

"So hot," I said.

He smiled a lopsided grin. "I get that a lot."

"What?" I asked, tugging at the bottom of my shirt and pulling it up toward my face. The dim-witted thought of what bra I had on flashed through my mind.

He pulled my shirt back down. "Whoa, whoa. What are you doing?"

"No air," I mumbled, trying to fan myself and wrestle my top off at the same time.

Yolanda appeared next to us. She batted my hands away from my shirt and slinked her arm around my waist. Officer Brooks joined her and together they ushered me toward a bar stool.

I wrapped my arms around their waists.

Wait! Wait!

My hand was right up above his back pocket . . . right next to the letter in his pocket. My finger grazed the paper.

Think, Maggie, think. Focus.

I tried to command my fingers to close on the paper, to grasp it, pinch it, whatever it took! But my fine motor—oh, who was I kidding, even my gross motor functions had totally shut down. We reached a bar stool and I flopped onto it, nearly toppling over.

Officer Brooks steadied me, then said, "Put your head down." Hands guided my head between my knees.

I gulped in air. My racing heart slowed a bit and my vision improved.

I chanced to put my head up, but a strong hand firmly kept it in place. "Not yet," the baritone said.

Oh, my hearing was better, too.

Now, how to get the letter?

I took a deep, calming breath.

Beepo appeared beneath my nose. We were eye to eye, nose to nose. He bared his teeth. I bared mine. He growled. I growled back at him.

The hand lifted from my head. "Did you just growl?" Officer Brooks asked.

I kept my head down.

"Jen said she was going to send an ambulance. Maybe they can give her oxygen or something when they get here," Yolanda said.

I raised my head. "I'm fine."

Yolanda's hand fluttered to her chest. "No, you're not. We've had a big shock and you nearly passed out."

I glanced at Officer Brooks and caught him studying me. I self-consciously smoothed down my wet hair.

A smile played around his eyes, and he said, "You're Rachel's sister?"

I nodded.

"Where is she?" he asked. "Have you called her and told her about Dan?"

I swallowed past the dry spot in my throat. "No," I muttered.

He nodded. "Okay, good. Let's keep it that way for a bit. This is a small town and I want to be able to control the information for as long as I can." He gave Yolanda a meaningful look. "Let me notify the next of kin before word gets out, okay?"

Yolanda stroked her collarbone, a strange expression on her face. As if she didn't know whether she should be offended at being called the town gossip or take it as a compliment. She seemed to decide on taking it as a compliment, because she reached out and squeezed Officer Macho's forearm. "You can count on me," she said.

I stood and crossed behind the bar, hoping to put some distance between them and myself. "I'm going to pour myself a drink now."

Officer Brooks raised a hand. "Hold on. I'm going to

have to ask you not to touch anything back there. This is a crime scene."

"Oh! I already poured one for her," Yolanda said, managing to look contrite while batting her eyelashes at him.

I picked up the half-full brandy and raised it toward her. "Thank you." I smiled at Officer Brooks. "Drinking a bit of brandy is not against the law, is it?"

Officer Brooks's eyes narrowed in response.

Beepo came around to the back of the bar. I expected him to snarl at me, but instead he sat down on his hind legs and watched me.

"So, where did you say Rachel was?" Officer Brooks asked.

I sipped the brandy, enjoying the smooth burn down my throat. "Uh," I hesitated. "She's out of town. I'm in charge of the bar. Um. Until she returns."

Officer Brooks frowned, and for a moment he looked like he was going to say something but then seemed to think better of it and simply nodded. He walked toward the body and asked, "Did either of you touch him?"

"Oh no, I didn't touch him. Why would I touch him?" Yolanda squawked.

Beepo's triangle-shaped ears perked up when he heard Yolanda and he immediately got up and moved out from behind the bar to go to her. I looked at the spot he'd left vacant. The Meat and Greet bag had been torn into and lay in shreds on the floor.

Figures the dog took advantage of our distraction and had himself a killer meal.

"Did you touch the body, Maggie?" Officer Brooks asked.

"I did. I took his pulse," I said.

"Oh! Yes, poor thing! You did! That's probably what sent you right over the edge," Yolanda said.

"Did you move him at all?" Officer Brooks asked.

"Uh . . . I just lifted his arm to try and take the pulse, that's all," I said.

Officer Brooks looked from the body to me. His eyes held mine for a moment, then I broke the connection and sipped the brandy.

"And I closed his eyes," I said. "They were open. He had a dead, you know, a dead glazed look." I sighed and shrugged.

Officer Brooks nodded. "Uh huh. What about the wine bottle? Anyone touch that?"

Yolanda and I exchanged looks.

"No," she said. "I didn't touch it."

I eyed her cautiously, a chill raising goosebumps on my arms. I hadn't seen her touch the bottle, that much was true, but she'd been standing over the body when I got here. She'd said the back door had been open. Why would both the back and the front door be left unlocked? It made no sense.

And what exactly had she said to Officer Brooks while I was trying to wash away past sins in the bathroom?

I realized that Officer Brooks was waiting for my response.

"I didn't touch it, either," I said.

The front door opened and a wiry man wearing spectacles popped his head inside. "Got a call from dispatch," he said.

Officer Brooks waved him in. "Come on in, Henry."

Henry was wearing coveralls, but he had such a young, fresh-faced boyish look that it was difficult to think of him as a crime scene tech. He nodded toward Yolanda and me, while he crossed the length of the bar toward the body.

"I'm going to cordon off the bar," Officer Brooks said

as he motioned to Yolanda and me to follow him out the
door.

"Wait! What do you mean cordon off the bar? I'm supposed to open in—" I glanced at my watch.

Crap! Almost 5:00 P.M. Yappy Hour!

"No, no. Bar is closed for tonight." Officer Brooks held
open the front door and peered out into the street. "Oh,
good. Backup." He turned to us. "Ladies, I'll need you to
give your statements to Officer Ellington."

I couldn't leave. I still had to the get the paper out of
his pocket.

Yolanda picked up Beepo and marched toward the front
door.

"Remember, please don't say anything about Dan yet,"
Officer Brooks warned Yolanda. "We need to notify the
next of kin first."

"Mum's the word," Yolanda said, making a dramatic
gesture of covering her mouth with her forefinger, then
waggling it at Officer Hottie-Pants.

Henry was getting busy with the body, taking pictures
and measurements and all sorts of things.

Officer Brooks quirked an eyebrow at me, no doubt
wondering why I wasn't beating feet right out the door.

"How long do I have to stay closed for?" I asked, stall-
ing for time.

"We'll be out of here tonight. You should be able to
open tomorrow. Leave me your number." He smiled slowly.
"I'll call you."

Just hearing the words, *"I'll call you,"* coming out of
his sexy mouth gave me a thrill, but I reminded myself that
he *wasn't* inviting me out to dinner.

I grabbed a Post-it pad from near the cash register, carefully avoiding the bowl of Bark Bites that was nestled
next to it, and scribbled my cell phone number down. As

I shuffled around the bar, a clamoring ruckus sounded from the street.

Officer Brooks stepped into the doorway and peered out. His back was to me, his attention momentarily distracted, and the dreaded paper was poking right out of his back pocket!

Now was the time for action!

I practically dove toward his pants, but restrained myself at the last moment. I gingerly plucked the paper out of his pocket and replaced it with the Post-it. He stiffened as he felt me brush against him.

I patted his back pocket and winked. "Yeah, call me."

Chapter Four

I squeezed past Officer Brooks's hulking frame, which was partially blocking the doorway, and instantly regretted it.

The cacophony on the street was coming from a group of people with small yapping dogs.

Yolanda was waving at me furiously. "Maggie, Maggie! Come meet the Roundup Crew. We *round* each other up each week and walk on the beach. They're some of the regulars at Yappy Hour!"

I involuntarily took a step back, right into Officer Muscular. The warmth of his hand on the small of my back shot heat right through my belly as he nudged me onto the street.

"Sorry lady," he chuckled. "Bar's closed."

The door banged behind me and I stuffed the paper I'd wrangled out of his pocket into my shirt.

Two women and a man were huddled around Yolanda. Each of them clutching a small dog on the end of a Day-Glo-green leash with the logo of The Wine and Bark on it. Across the cobblestone path was the doorway to

DelVecchio's. The door was partially open, and a dark figure seemed to be hovering beyond the entrance. In the front window, next to what seemed to be the menu, was a prominently displayed No Dogs Allowed sign.

No dogs? Could it be that I'd just found a place after my own heart?

Suddenly I felt hungry.

The woman next to Yolanda, an attractive brunette wearing short shorts and cuddling a Chihuahua, said, "Hi, I'm Brenda." She stroked the dog's head. "And this is Pee Wee."

I nodded at her.

"You're Rachel's sister?" she asked.

I nodded again, while the other woman said, "Oh! Rachel's told me so much about you! I'm Abigail, and this is Max." She was wearing a flowered sundress, her dark hair pulled back in an elegant French braid, and holding fast to a white Shih Tzu with a rhinestone bow on the top of its head.

I glanced at the dog, but then realized she was introducing me to the man standing next to her, who was attached to a beagle chomping on a plush pink bunny. The man was tall and had a classic boy-next-door friendly face and wavy sandy-colored hair.

Brenda eyed the yellow police tape in front of The Wine and Bark. "What's going on?" she asked. "Was there a break-in?"

Yolanda waved her hands around dramatically. "Something really awful has happened, but Maggie and I have been sworn to secrecy, right Maggie?"

Before I could answer, Yolanda leaned into the group and said, "We probably shouldn't talk about it here, in front of . . ." She made a motion with her head toward DelVecchio's. "Well, you know."

All eyes glanced toward DelVecchio's. The shadowy figure was gone, but the group seemed to stiffen and everyone stood straighter as if on high alert. Even the dogs seemed to come to attention.

"Well, we can't go into the bar, right?" Brenda asked.

I shook my head. "It's closed for tonight."

A hush came over the small group, and I noticed they were all staring at me now, both the people and the dogs, except for Max. He was looking over at Brenda with a sort of long-lost puppy dog expression.

Ah, unrequited love.

"Well, we may be open tomorrow, but I don't know . . ." I looked toward the street at the parked police cruisers and several officers that were hovering around their vehicles. With any luck, the cops would have the bar closed until Rachel got back from wherever she was, and I'd be off the hook from tending bar and dealing with dogs.

"You have to be open tomorrow!" Yolanda squawked. "We've invited Mrs. Clemens; she's scheduled to come and get the paw paintings going. It's a practice run for the fund-raiser next Friday. People are paying over a hundred dollars to get their paw-cassos. You have to be open!"

"Paw-casso?" I asked.

"Mrs. Clemens brings canvas and all different color paints, then she lets our little babies dip in," Abigail said, wiggling one of the Shih Tzu's paws at me as if she was waving. "They create one-of-a-kind paw paintings. But don't worry; the paint is completely pet safe."

"I was really looking forward to the paw-cassos," Brenda said. "Pee Wee is supposed to be the first one, right?"

"And I'm bringing the baby pool. We're going to set it up out here," Abigail said, motioning to the patio landing in front of the bar.

"Uh . . . a baby pool?"

"Don't worry," Abigail continued. "I'm bringing some fun float toys for the dogs to play with. It's all been taken care of."

"I think Rachel got some Wine and Bark towels printed up for the dogs," Yolanda said.

I was starting to feel like I'd entered the twilight zone, or at the very least an alternative doggie universe.

"Do you know where the towels are?" Yolanda asked. "Are they inside the bar? Or at Rachel's apartment?"

I knew Yolanda was waiting for an answer from me, but I simply couldn't get my brain to form words. A man had been pummeled to death inside the bar, and yet all she seemed concerned with was throwing some dog extravaganza.

The door to DelVecchio's opened and a uniformed waiter began setting up the patio seating. He glanced at our group a few times and then toward the street at the police congregating around their vehicles, but mostly worked efficiently.

He probably didn't know about Dan yet. And neither did the Yappies, I reminded myself. Except, of course, Yolanda. . . .

What else did she know? Did anyone know about Dan threatening Rachel? Did anyone know about the letter? Who else had a copy of it?

Another police cruiser arrived and parked. The officers who had been shuffling about jumped to attention.

The beagle with the pink bunny in his mouth began to sniff around my feet.

That's it! Time to go, before another one decided to leave his mark on me.

I took a step back. "Uh, guys. I'd love to stay and chat, but the bar's closed and . . ." The police began making

their way down the cobblestone path toward us. A uniformed officer was in the front, and behind him were several other men, two in uniform and two in coveralls. "We
should let the police do their job."

The group around me turned to look at the officers.

Yolanda waved madly at the man in front. "Sergeant
Gottlieb!"

Sergeant Gottlieb was completely bald, with a promi-
nent nose and dark bushy eyebrows. He looked intense and
gave me the impression he would find the person responsible for the crime. At the same time that relief flooded my
body, a chill ran down my spine.

Before I could be happy about justice being served, I'd
need to make sure Rachel was in the clear.

Sergeant Gottlieb motioned to his crew to go inside The
Wine and Bark. I turned to watch them as they disappeared
into the darkness of the bar.

Yolanda introduced me to Sergeant Gottlieb, and I
found myself shaking his hand almost on autopilot. She
told him we'd already given our statements to Officer
Brooks.

Had I given a statement?

Sergeant Gottlieb patted my arm and said, "We'll be in
touch." He turned and followed his crew inside the bar.

The dark figure appeared again in DelVecchio's
doorway.

I needed to get home and try to reach Rachel again. At
the very least I needed to figure out what kind of statement to give Sergeant Gottlieb when he realized that I
hadn't actually given one.

Brenda made eyes toward DelVecchio's, clearly indicating to the group something I wasn't in on. "Should we go
someplace else so we can talk?" she whispered.

"We can go to my place," Yolanda offered. "The pool's

open and our complex manager is fine with animals. It's a good thing that most of the group is in Carmel at the pet show, otherwise, it wouldn't work."

They started to pull away from me, then suddenly Yolanda linked her arm through mine and Beepo yapped at my heels. "Now we'll have time to visit and you can tell us all about yourself."

"Oh, uh. I don't think so. I have to get back," I said.

"Back to what?" Yolanda pressed. "You've had a horrible shock. I'm not letting you out of my sight until I know you're okay."

"I'm fine," I said.

"Don't worry, I have an extra swimsuit at home you can borrow," Yolanda continued.

"I'm fine," I repeated, stepping away from her and tripping over Beepo. The dog yowled and I fell onto the cobblestones, scraping my bare knees.

Hands pulled me to my feet, wet noses rubbed my ankles, the group making a tremendous fuss over me, the yapping and yipping both human and canine rising to an ear-shattering crescendo.

"I can't go with you," I said.

The group continued to make noise, cries of "Don't be silly" and "You must!" The beagle dropped the sopping pink bunny on my foot and Pee Wee nipped at my toes.

I shuffled my feet away from the dogs and held my hands palm-side up toward them. "I'm not . . . I'm not . . . a doggie person." Air filled my lungs and I let out a huge exhalation.

There! I'd said it!

A collective gasp came from the group.

Then blessed silence descended upon them, but the look they gave me was what they'd give the devil incarnate. Even the dogs seemed to have the same expression.

I dropped my hands. "I'm . . . I'm sorry," I mumbled.

"Well," Yolanda said, smoothing down her skirt. She gave a little flick of her wrist as she did it, as though she was whisking away the thought of my words, better yet, the thought of *me* and my kind with the motion.

"Not a doggie person?" Brenda asked incredulously, her hand over her heart, a look of shock on her face. Even her Chihuahua, Pee Wee, whimpered and skirted around behind her feet, hiding from me.

Suddenly I felt the need to defend myself. "I don't *hate* them," I said, probably lingering a little too long on the word hate, so it sounded like I meant the exact opposite of what I'd said. "I mean, you know, I just don't—"

"Hey, not everyone's a dog person," Max said.

Brenda cut him a look that seemed to communicate he'd gone down two notches in her estimation, then turned on her heel and pulled the leash of her Chihuahua. Max picked up the beagle and hurried to walk alongside Brenda.

The pink bunny still lay at my feet, and the beagle howled in agony as Max rushed off without it.

I stooped to pick up the bunny. "Uh . . . wait!" I called after him, but Max didn't hear me. The bunny was missing an eye and losing some stuffing out his side. I knew exactly how he must feel.

The dark figure from DelVecchio's had settled himself in the doorway. He was tall, wearing tight jeans and a snug black shirt. His arms were folded across his chest as he watched us. He radiated animal magnetism, and for no good reason I blushed.

How long had he been standing there?

Yolanda patted my arm. "I know we had a terrible shock today. But we are counting on you for tomorrow. After all, Rachel left you in charge of her business." Yolanda's eyes narrowed at me. "And you don't want to ruin that, do you?

Perhaps you *should* get home and get some rest. Things will be better in the morning." She turned to follow Brenda and Max.

What things would be better? Certainly nothing would be better for poor Dan.

Abigail cast a worried glance over at the man in the doorway at DelVecchio's, then leaned into me. "We need to talk," she whispered.

"What?" I asked.

She gave me a look I couldn't read and said into my ear, "I know what Rachel's done."

Chapter Five

Between the dead body, the dogs, Rachel being MIA, and the guy watching me in the doorway, I feared a nervous breakdown, if not at the very least another panic attack.

"Where can we talk?" I asked Abigail.

Abigail, who was clutching her Shih Tzu, brought it up to her cheek, giving the impression she was seeking counsel from the dog. I waited as she blew lopsided kisses toward it. She was deliberating something, and I hated waiting.

"Want to go my place? I'm over at Casa Ensenada."

She made a face as if I'd told her I was living in a dungeon.

"I have the keys to Rachel's place and it's close by. How about we go there?" she asked.

Why did she have keys to my sister's house?

Even though I found this annoying, I agreed to go. Perhaps there'd be a clue at Rachel's apartment about where she was, when she was returning, and if she had anything to do with poor Dan's unfortunate demise.

As we walked down the street toward Rachel's place, Abigail said, "I want you to know I was against it from the start."

Against it? Against what?

Oh great.

What had Rachel done this time? Please God, let it be something I could fix. Please don't let her be involved in Dan's death.

"Against what?" I managed to squeak.

Abigail whirled around to face me. "Against Chuck, of course."

Chuck? Who was that?

"I don't know a Chuck," I said.

Abigail's eyes grew wide. "Oh, you didn't know him?" she whispered, half to me and half to her Shih Tzu, which seemed to be permanently lodged under her arm.

"Who's Chuck?" I asked again.

"Her latest beau," Abigail said. "Don't get me wrong. He's very nice. It's just that, we don't . . . we didn't like him for her, you know?"

"Uhh . . ."

"Missy and I are very protective about Rachel."

"Missy?" I asked.

"This is Missy." Abigail gestured to the Shih Tzu, whose ears cocked at her name. She let out a little yelp, seemingly a greeting.

"Oh. Yeah, hi, Missy," I said.

We turned the corner to Rachel's street and then climbed up the wooden stairs to her apartment. Rachel lived in two-story stone building that dated back to the early 1900s. Legend had it that the stones had been arduously gathered from Pismo Beach. The building included huge wraparound windows that must have had a wild view of the Pacific Ocean. Poor Rachel could only afford the east side, no view and a tiny cramped one-bedroom.

The main door to the building was unlocked, so Abigail, her dog, and I walked in without a problem. We climbed the interior staircase to the second floor, then Abigail dug out a key from her pocket and stuck it into Rachel's door.

"Anyway, I'm supposed to water her plants while she's gone."

Oh, this was rich. Missy and Abigail got trusted with Rachel's houseplants and I got stuck with the bar? Seriously? Who was this woman anyway? How close was she to my sister?

I suddenly felt ashamed about my jealousy.

Why did it bother me that she got the houseplants?

While it was true I didn't have the greenest thumb, still, I felt slighted somehow.

"So where is Rachel? And when is she coming back?" I asked.

Abigail pushed open the door to the apartment, and Missy shot in like a cannonball, making a beeline to the back bedroom. Abigail gave a halfhearted call, "Missy!" Then she turned to me. "She's on a Mexican Riviera cruise."

Heat flashed through me and I was immediately livid. I was stuck here in Pacific Cove, watching my harebrained sister's dog bar and stumbling over dead bodies, while she was off traveling! She had to be on Soleado Cruise Line, as they were the only one in town, the same company I was soliciting for a job.

Was there no justice in this world?

I should have been on that cruise. Rachel was downing margaritas and I was going to be stuck serving mutt-garitas.

"Are you okay?" Abigail asked. "You look a little peaked."

Even though I was furious with Rachel, I was still too much of a type-A personality to air my sister's dirty laundry with a stranger. So I said nothing and sat on Rachel's couch in a huff.

My entire relationship with Rachel seemed to flash before my eyes. Why did I have to run the bar? I wasn't even a good bartender. Sure, I could handle the cash and make sure the till added up every night, but really . . . ?

Couldn't she have told me she was going to Mexico?

At the root of it, I was probably just plain jealous that this woman in front of me was a closer confidant for my sister than I was.

Abigail got busy tending to the houseplants. She quietly watered an orchid perched on the windowsill, patiently dusting around it. Next she moved to a plant by the door. She picked off the dry leaves and even muttered something to it.

The woman was talking to the plants!

Okay, she was the right person for the job.

I watched Abigail as she stooped to scoop the mail out of the small box on the backside of the door.

The mail!

I jumped up from the couch and snatched the mail out of her hand. "I'll take that!"

Abigail looked at me, startled. "Oh, yeah sure. I was only going to put it on her kitchen counter, next to the cordless phone, that's where she likes it."

I nodded and flipped through the letters. It looked like ordinary mail: the power bill, the supermarket circular, and a flyer from Flab-U-Less, a new yoga studio opening up near Rachel's bar.

Nothing from Dan.

That much was good.

"When did Rachel start dating Chuck?" I asked.

Abigail pressed her lips together, looking considerably worried. "Well, that's the thing. They just haven't been dating all that long."

"What happened between Rachel and Dan?" I asked.

I felt like I was walking on eggshells. I couldn't let Abigail know that Dan was dead. And yet, I remembered that when he and Rachel broke up, it was quite bad. Did Abigail have more information than I did?

Abigail shuffled over to the next houseplant. "Oh Dan. He was perfect for Rachel. I don't know why she didn't see that. I kept telling her to give him another chance."

"She was the one who didn't want to be with him?" I asked. Somehow I remembered the story differently, but now I doubted how much Rachel actually shared with me.

Abigail shook her head. "He was ready to settle down. I think he would have made a great catch for Rachel. He knew the business backward and forward—"

"But he didn't like her business, right? The dogs?"

Abigail frowned. "Really?"

Ack. Had I just stepped in it? Clearly she didn't know about the letter. That much was good.

"Uh, well, there's a no-dog sign in front of DelVecchio's," I said.

Abigail nodded. "But that's not because Dan doesn't like dogs. He's always been kind to Missy." She looked around, realizing Missy wasn't in the room with us. She called out, "Missy? Missy?"

"Why then?" I asked.

Abigail looked confused for a moment. "Oh, the no-dogs sign? That's Gus DelVecchio. He's the chef there. He has a thing about dogs near his food. He's a bit of a crazy, if you ask me."

I hid my smile. That was the first thing that had sounded sane to me all day. What was crazy about a chef not wanting animals near the food he'd labored over? Plus, restaurants were so expensive to run. He was probably fighting tooth and nail to stay in business, and likely the last thing a fine-dining Italian restaurant needed on its shared patio was a doggie happy hour . . . well, doggie anything, really.

"Anyway, I wish I could have convinced Rachel to give Dan another chance. He really loved her."

"I didn't know they were that serious," I said, feeling removed. Why hadn't I known what was going on in Rachel's life?

I'd been too wrapped up in my own life, my New York life: long hours at the office trying to make it as a financial advisor. I was glad now that I'd come home. Rachel needed me. She was my little sister, and I'd do whatever was necessary to protect her. But first, I had to figure out what happened to Dan.

"When did Rachel leave?" I asked, thinking back to the text she'd sent me early in the day.

Certainly the coroner would peg a time of death, and hopefully that would rule her out immediately.

"The cruise left this afternoon," Abigail said.

Darn. Oh well, there'd be something else to clear her from suspicion entirely. I was sure of it.

And what about this Chuck guy? This new man in her life. Was it possible that he and Dan had fought over Rachel? Could she have fled with him, thinking she was protecting him somehow?

Why else would she leave on such short notice?

"When did you know she was leaving town?" I asked.

"I only found out this afternoon. She sent me a text. I tried to talk her out of it, but she wouldn't hear of it. She wanted me to promise to pick up the mail and water the plants."

"You tried to talk her out of a vacation?" I asked.

She frowned. "Vacation? No, not that. I tried to talk her out of eloping."

Chapter Six

She's eloped?

I staggered back and sat on the couch. Missy materialized from Rachel's bedroom and seemed to sense my distress, because she beelined toward me and pressed her wet nose into my ankle.

Abigail watched me. "You didn't know?"

"What do you mean *eloped*? She *married* this Chuck guy? Who is he? How long have they been dating?"

"About two weeks," Abigail said. "I'm sorry to have sprung it on you, I thought you knew."

Which begged the question, why didn't I know? Rachel didn't feel she could confide in me, obviously. Disappointment weighed down my shoulders. After our parents passed, Rachel and I were left with only Grunkly, so it's not as if I imagined she wanted a huge family wedding, but I had always envisioned standing by her side on that big day.

Abigail picked up the dog. "Come on, girl, leave Maggie alone." She looked around the apartment. "Do you think we should do anything else around here before we go?"

I glanced around, noticing the dust and general disarray of the place. "I'll tidy up a bit," I said. "You don't have to stay."

"We should look around for The Wine and Bark towels for the rehearsal tomorrow," Abigail said.

"Don't worry about that. I'll look for them," I said.

Perfect.

That way I could nose around Rachel's place and try to figure out why she'd married this guy. Who was he? Did she love him? Not to mention, I could poke around and see if there was anything tying her to the unfortunate death in her establishment.

I shuddered to think what I would do with anything should I find it.

"Do you know how I can reach her?" I asked.

"No, she's supposed to call me when they get to port. There's no cell phone coverage onboard."

But the ship certainly had phones or radios.

Maybe there was a way to reach her after all. I'd have to go ask around at Soleado Cruise Line for a number. Surely that would endear me to whoever was interviewing applicants for the purser position. I could see it now: *"Please, I have to get an urgent message to my sister—who's eloped and said nothing to me—that a man was found dead in her bar. Oh, and, by the way, have you had a chance to review my résumé yet?"*

I pressed my fingertips to my temple, trying to fend off the headache that threatened.

"It was very nice to meet you, Maggie," Abigail said, reminding me she was standing in the doorway.

I stood. "Right, right. Sorry. I was distracted. Thank you for taking care of the plants for Rach."

Abigail nodded absently. "What happened at the bar tonight? Why were the police there?"

I bit my lip. I was under strict orders not to talk about Dan, but really, what would it harm? Maybe Abigail knew something. As I was about to speak, someone knocked on the door. Abigail gave a start and Missy began to bark.

I crossed the room and opened the door. Officer Brooks filled the hallway. "Good evening, Maggie. Is Rachel here?"

Abigail peeked out at him and Missy gave him an appraising sniff. "Hi Brad," Abigail said.

He nodded at her.

"Rachel's out of town," I said. "I thought I told you that already."

I suddenly felt protective about her again. Why was this cop, handsome or not, snooping around her place?

"She's off and eloped," Abigail chirped.

The fact that Abigail was so willing to spread gossip about my sister irked me. Although, if it was technically true, did that make it gossip or news?

Either way, I didn't like it. The elopement was Rachel's business, not this Officer What's-His-Name's or Abigail's.

Brooks raised an eyebrow. "Eloped, eh? When?"

"First thing this morning, they took off on the Mexican Riviera Cruise," Abigail said.

"Who's the lucky guy?" Brooks asked.

"Chuck Hazelton," Abigail said, proceeding to chat at length and fill Officer Brooks in on Rachel's private dealings.

I fought the overwhelming desire to throw them out into the hallway. Did I really have to stand here and listen to my little sister's love life be dissected?

"They'd only been dating a few weeks, can you believe it?" Abigail said.

Was it my imagination or was Abigail suddenly standing

taller? Almost as if she was thrusting her well-endowed top half right under Brooks's nose.

"A little wild and crazy, wouldn't you say?" Abigail continued. "I don't suppose you do that sort of thing? Hey?" She poked at Officer Brooks's shoulder.

His eyes were on mine. He didn't seem to hear Abigail when she said, "Anyway, if you ever want to do coffee, let me know."

At that Missy barked—she probably didn't want Officer Brooks in her life. Could dogs sense flirting?

"Hush now, baby," Abigail said, then she regarded Brooks and me for a moment and realized that neither of us were speaking.

"May I come in?" he asked. "I'd like to ask you a few more questions."

"Oh? Is that about what happened at the bar?" Abigail asked. "What did happen? A robbery? Are we unsafe here in Pacific Cove?" She clutched at his bicep.

He looked at her and said politely, "If you don't mind, Abigail, I'm not at liberty to discuss the details of an ongoing investigation."

Abigail's eyes widened, but to her credit she didn't shriek like I figured Yolanda might when she repeated, "Ongoing investigation?"

Officer Brooks broke free of her hold and stepped in through the apartment door, smiling tightly at Abigail as he firmly closed the door behind him.

He pressed his back against the door and stayed next to it like a stanchion. "I came to inquire about Rachel. Do you have a way to reach her?"

"No, not yet," I admitted.

He nodded. "Also, you left without giving Officer Ellington your statement." Something flashed through his eyes that I read as anger. I only hoped it was directed toward Ellington and not me. "I can take that now," he said.

I hesitated. I still didn't have a great statement to make. What did I know?

Not much.

Brooks seemed to read my hesitation.

"It doesn't hurt. I promise." He pulled out a notebook from his front chest pocket and flipped to a blank page.

"Do you want to sit down?" I asked, motioning to the couch.

He shook his head. "Not necessary. I'd just like you to take me through your paces starting with last night."

"Last night? Do you have the time of death already?" I asked.

He poised his pen over the blank page. "Could you kindly tell me your whereabouts last night?"

Now I felt like a loser. For some strange reason I wished I'd had a hot date to report to him, I wanted to see if jealousy would flash across his masculine face, but my love life was deader than Dan.

"I was home last night," I said.

"Did you have any company? Talk to anyone? Can anyone vouch for you?" he asked.

"Am I a suspect?" I replied.

"Well, I'm not putting you in handcuffs yet."

A shocked expression must have crossed my face, because he gave a little self-satisfied smile, then said, "These are standard questions, miss. I'm not accusing you of anything. I'm only getting the facts."

He was calling me *miss* now. We'd backtracked.

"Would you like something to drink?" I asked. "Coffee?"

He shook his head.

The thought crossed my mind to offer him a doughnut, but I figured it was too cliché.

"Mind if I have one?" I asked. Then immediately regretted it. Why was I asking for permission?

He didn't answer my question, though, just repeated his. "Did you talk to anyone last night? From your house?"

I hadn't talked to anyone. I'd stayed up late, cooked a frozen pizza, and watched a cheesy Hallmark movie where the man and woman fell in love and were torn apart when her past came to haunt her. Only I was too embarrassed to tell Officer Brooks that I was a sucker for romance plots. So I lied and said, "My uncle, we chatted last night."

I made a mental note to tell Grunkly to cover for me. I crossed to the kitchen. I was sure Rachel had something in her kitchen that might take the edge off. Why was I so nervous talking to this man? There were several boxes stacked in a corner of Rachel's kitchen.

I grabbed a kitchen knife and sliced into the first cardboard box. Officer Brooks watched me without saying a word.

Ah! The Wine and Bark towels.

"One mystery solved," I sang out, then immediately regretted it upon seeing the serious expression on Brooks's face.

Moving the box aside, I sliced into the next, a case of Stoli. It must have been for the bar. I picked out a colored tumbler from Rachel's cabinet and filled it with ice. "It's not too late to change your mind," I said.

"I'm still on duty."

"After I give you my statement, will you be off duty?" I asked.

He shook his head stoically.

I poured a healthy dose of vodka into my tumbler. "Okay, what else do you want to know?"

"Did you know Dan?"

"No, I knew of him. I know he and Rach dated for a bit."

He nodded. "How did it end? Was she angry with him?"

"No!" I said, suddenly defensive for my little sister again. "They just dated and then they ended it. Rachel was busy with the bar. She didn't want to get too serious with anyone."

"But now she's married. Very suddenly, I might add."

Yes, that did seem like a big fat inconsistency.

I shrugged. "I didn't know about it until Abigail told me just now. I have to verify it."

"Are you saying it might not be true?"

I sipped my vodka. "Well, I'm not calling Abigail a liar or anything. It's just strange that my own sister didn't mention it to me."

"Maybe she thought you wouldn't approve of the guy," Brooks said.

"Do I look like the type of person who judges other people's relationships?" I asked.

He shrugged. "From the little I know about your sister, your opinion is very important to her."

I twirled the tumbler in my hand and thought about it a moment. Yes, it did seem strange that Rachel would elope without even a word to me about it.

It smelled of trouble.

Like she was hiding something.

I only hoped the something she was hiding didn't have anything to do with poor Dan.

"How about today? Can you take me through your steps please?" he asked.

"This morning I went to the beach, then shopped at The Meat and Greet, before getting a text from Rach about helping out at the bar." I finished my vodka and poured another. "You should talk to Yolanda, though. She's the one who found Dan, you know. She was at the bar before I was."

He nodded. "All right, one more thing. Why did you steal the fund-raiser flyer out of my pocket?"

I reddened, embarrassed about being caught, but relieved that it hadn't been a copy of the letter from Dan.

"I didn't want you to go as Yolanda's date," I said.

He chuckled. "I thought maybe you wanted a first crack at the pets that would be up for adoption," he said.

I laughed. "No."

We stared at each other for a moment, suddenly silent. A nervous energy fluttered in my belly as I held his gaze.

"Can I get a rain check?" he asked.

"Rain check?"

"On the drink?"

I nodded dumbly. He made his way to the door. "I have to talk to the people at DelVecchio's tonight. And I work tomorrow as well, but I'm off on Sunday."

Was he asking me out on a date?

My heart began to race.

"Sunday works," I said, before realizing that I'd probably have to tend Rachel's bar on Sunday. With any luck, maybe the bar would have to be closed until Rachel returned from her trip.

Officer Brooks had his hand on the doorknob, and as if reading my thoughts turned and said, "My crime scene team is still working at The Wine and Bark. I'll let you know when you can reopen."

"No rush," I said.

He chuckled, then wiggled his fingers at me as he waved good-bye.

Chapter Seven

First thing I did when Officer Hottie-Pants left was down my vodka, then I tried Rachel's cell phone again. It went to voice mail immediately, which told me she had either turned it off or it was out of battery. I left her a message to call me ASAP, then sent her an e-mail in case she had access somehow to that account.

I poured myself another drink and then searched the kitchen, each cabinet and cupboard, even the sugar bowl for evidence of what she'd been up to.

When I came up dry, I decided to scour the rest of her apartment, including the desk she kept in her bedroom that held a laptop computer. The laptop was password-protected, but I tried my hand at hacking my way into it. It wasn't as difficult as I thought. Her password for everything was Wineandbark. I'd have to talk to her about Internet security. She was ripe for identity theft.

I found cached searches on her computer for "disorderly house," which was the violation Dan had referenced in his letter. So, it seemed that Rachel had been aware that Dan was threatening to file a complaint.

But I didn't, however, find another copy of the letter, so as far as I could tell, she'd either heard about the threat from him or someone else at DelVecchio's.

Additional poking around yielded me some online chats between Rachel and a Mr. Chuck. It seemed that Mr. Chuck was a computer engineer. Really? That was a first. Rachel never went for the nerds.

How could she have eloped with the guy?

I searched her computer cache for anything related to elopement: bridal dresses, floral bouquets, or wedding cakes—and found nothing. I glanced around her room; there were no photos, no evidence of a new relationship. I walked to her closet and examined the clothes. All were hers; there was no man's anything anywhere. It was hard to believe that she was in a relationship with this Mr. Chuck at all, much less a relationship serious enough to elope.

Sadness bore down on me. Why would she not confide in me? After all, if she didn't trust me enough to tell me she was getting serious with a guy, how likely would it be for her to reach out to me if she was in trouble?

I went to pour myself another drink and was shocked to see the dent I'd put in the bottle. How many drinks had I guzzled? All right, it wasn't every day you found a dead guy, but still, I didn't need a hangover in the morning.

I put the bottle away, disgusted with myself, and staggered to Rachel's door. It was late now, time to go home. Tomorrow would be another day. I'd start with a fresh slate, bright eyed and bushy tailed, determined to locate my sister.

My stomach rumbled and I remembered with a sigh the way the evening was supposed to have gone down: a nice steak dinner at Grunkly's. Now, I'd kill for a steak.

Did Pacific Cove do takeout? There were some things about New York I'd never get over missing.

Why had I even left? I sighed as I pulled open the front door and stepped out into the darkened hallway. Before my vision could adjust, I heard a rustling. A chill zipped up my spine, my senses going on high alert.

Who was here?

I froze, pressing myself against Rachel's apartment door, feeling vulnerable. There'd already been one murder tonight. What if . . .

Heavy footsteps sounded on the floor and my blood pressure skyrocketed. I was a sitting duck! What would I do if this person attacked me?

Then the inevitable happened.

My stomach growled.

A man's voice called out. "Rachel?"

The voice was deep, low, and very manly indeed.

I was silent, speechless.

Suddenly the man approached. "I can't see. Who's there?"

I cleared my throat. "Not Rachel."

The man fussed with something. "Sorry, it's dark."

"I'm Rachel's sister," I said.

The man was upon me. He had a cell phone in his hand and waved the light at me. "Ah! Rachel's sister?"

I couldn't make out his face. Only his form. Tall and imposing. He wore dark clothes. Was this the man who watched me from the doorway of DelVecchio's? Goose bumps rose on my skin and I shivered.

Was I in danger?

Could this man be the murderer?

The vodka was making the hallway spin. Why had I drunk so much?

I couldn't think of anything to say, but my stomach rumbled again.

"You hungry? I always cook for Rachel after the bar

closes. You must be hungry now, too." He took hold of my arm and pulled me toward his apartment. "How about veal piccata?"

I staggered along the corridor, leaning a little too much on him. "Whoa," was all I could muster.

He chuckled and steadied me by grabbing my arm. "Did you have a few too many greyhounds tonight?"

I suddenly giggled uncontrollably. "Sorry, I . . . I've had a rough night."

"Me too," he said. "I just closed the restaurant, but I have a good bottle of Chianti here. It goes nicely with the veal. You'll love it."

Some part of my mind was warning me off. I didn't even know this guy; why in the world was I following him into his apartment? And yet, the lure of food was too great. Veal and Chianti, no less?

Bring it!

"I'm Gus, by the way. Gus DelVecchio." He stuck out his hand and I shook it.

"I'm Maggie."

His hand was warm in mine and I realized he wasn't letting go.

"What about Rachel?" he asked. "Is she hungry?"

"Uh . . . no . . ."

He let go of my hand and pulled a key from his pocket. He unlocked the door and held it open for me. I walked into his apartment.

The apartment was the mirror image of Rachel's, only his was tidy and masculine, the décor a sexy red and brown with leather chairs and glass tables. There were a few framed art pieces on the wall: still lifes with fruit, ham, cheese, and wine.

My empty belly was about to howl out a complaint, so I clamped my hand over it and pressed.

Gus looked over at me with a curious look on his face. "Are you okay?"

I gave him a tight smile.

"What happened at the bar tonight?" he asked. "There were police there and it was closed for Yappy Hour."

He didn't know.

I was still sworn to secrecy, wasn't I? I wasn't supposed to say anything until next of kin had been notified. Had Brooks already done that?

"I'm not supposed to talk about it," I said.

Gus immediately uncorked a bottle of wine. "Don't talk about it, then." He smiled, a disarmingly charming smile. "I don't want you to talk anyway. Just eat."

"I bet you say that to all the girls."

He laughed. "Guilty as charged."

He poured the wine and walked to the kitchen. I followed him, sipping on the fragrant full-bodied wine.

The kitchen was set up for a professional chef, complete with a commercial oven and a million steel-bottom pots and pans hanging overhead.

Gus pulled the meat, a couple of eggs, a lemon, a jar of capers, and a fresh bunch of parsley from the fridge.

"Can I help?" I asked.

He put a large sauté pan over medium heat and added some olive oil. "Can you cook?"

I smiled. "Do frozen dinners count?"

A horrified expression crossed his face. "No. Have a seat." He pulled out a kitchen chair for me and proceeded to coat the veal cutlets in flour and egg. They sizzled when he popped them into the pan. In no time, the kitchen was filled with the heavenly scent of frying meat.

He whipped up the sauce, then plated the food and topped off my wine. "Eat," he instructed.

I didn't exactly do as I was told, I more or less *inhaled* the food.

He chatted as I chewed, telling me about his stint at the Culinary Academy in San Francisco. After a bit, he asked, "Where's Rachel?"

"I'm not sure," I confided.

Gus got a wicked little glint in his eye. "You know, my business partner, Dan, didn't show up for work today. Maybe they're together."

I almost choked on the veal. "Uh . . ."

"You know they were dating, right? I thought they broke up a couple weeks ago. At least that's what Dan said. And he sure moped around enough about it. But today, when he didn't show at work, I figured maybe they—"

"No!"

"What?"

I bit my lip. "Uh . . ." What now? I knew I wasn't supposed to say anything and yet . . .

When I hesitated, Gus repeated, "Well, anyway, I figure they were probably together tonight—"

I thumped the table with my hand. "No!"

Gus lurched back, startled. "What is it? Is something wrong with the food?"

Suddenly my hands were shaking. I couldn't go on letting this man think that his partner was alive.

"Dan is dead," I blurted out.

Gus's eyes grew to the size of saucers. "What do you mean?"

"This afternoon. That's why the police were at the bar."

Gus stared at me, one hand clasped over his mouth.

"Dan was killed inside the bar. I found him. I'm sorry I didn't tell you earlier. The police asked me not to say anything. They wanted to notify the next of kin before—"

Gus shook his head. "Are you sure? It can't be. Do you even know Dan? Maybe it wasn't him."

"Yolanda identified him. Officer Brooks confirmed . . ." I reached for Gus's hand, but he stood, pulling away from me.

"I'm so sorry," I said.

"How? How did he die?"

"I really don't know. I found him on the floor. I'm sure the police . . ."

Gus looked around the room as if suddenly lost. "I . . . Excuse me one moment, Maggie, I want to call his folks." He glanced at his watch. "They live back east. It'll be early morning there now . . . but . . ."

I stood. "Of course. I should go."

He grabbed my shoulders abruptly. "No. Please. Stay. I just . . ."

"Okay, no problem. Go ahead and call them."

He left the room, and a heavy sadness enveloped me. I hated to have been the one to break the news to him. I should have listened to Officer Brooks. Why did I have to stick my nose into it? Let the professionals handle it.

As I waited for Gus, I finished my veal piccata. I was tempted to lick my plate, but figured that was in extremely poor taste. I mean, who even had an appetite after finding a dead guy?

Me, apparently.

I poured myself some more wine and sipped, waiting for Gus to return. When he did, it was evident he'd been crying.

"I'm sorry, this is really a shock. Dan was my best friend. He was like my brother." Gus looked away from me, his eyes searching the room, his shoulders slumped.

"I understand," I said, feeling the sadness grip my heart. What would I do if something happened to Rachel?

"Were you able to reach his parents?" I asked.

Gus shook his head. "I got their voice mail. I didn't have the heart to leave a message." He dragged a hand through his dark hair. "I cook Thanksgiving dinner for these people . . . they're like my family." He took a deep ragged breath. "I'll try them again later."

He sat at the table next to me.

"Dan and I met at the Culinary Academy. It was his idea for the restaurant. He'd run it and I'd be head chef, because he couldn't cook to save his life—" Gus paled and his voice hitched. "I mean . . ." He shook his head. "I can't believe he's gone."

We sat in silence for a moment, letting the gravity of it sink in.

Gus poured himself a glass of wine. "Well, Dan wouldn't want me sitting around crying, that's for damn sure." He pressed his lips together and seemed to pull resolve from within.

I fidgeted in the chair and determined to pull on the same internal resolve Gus had reached. I cleared my throat. "What made you think Dan was with Rachel?" I tried to ignore the pit that formed in my stomach as I asked the question.

Gus frowned. "What?"

"Earlier you said you thought Dan might have been with Rachel. Why did you think that?"

Gus shrugged. "He talked about her constantly. Said he was going to win her back."

By threatening to bring Alcohol Beverage Control down on her?

Or had the letter been a ploy? Perhaps an excuse to see Rachel?

I wondered if Gus even knew about the letter.

"What do you think happened?" Gus asked. "I mean,

what strikes a man down in his prime? Did he have an aneurism, a heart attack or . . . ?" He shook his head, frowning. "He was so healthy."

"Gus, no. I don't think it was a natural cause."

Gus blinked at me rapidly. "What do you mean? Not a natural cause . . ."

An image of the magnum bottle beside Dan flashed across my mind and I felt nauseous. "I think someone killed him, Gus."

Gus shook his head, clearly in denial. "No, no, that can't be. Who would hurt Dan?"

"That's what I wanted to ask you."

"Everyone loved Dan," Gus said.

Clearly not everyone.

In the silence that followed, Gus abruptly stood and then sat again. He drummed his fingers on the table, and then fixed his eyes upon me. "Maggie, you have to help me. The police are going to think I killed Dan."

Chapter Eight

I woke up with a throat as dry as sandpaper and a pounding headache. I glanced around the room, completely disoriented. Where was I?

And then suddenly it came flooding back. I'd found a dead guy, Rachel was missing, and I'd passed out at the hot Italian guy's place—the guy who thought he might be suspect numero uno.

My head throbbed out a rhythm similar to Beethoven's Fifth.

Good God, why had I drank so much? It certainly didn't solve any of my problems.

On the night table was a tall glass of water. Apparently, Gus had left it for me. What a nice guy. Still, I couldn't be too careful. If what he'd blurted out last night was true, he had a lot to gain from Dan's death.

Like half ownership of DelVecchio's.

We had talked into the late hours of the night. He'd been emotional about losing his friend and, let's face it, I wanted the company.

But what had I agreed to? He'd asked me to help him

find out who killed Dan. But I wasn't qualified to investigate anything. That's what the police were supposed to do, right?

And what about Rachel? Where was she really? I wasn't buying the elopement story. That seemed crazy. There's no way she'd eloped because, if that was true, I would have found something on her computer. Searches for a marriage license, or a list of best places to elope, even a search on Vegas, but I hadn't found a thing.

I just couldn't believe it.

If she had met someone online, then I certainly would have found evidence of him; aside from the few chats, there were no texts, photos, or even a sweater he'd left in her closet.

Then a terrible thought tugged at my consciousness. What if the person who killed Dan had kidnapped Rachel?

Or worse . . .

I shuddered to think about it.

I thought back to the last communication I'd had from Rachel. A text . . . How did I even know it was from her? Anyone could have sent it. All I really knew was that it had come from Rachel's phone, but if she'd lost it or someone had stolen the phone . . .

I groped for my cell and tried her number again.

Voice mail!

The smell of bacon wafted through the apartment.

Oh goodness. Gus was cooking me breakfast.

I slipped out of the covers and found that I was fully clothed—wrinkled, but clothed nonetheless. There was a bathroom attached to the master bedroom, and I took advantage of the chance to wash my face. Gus had left a new toothbrush alongside a fresh set of towels. He was thoughtful, I'd give him that. Then a nagging little voice reminded me that a murderer had to be thoughtful to commit a crime and get away with it.

I couldn't let my guard down until the police had arrested the killer. I pushed the thought from my mind that my own sister had plenty of motive and her disappearance could also be self-imposed.

Was she on the run?

I stepped out of the bedroom and peeked into the living room. A rolled-up blanket and pillow were on the couch. Obviously, Gus had given up his room to me. He'd fed me and made sure I'd been comfortable last night and this morning. How could I think this man could have anything to do with Dan's death?

I crossed into the hallway and called out, "Is that bacon I smell?"

"No!" Gus answered. "Pancetta."

Murderers didn't cook pancetta for their guests for breakfast!

He smiled as I came into the kitchen. He looked refreshed this morning. His eyes were bright and clear; gone were the red rims from the weeping he'd done the night before.

He picked up a pair of tongs and placed the pancetta on a plate for me, then he slid an omelet alongside it and handed me the plate. "Did you find the towels and toothbrush?"

"Yes, thank you. I appreciate you letting me stay the night."

He grinned and my knees went a little jelly and weak. Did he have to have such a killer smile?

"Don't worry about it. You weren't in any shape to go home last night. It was my fault anyway. I shouldn't have given you Chianti in your condition."

"You didn't make me drink it," I said.

He chuckled. "I'll make you drink this though. It'll cure anything." He steamed some milk in a small aluminum pitcher, poured it into a cup, then added some espresso with a flourish. When he handed me the demitasse cup and saucer, I saw that he'd made a heart on top of the coffee for me.

I laughed. "It smells heavenly!"

From an overhead cabinet, he pulled out a small bottle of pain relievers and shook out two brown pills. "These are just backup."

"Are you part angel?" I asked.

He chuckled. "No one has ever accused me of that."

"Well, you're acting the part this morning," I said, digging into my omelet. After one bite I stared at Gus.

"Is something wrong?" he asked.

"This is the best omelet I've had in my life."

He smiled. "I don't do breakfast at DelVecchio's yet, but I'm thinking about opening for a Sunday brunch soon." His handsome face grew serious, almost sad. "At least that's what Dan had wanted to do. He had big plans for us, but now . . ." He waved his hands around as if he didn't know what else to say and wanted to drop the topic.

"Have you been able to reach his folks yet?" I asked.

Before Gus could answer, there was a knock at the door. Gus looked puzzled. "Excuse me," he said, walking out of the kitchen toward the living room. When he opened the front door the voice of Officer Brooks floated down the hallway.

Oh no!

How was I going to explain the fact that I'd spent the night at Gus's place? It had been completely innocent, that was true—Gus was a perfect gentleman—but still, it looked awful. At the very least, I showed poor judgment in drowning my stress with vodka last night.

This was sure to get Officer Brooks and me off on the wrong foot. Inanely, the thought of hiding under the table crossed my mind.

No! Ridiculous!

Behind a kitchen swinging door?

Don't invite him in, Gus, I thought, hoping to send him the message telepathically. Don't invite him in!

The voices were getting louder, aka closer.

"Smells good in here," Brooks said.

I stood, then sat. Panic flooded me and my legs began to shake.

Could I dash back into Gus's bedroom? No! That would look even worse!

"Come on in," Gus said. "I'll make you an espresso."

Darn it!

The kitchen doorway filled with Officer Brooks's form. A look of surprise crossed his face, then passed as he quickly composed his features back into a neutral expression.

"Maggie," he said by way of greeting.

I stood. "Hello, Officer."

Did my voice sound warbly? A little guilty?

Now not only had I been caught at Gus's, but soon he'd find out that I'd spilled the beans about Dan.

Gus entered the kitchen and looked between Brooks and myself, assessing the situation.

As they stood next to each other, I realized they looked like complete opposites. Brooks was an all-American guy, with blond hair and blue eyes and an open stance—the kind that said, what you see is what you get. Gus, on the other hand, was the Latin-lover type: dark hair, dark eyes, and an aura of mystery surrounding him.

"What are you doing here?" Officer Brooks asked me.

Gus turned his back to Brooks and began to steam milk

at the espresso machine. "She came to ask me about Rachel," he said smoothly. "I haven't seen her since Thursday, though."

My shoulders eased down from around my ears. Gus was going to cover for me.

Brooks looked from me to Gus.

I did my best to keep my eyes wide and look innocent. After all, I was innocent! The worst that I could be accused of was telling Gus about Dan. Could that mess up an investigation?

Gus handed Brooks the small, white espresso cup; he'd made a little picture of a smoking gun in the steamed milk. Brooks ignored the design and gulped the espresso down.

"Thank you, Gus. I'm sorry, I didn't know you had company, but I'd like to speak to you about something rather unpleasant. Can you come down to the station?"

Gus's brows flew up. "The station? What's going on?"

Brooks glared at me. "I'm not at liberty to say."

Why the glare? Did he suspect that I had told?

I scooped the final forkful of omelet into my face and tried to hide my no-doubt guilty expression.

Gus cleared my plate and loaded it into the dishwasher. "I'm sorry that I have to go now, Maggie. Come by the restaurant tonight. I'll make you dinner."

Brooks watched me, presumably assessing my reaction to Gus.

"Oh, Gus. Thank you for the offer," I said. "But I think I have to work." I looked at Brooks. "Can we open The Wine and Bark tonight?"

"Yes, my crime scene tech is done. You're clear to reopen this evening," Brooks said.

Gus pressed his full lips together. After a moment he said, "A rain check, then."

I cringed.

Really? Did he have to say the same thing Brooks had said only last night?

I shifted uncomfortably in my chair.

The man had made me a superb dinner the evening before, saved me from stumbling home in the dark drunk, and now had just filled my belly with the best omelet of my life, and here I was, completely ungrateful.

"Who could turn down your cooking, Gus?" I said, attempting to sidestep the awkwardness.

Gus smiled, while Brooks's eyes narrowed.

"Are you ready to come to the station now?" Brooks asked.

"Yes," Gus said. "Can I drive myself? Or . . ."

"You can ride with me," Brooks said.

Gus stiffened. "Right. Okay, then. Let's go."

I stood and we marched out of the kitchen and into the apartment hallway.

"Do you want a ride home, Maggie?" Brooks asked.

"No, thank you," I said. "I need to go check in on my great-uncle."

Brooks nodded, then said rather possessively in front of Gus, "We're still on for our date tomorrow, right, Maggie?"

My heart surged.

We were still on for tomorrow and he'd just called our "drink" together a "date"!

Gus flashed me a look, and then I was immediately nervous and felt guilty that Brooks had said it in front of him.

"Right," I said self-consciously.

What was going on? How had I managed to get the attention of these two handsome men in such a short time in California, when in New York, I'd been invisible?

Must be the fresh air.

Chapter Nine

I walked on the beach toward Grunkly's house, hoping the salt air would clear my head. Instead, the constant pounding of the tide seemed to increase my headache. It was early enough that only a few joggers were out, but their footsteps were hammering such a steady beat that I thought I was going mad. My agitation grew as I noticed it was a rising tide, and the water level kept getting closer and closer, finally soaking my feet.

It seemed the world was closing in on me.

When I arrived at Grunkly's, I knocked on his door and waited.

"It's me, Uncle Ernest. Maggie!"

No answer.

I knocked again, worry snaking around my shoulders. Where was he? Why wasn't he answering the door? Had he fallen? Was he hurt?

I extracted my cell phone from my pocket and dialed his number.

He picked up on the third ring. "Is that you at the door, Magpie?" Grunkly said.

Relief flooded me at hearing Grunkly's voice. "Yes it's me. Are you all right? Can you get to the door?"

"There's a key under the mat," he said.

I hurried to hang up and dig the key out from under the mat, panicked to see Grunkly's face. A fierce love for him suddenly overwhelmed me. Aside from Rachel, he was my only living relative, and now Rachel was . . .

I let myself inside and rushed to the living room only to find him glued to the TV. While Grunkly owned many horses, his recent favorite, Winged Arrow, was racing today. The beautiful stallion filled the screen.

I stared at Grunkly, taking in the scene. The architecture of his house was gorgeous: rock walls, exposed wooden beams, and high ceilings, but his housekeeping was abysmal. The living room was littered with stacks of paper, electronics on the floor, and a broken fan. A table had been shoved aside, cockeyed, to make room for his big-screen TV, which his leather easy chair was parked in front of.

There was also a graveyard of old TVs, VCRs, DVD players, and AM/FM radios along the west-side wall of the dining room. Grunkly flat out refused to throw anything out. Even if it no longer worked or was obsolete, he could always find a use for it, like, say, as a paperweight.

"Is that why you couldn't open the door?" I demanded, pointing to the TV. "I was worried about you, and you're watching a horse race!"

"Shhh. I have five hundred on Winged Arrow to place," he said. Grunkly was wearing an old blue ball cap, which I knew he wore for luck, along with a flannel shirt. Never mind the fact that it was already eighty degrees outside, Grunkly was always cold, and now that he was so thin, the problem seemed even worse.

"Hand me that blanket, would you, Mags?" He pointed

at a wool blanket that was haphazardly thrown on the arm of the sofa.

I stepped over three stacks of newspapers and crossed to the sofa. I handed him the blanket, which he wrapped over his legs. I looked longingly at the window. I wanted to pry it open, but knew that Grunkly hated fresh air. He'd only tell me it was making him cold. As it was, the house smelled of stale cigarettes.

There was no place for me to sit, except the couch, which was bulging with mail, some flimsy cardboard boxes, and a few soiled t-shirts. I picked my way through some items and moved a few things to the floor to clear a spot for myself in order to sit down. "Grunkly, do you know where Rachel is? Do you know anything about a cruise or her eloping?"

Grunkly waved the remote control at me. "Two minutes to post, Magpie."

"Grunkly! I found a dead guy yesterday, at Rachel's bar!"

He shook his head. "That's terrible," he said, in the most insincere tone possible, which clearly telegraphed he wasn't listening at all.

"Grunkly—"

"Ah ha."

"Is that all you have to say?"

"It certainly is exciting." He held up a finger to silence me.

I fidgeted on the couch. I knew I had to either turn off the TV and risk his wrath or just wait the three minutes for the race to finish. The bugle sounded and the horses were off. Grunkly's pick, Winged Arrow, started out strong.

"Go, baby, go!" Grunkly yelled.

Winged Arrow rounded the first lap fast, neck and neck with Zesty Marzipan. The announcer's voice blared out through the speakers: "Zesty Marzipan is favored to win, but Winged Arrow is making a good show."

"Go Winged Arrow," I cried, getting caught up in the excitement.

Winged Arrow lurched forward, pulling into the lead.

Oh my God, Winged Arrow was going to win!

"Come on, Winged Arrow, come on!" I yelled.

Another horse rounded out the top tier and Winged Arrow fell behind a bit, neck and neck with the other horse.

Grunkly stood and shook his fists at the TV. "Go, Winged Arrow, go!"

Another horse approached, and Winged Arrow fell to third.

"Oh no!" I said.

"Get the lead out!" Grunkly screamed.

Suddenly they rounded the last corner and another horse passed Winged Arrow. Then another.

"No! No!" Grunkly said.

Winged Arrow gave it all he had, but it looked like he was running out of steam. One by one, each horse passed him.

Grunkly clasped his head in his hands. "No, no, no!"

"And Zesty Marzipan wins by a nose, followed by Night Runner in second and Daisy Mama in third. Winged Arrow brings up the rear," the announcer said.

Grunkly slumped back into his chair; his shoulders caved in and he looked completely defeated. "Dead last!" he said.

"Yeah, sorry about that, Grunkly." I surprised myself by actually caring. Watching the horse race had been exciting, not to mention a stress release, but winning would have been much better—now it was just more of a damper on my mood.

We sat in silence for a moment, and then Grunkly flicked off the TV. He turned to me. "So, how are you doing, Magpie? Any news?"

"Well, yes, thanks for asking. The manager at DelVecchio's is dead. And Rach is missing. One of the doggie ladies said she thought she eloped."

Grunkly scratched his chin. At his age, he was pretty hard to shock, but I got the distinct impression I'd done just that. After a moment, he said, "I can't believe that. Missing? Eloped? That's nonsense!"

"But I don't know where she is. I can't explain it. And worse, I think the manager from DelVecchio's was threatening Rachel about bringing in the health department . . . it makes it look like she had motive. . . ."

Grunkly frowned. "No! Rachel wouldn't hurt a fly."

"Did she say anything to you about leaving? About where she was going?"

Grunkly's eyes flicked over to the TV's dark screen. I got a bad inkling that it was likely she'd told him something, only now he couldn't recall because he'd probably been caught up watching something on the TV. He shrugged. "I don't think so."

I felt completely deflated. I looked around the house at the mess and clutter. "Okay, well, let me help you clean up a little, and if you remember anything—"

"Whoa! Clean up?" He held up a hand and waved me off. "No, no. I know where everything is, don't bother."

"It's no bother."

"Please!" he said.

"I can't leave you while the house is in such disarray, Grunk, let me at least vacuum."

He glanced around the floor, cluttered with objects. Of course, to vacuum we'd have to move everything. He hesitated, but I jumped into action, lifting a couple stacks of paper onto the dining room table.

"Wait, wait," Grunkly cried. "Those are my to-be-paid bills; if you move them around I won't be able to find them."

I placed the mail on the table. "Grunk, we gotta start someplace."

A sour expression crossed his face. He didn't agree with me. After all, if you live eighty years in a place and all is well, why change anything?

"I can't let you keep the place like this. No nurse is going to want to work—"

"That's right!" he said adamantly. "No nurse!"

I flipped through his mail. "Do you need help paying these? Where's your checkbook?"

He smiled. "Now you're talking! Leave the vacuum for next time. Help me with the bills. It's getting so hard to read those things. Is the print getting smaller?"

"No."

"I think it is." He shuffled across the room and pulled out a checkbook from under another stack of papers. "I think they're printing smaller to save paper. Be green. Isn't that the latest thing?"

We sat together in the dining room and walked through his bills step by step. When we got to an insurance statement, I asked, "What's this?"

Grunkly took the paper from me and squinted at it. He tried on several pairs of glasses, one without an arm that he had to hold in place, one pair that were bifocals, and then a third pair with black rims. "Ah!" he said. "These are the good ones."

"If you throw out the other two pairs, you won't get confused," I said.

He scowled at me. "Those are my backups!"

"Right."

He looked at the statement again. "Oh, yeah. This is the building insurance for The Wine and Bark."

Grunkly owned the building and Rachel rented out the space from him. "It's past due, Grunk."

He scratched at the stubble on his chin. "That's because I was in the hospital. Let's pay it now."

The date on the notice indicated it'd been mailed far after Grunkly's heart attack, but he'd just as soon have another heart attack before he admitted it actually got lost in the clutter here.

We proceeded through the rest of the mail and sorted all the bills out. There were several calculators on the table. Each one had a different company logo, all freebie promotional items that he'd collected throughout the years. I punched the number nine on one of the calculators and it stuck.

"I think you can toss this one, Grunkly."

He picked up the calculator and put it to the side. "Oh no, Mags, it's perfectly fine."

"The nine sticks."

He fondled the calculator possessively. "I'll use it for figuring out lower sums."

I sighed. Getting Grunkly to throw anything away would be a miracle.

When we were done paying the bills and balancing his checkbook, Grunkly looked out at me over his reading glasses. "You know, Maggie, just between you and me, I think if Rachel were in trouble she'd go to Stag's Leap."

Stag's Leap was a cabin in the woods that Grunkly owned. When Rachel and I were young girls we spent our summers there.

"Do you still own Stag's Leap?" I asked.

He glared at me. "Magpie! You know I don't ever sell my real estate! That's for you and Rachel when I kick the bucket."

I wrapped my arms around him and pressed my cheek to his. "Thank you, Grunk. I know."

He patted my back. "Do you want to take a drive out to Stag's Leap and see if we can find her?"

"You don't believe she's eloped?"

Grunkly shook his head.

"Me either."

My shoulders relaxed. Grunkly was right. Rachel was likely at the cabin. She had probably given Abigail a tall tale about eloping to cover up the trouble she was having with Dan. It was just like Rachel to run off instead of heading things off.

"Whatdya say? Road trip?"

"I don't have a car."

"We'll take the Cadillac!" he said.

I laughed. Grunkly's Cadillac was over forty years old. "Does it even start?"

"Sure! I turn it over every week. Otherwise, the battery dies." He coughed suddenly, and his face took on a gray pallor. I realized that visiting with me and paying the bills was taking its toll on his stamina.

"I have to work at Rachel's bar tonight. Whatdya say I find a ride to the cabin and I'll report back to you?"

He shook my hand. "Deal!"

Chapter Ten

I headed over to The Wine and Bark early. A creepy sensation was crawling up my skin. I couldn't shake the feeling that I would find another dead body. I knew, of course, that it was highly unlikely, but the memory of finding Yolanda standing over Dan lingered.

Today the "happy vibe" front door didn't look so happy with the yellow crime scene tape across it. I yanked the tape off and wadded it up. I tried the handle on the door. It was locked, and I was glad of the fact.

No surprises.

The bar was dark and I immediately flicked on the light switch before stepping foot inside. It was eerily empty, only the hum of the ice maker to keep me company. I tossed the wadded-up tape in the trash can behind the bar and crossed to where Dan had been on the floor the day prior. The spot where the blood had pooled hadn't been cleaned.

Really? The police had left this for me?

The crime scene technicians must have taken samples, and off they went, leaving a mess in their wake.

I prepared a bucket of hot, soapy water and went to work. I bit back the bile that threatened as I mopped the floor. As I was rinsing the mop, a woman with pink spiked hair stuck her head into the bar.

"Hiya!" she said, entering and approaching me. "Are you Maggie?"

"Yes."

"Yolanda told me about you. I'm Evie Xtreme. My band the Howling Hounds is playing tonight. It's sort of a dress rehearsal for the Tails and Tiaras fund-raiser next weekend."

I glanced at the mop bucket of bloody water and wondered what else Yolanda had told her.

Her eyes followed my glance, and she gasped when she realized there was blood in the water. She covered her mouth in shock, then dropped her hand and asked, "What happened? Was there an accident?"

"Yes," I said, not sure what else to add.

"Oh God, I hope everything is all right," Evie said.

I shrugged, unsure what I was supposed to say. Certainly, publicizing the fact that someone had been found dead in the bar wouldn't help business.

Evie looked away from the mop water and said, "My band will be here in a few. Mind if I start setting up?"

"No, that's fine," I replied, glad not to have to explain about Dan. "Do you need help setting up?"

"Nah," she said. "I'll just move some of the tables over there so we can get our amp system going. Where's Rachel? Will she be back in time for the fund-raiser next weekend?"

The question of the day.

The more I considered what Grunkly had said, the more likely it sounded. If Rachel needed space, she would have found solace at Stag's Leap. It seemed more rational than eloping . . . but then again, *rational* wasn't a word I'd used to describe Rachel.

I watched Evie as she pushed the chairs and tables aside. She was rail thin and barely seemed to have the strength to move the tables, which all had wide wooden bases. I helped her push one of the tables, and she flashed me a big crooked-toothed grin.

The bar door pushed open and a man in dark clothes and combat boots stepped in. Involuntarily, I stiffened.

"Hey Bish," Evie said. She turned to me and said, "Bishop is our guitar player. Stage name, The Burning Bishop."

He grunted at us. He had a piercing in his lip and bulging biceps. His stance was imposing and I felt vaguely threatened.

Suddenly the bar seemed too dark, and I rushed to prop open the door. While I searched around on the patio for something to secure the heavy door, I saw Gus DelVecchio approaching. He waved at me enthusiastically.

"Hi, Maggie! Getting the bar ready?"

"Yeah, we have a band tonight," I said. "It's a dress rehearsal for the big fund-raiser next weekend."

Gus walked over to me. "I'm sorry our breakfast was interrupted this morning."

He grabbed my hand and a jolt of electricity coursed through me, which I tried to ignore.

"That wasn't your fault. What did Officer Brooks tell you? Do you have any more information about Dan?"

Are you a suspect?

"He told me about Dan. I remembered you weren't supposed to have told me, so I pretended I didn't know, but then somehow he knew that I'd called Dan's parents last night, so he called me a liar. I'm afraid it didn't go well."

"I'm sorry. I feel like it's my fault," I said.

Not only had I gotten Gus into trouble, but now Officer Brooks would think I was a blabbermouth. It seemed like I'd gotten off on the wrong foot with practically everyone in town. A heaviness settled into my belly.

"It's not your fault. How could it be your fault?" He sighed. "Anyway, I managed to walk out of there without having to hire a defense attorney. So that's a bit of an accomplishment. But it doesn't bring Dan back." He ran a hand through his thick dark hair and for a moment looked like a lost little boy. I fought the impulse to hug him.

Across the patio, Yolanda and Beepo clicked and clacked toward us, Beepo on his Day-Glo leash and Yolanda sporting leather pants and leopard halter top.

Gus watched her approach and suddenly made himself scarce. "I'll catch you later, Maggie," he said, giving my hand a final squeeze and retreating into the restaurant.

So he wasn't friendly with Yolanda.

"Wow, that's some outfit," I said to her when she reached me.

She flicked her hair. "It's my dancing outfit."

Beepo snarled at my feet and I inched away from him.

"He won't bite you," Yolanda said.

But he might relieve himself on my shoes!

"Yolanda, do you know if Rachel was dating someone?" I asked.

Yolanda crinkled her delicate nose. "As far as I know, she wasn't. Why?"

I shrugged. "It's not important." I wasn't ready to confide in her. First, I didn't know her all that well, but more importantly, she didn't seem all that trustworthy at the moment, what with the fact that I'd found her hovering over Dan less than twenty-four hours ago.

Yolanda, Beepo, and I walked together toward the painted blue and orange door of The Wine and Bark. I must say the bar door looked decidedly more cheerful without the crime scene tape.

Before pushing open the door, Yolanda leaned in to me and said. "Do you know if we've been given the all clear about Dan?"

Beepo yapped at the front door of the bar, clearly indicating he wanted in.

I shrugged. "I don't know any more than I did yesterday. Do you?"

She nodded. "I went to the station to give my statement to Officer Gottlieb." She quirked an eyebrow at me. "Did you do that?"

"Yes. I gave my statement to Officer Brooks."

A disapproving look crossed her face, and Beepo barked at me. Evidently, she was irritated with me, and Beepo wanted to make sure I knew it.

Did Yolanda have the hots for Officer Brooks?

I refrained from asking, but if one odd look from her caused Beepo to bark, I hesitated to think what he'd do if she suddenly raised her voice at me.

"I think Dan's next of kin have already been notified," Yolanda said.

In other words, she meant we were at liberty to gossip.

"What do you think happened?" I asked.

"Well, obviously someone whacked him over the head with that magnum bottle," Yolanda said.

"Right, but who do you think did it?" I asked. "Any rumors?"

Yolanda made an exaggerated head gesture toward DelVecchio's. Anger coiled around my middle. So that was it, everyone was going to blame Gus. Forget about innocent until proven guilty.

Suddenly a middle-aged woman, dressed in turquoise from head to toe, sauntered down the cobblestone path toward us. Under one arm she carried a roll of canvas, and in the other hand was a wooden box.

Yolanda shrieked, "Mrs. Clemens!" She took off at a mad dash toward the woman, with Beepo in hot pursuit.

Ah, the paw-casso practice run, how could I forget?

Across the street, a woman and a man, both with small dogs, huddled around Mrs. Clemens. My clientele was arriving, better get back to work.

I entered the bar and found that Evie and the guitar player were in a heated argument. They immediately got quiet when they saw me.

"Hi," I said. "Looks like we're about to get busy. Do you need anything before I get to work?" Evie shook her head, but the guitar player approached the bar.

"How about a fire hydrant?" he asked.

"What?"

"It's a cocktail. Get it? Fire hydrant for The Burning Bishop?" I must have flashed him a look, because he laughed and said, "I'll tell you how to make it."

"Oh, right." I put on the Day-Glo apron with the logo of The Wine and Bark on it and crossed to behind the bar.

"Gin, pineapple juice, and cranberry, and a splash of grenadine," he said. "You never made one of these before?"

I shook my head.

I wondered if Rachel had left me a cheat sheet with her specialty cocktails anywhere. I rummaged around behind the bar, but found nothing, which of course was no surprise. Leaving me instructions would have taken planning on her part, and Rachel never planned.

The Burning Bishop emptied his drink in one pass, then burped. He slammed the glass down on the bar and said, "Another, Mother."

"Bish," Evie whined. "No more. We got to play."

He waved a hand at her. "You're not the boss of me."

I felt like I was witnessing children on a playground on the verge of a fight. The door to the bar swung open and a tall African American man stepped in.

"Hey, there Smasher," Bishop said. He turned to me. "This here is our drummer. Smasher, this is Maggie."

The man graced me with a charming smile as he thumped Bishop on the back. "Are you staying out of trouble?" He winked at me as he ushered Bishop back to the makeshift stage. "Ready for a sound check, Evie?"

Through the window of the bar, I could see a crowd forming on the patio. Mrs. Clemens, Yolanda, and several of the crew from yesterday, including Brenda, Max, and their dogs. The door flung open and they poured into the bar like a waterfall, loud and continuous.

Oh God! Was I ready for this?

Brenda flanked the bar. "Two greyhounds! One for me and the other for Mrs. Clemens."

"How about a pitcher of saltys?" Yolanda asked the group. "We can take it to a table."

The dogs swirled around, barking and sniffing. Max appeared behind the bar. "Do you need some assistance? I sometimes help Rachel out."

I refrained from throwing myself at him, but my voice said it all as I yelled a grateful "Yes!"

He chuckled. "Okay, ladies, have a seat. I'll bring the drinks." He motioned to them and the throng backed away. The beagle poked its nose around the bar.

"Oh, I have your bunny," I said to the beagle.

The beagle kept his eyes on me while Max said, "Do you? Ah, Bowser and I wondered where that went."

I pulled the pink plush bunny out of my bag and tossed it to Bowser. He caught it midair, his tail swinging back and forth contentedly. After a moment, he dropped the bunny at Max's feet. Max tossed the bunny on the floor near the table the gang had commandeered, and the beagle obediently went to be with the gang.

I looked around at all the bottles and glasses and felt short of breath.

Max studied my face. "It gets easier," he said. "I tended bar in college."

I nodded numbly.

"Pitcher of salty dogs. Do you know how to make that?"

"Greyhound with salt, right?"

He smiled as he pulled a bottle of Stoli out from the rack. "That's right."

I salted the rims of the glasses. "I thought this was a wine bar. Why all the fancy cocktails?"

"Ay, we usually drink wine only during the work week. Friday Yappy Hour kicks off our weekend celebrating. We love Rachel and the bar. It's super that she provides a place for everyone to hang out with their pets . . . we missed her yesterday."

I nodded.

He poured the vodka over ice and gave me a sidelong glance. "What happened yesterday, by the way?"

I pressed my fingertips into my temples. It would be the never-ending question. Each person would ask me, one by one, until the news had snaked its way into every ear in Pacific Cove. I wondered if posting it on the Internet would be faster.

Before I could say anything, Brenda, followed by her Chihuahua, made her way back to the bar. Max seemed to stand up straighter and puff out his chest. Brenda was dressed all in black save for a pair of teal Manolo Blahnik sandals.

"Maggie, sorry to be a bother, but can I have a treat for

Pee Wee?" Brenda asked. She picked up the small dog and stroked his ears. "We've been out all day and he's been such a dear."

I grabbed a Bark Bite from the bowl nestled near the cash register. No sooner did I hand her one than all the dogs began sniffing wildly and rushing over. I handed out treats to each one.

Brenda patted her flat stomach. "How about for us? Any dogs in blankets ready?"

I glanced at Max for help.

"Oh, we'll get right on that," Max said.

Brenda wiggled her fingers at us and waltzed back to the crowded table. The band started up and the noise level increased, complete with the dogs barking to the Howling Hounds' music.

"I'm supposed to do food, too?" I asked Max.

"Only arf d'oeuvres," he said.

I rolled my eyes and he laughed.

"Don't sweat it. The dogs in blankets are just hot dogs rolled in mini-croissants. Rachel has a ton frozen in the back fridge. All you have to do is turn on the oven."

"That I can handle," I said, heading to the rear of the building and preheating the oven.

I felt like an alien in my own skin. Everyone here seemed really kind and funny, and yet someone had been murdered hours ago in this very building. Was I even safe around these people?

I pulled the dogs in blankets from the freezer and popped them onto a baking sheet. I was hungry and laughed to myself thinking about what kind of meal Gus was cooking up next door at DelVecchio's. Certainly not dogs in blankets.

A warmth filled me as I remembered him squeezing my hand. When I emerged from the back after having put the dogs in blankets in the oven, there was a hubbub at the bar.

Brenda and another woman were huddled with Max, and their respective dogs were circling their feet. The look on the woman's face was a mixture of shock and sadness. When they saw me they immediately descended upon me.

"Yolanda just told us the news about Dan," Max said.

"Why didn't you tell us?" Brenda demanded, her delicate brows furrowing together.

"We . . . uh . . . the police told us not to—"

"I can't believe it!" she said. "Poor Dan! Any ideas who did it, Maggie?"

"It's gotta be Gus," the woman standing next to Brenda said. "He'll be in charge of the whole business, now that Dan's gone. What better motive?"

My heart lurched at the thought that Gus was already tried and convicted by the town. Even the police were looking into him. I suddenly felt conflicted; while I was upset that Gus was being accused of such a horrible thing, a small part of me felt relieved that the police weren't prodding into Rachel's business. Gus had been right—they were going to try to pin it on him. But he didn't strike me as a cold-blooded killer. With the police barking up the wrong tree, *someone* had to figure out who was responsible for Dan's murder.

A sharp beeping sounded throughout the bar, rattling the patrons.

Ack! The smoke detector. I had forgotten the arf d'oeuvres in the oven. I ran toward the back as smoke billowed through the bar.

Darn! I'd burned the arf d'oeuvres.

Chapter Eleven

Beepo appeared at my side; he seemed to be whining about the burnt snacks.

"Thanks for the company, pal," I said, "but I think I got this."

In the main room, the band finished their song and I heard Evie say into the mic, "All right, ya'll, we'll take a little break and be back before you can howl." With that, she let out a long howl that got all the dogs to join in. They were in perfect pitch with the smoke detector.

If I wasn't panicked, I'd have laughed, but as it was, I wanted to tear my hair out and stick a muzzle on the howling dogs.

I pulled the tray of burnt arf d'oeuvres and tossed them into the trash. As I fanned the alarm with a bar towel, Beepo overturned the trash and stuck his nose in it.

I let out a scream and Yolanda materialized at my side.

"Beepo, get out of there," she scolded.

I began to reload the baking sheet with more frozen arf d'oeuvres.

"Maggie, Mrs. Clemens wants to set up now for the paw-cassos," Yolanda said.

"Yeah, okay." I slid the tray back into the oven.

Beepo chewed on an arf d'oeuvre, growled in distaste, and spat it out.

Apparently my cooking was not even fit for a dog.

"She wants to do the paw-cassos on the patio, of course, but . . ." Yolanda looked toward the door, hesitating.

I set the timer for the dogs in blankets and waited for Yolanda to get around to whatever she was hedging over.

She glanced back at me and, in dramatic whisper, said, "It is okay with DelVecchio's?"

Was I supposed to get permission? Hadn't Rachel cleared all this with the restaurant?

The Wine and Bark shared a patio with the restaurant. I couldn't imagine that she wouldn't have already discussed this with them, but knowing that my sister was so spontaneous it didn't surprise me.

I suddenly found myself grateful that Rachel wasn't here, otherwise I might have strangled her.

"Let me guess," I said. "No one asked them?"

Yolanda offered me a tight smile. "Well, I don't know . . . but . . ."

I sighed and breezed past her back to the bar. Max was holding down the fort, pouring wine and cocktails like a pro.

"I have to go next door, Max, and talk to them about using the patio. Can you manage?"

He nodded distractedly. He seemed eager to eavesdrop on Brenda and her friend. That was one benefit to working the bar. Nothing loosened tongues faster than a few doggie-themed cocktails.

I walked out onto the patio and noticed that Bowser had followed me. "No, go back inside," I said.

He dropped the pink plush bunny at my feet.

I stooped to pick it up, and as I did so, his teeth clamped down on it. I released the bunny and so did he. The bunny flopped to the ground.

"Ah, you want to play, huh?"

The sound of hurrying footsteps clicking on the cobblestone path alerted me to company. Abigail strutted down the path with a bright blue baby wading pool tucked under one arm and her Shih Tzu, Missy, tucked under the other.

"Maggie! I'm so glad you're out here. Can you help me with this?" She thrust the pool at me, nearly toppling me over as she rushed to pull the bar door open. "I can't wait to down a few mutt-tinis, what a day I've had!"

She disappeared inside without even so much a second glance back at me.

Who did she think was tending bar? Maybe Max was a regular helper?

I dropped the empty wading pool outside The Wine and Bark. Bowser jumped in and dropped his bunny, barking at me. I laughed as the same waiter from the night before emerged from DelVecchio's onto the shared patio. He wore his uniform, but had a windbreaker still on. He looked like he was ready to leave. He glanced at me, then at the baby pool. He frowned, but said nothing, then turned away toward the cobblestone path.

I hurried after him. "Excuse me. Do you know if Gus has approved—"

The door to The Wine and Bark opened, and Evie and the Howling Hounds, Bish and Smasher, stepped out onto the patio. Evie pulled out a cigarette holder from her jeans pocket; she selected a cigarette and Smasher leaned in to light it for her.

The waiter looked from them to me and said, "Follow

me," as he hurried back into the restaurant. "We're closed tonight," he said by way of explanation for the empty dining room. He ushered me toward the kitchen. I'd been expecting red-checked tablecloths and used Chianti bottles with wax dripping down the sides as candleholders, but instead there were white linen tablecloths and crystal candleholders. There was even a hearth at the far side of the main dining room that looked like it doubled as a pizza oven.

This was one fancy operation.

No wonder Dan had heartburn about sharing the patio with The Wine and Bark.

The kitchen was deserted.

"I thought Gus was back here," the waiter said. "Last night . . . our co-owner . . ." He glanced around the empty kitchen.

"I know."

"Gus called all the staff in to let us know. We're going to be closed this week. But I thought for sure he was still here. He was going to lock up after me." He shrugged. "You can talk to him later. I don't think the pool out there will be a problem tonight."

"Are you looking for me?" a voice called.

"Ah, the office, of course!" the waiter said. He walked me out of the kitchen and pointed down a narrow corridor, where the men's and ladies' rooms were. Past the restrooms was a dimly lit little office.

Gus was seated at an immaculate metal desk. On the desk was a computer, a black touch-tone phone, and a small tensor lamp. Several letters and spreadsheets were lit up in the spill from the lamp. There was a plush blue loveseat across from the desk.

Gus had his hands folded behind his head, his eyes red rimmed and looking strained from sifting through the documents on the desk. He sprang to his feet when he saw me. "Maggie!"

"I'm sorry to disturb you, Gus." I explained to him about the paw-cassos and the baby pool. While I spoke, he surreptitiously slipped the papers into a folder and quietly slipped them into the top drawer of the desk.

When I finished my explanation, he said, "It's no problem, Maggie. We're closed for the week. I gave my staff the time off. We all need to grieve."

What had he been looking at?

I prayed it was nothing that would incriminate my sister.

◇◇◇

By the time I returned to The Wine and Bark, the rehearsal was in full swing. Dogs were playing in the baby pool with chew toys and rubber duckies galore. A photographer had materialized out of nowhere and was taking multiple shots of the dogs in and out of the pool, wrapped in the Day-Glo towels with the Wine and Bark logo embroidered on them.

There was a crowd around Mrs. Clemens, clamoring for paw-cassos. There were pitchers of mutt-tinis flowing, and even the arf d'oeuvres had made it to the tables. I hustled back into the bar to the relative safety of pouring mutt-garitas. Max was tapping his foot along with the Howling Hounds and swinging around bottles of gin as if he were a pro. Thankfully, he seemed happy behind the bar.

"I'm sorry to have abandoned you! I didn't think I'd take so long. You're a lifesaver."

He waved a hand around and grinned. "You can pay me in drinks." He picked up a cocktail that was nestled next to the cash register and held it up in a toast.

"I'm glad to see you're already paying yourself."

"What's your poison?" he asked.

"Nothing today. I overindulged last night."

"I don't blame you after the shock you had." He shook his head. "It's pretty spooky to think that someone was killed right here. Right under our noses."

A woman holding a white Pomeranian ordered a glass of pinot, and I was glad to only have to uncork the bottle and pour. My thoughts slipped back to Rachel. Could she be hiding out at Grunkly's cabin? I hadn't been there since I was a kid. There was no way his Cadillac could make the drive. I'd have to find another ride up there. And then there was the matter of my date with Brooks. I'd have to get up to Stag's Leap and then back home by afternoon. It would mean an early departure.

"Do you have a car, Max?"

Max laughed. "I wish. Don't really need one here, though. It's such a small town."

"Yeah, I have to run an errand in the morning . . . I need a car. . . ."

At that moment, Yolanda sashayed up to the bar, cradling Beepo in her hand. Beepo was wrapped in a Wine and Bark towel, and someone had managed to put a beret on his head, making him look absolutely ridiculous.

"Maggie!" Yolanda screeched. "Everything is going smashingly well. Just divine!" She slurred, "Thank you so much for pulling it off. I had my doubts." She leaned in close to me. "You know, after your . . . ehem . . . confession." The last word she enunciated slowly. Certainly she was referring to my admitting that I wasn't a doggie person.

Beepo let out a string of half barks and yelps as if to agree with her.

I glanced at Max, signaling him to cut Yolanda off. He nodded and filled a tumbler full of ice water for her. She frowned upon seeing it, but gulped it down nevertheless.

Abigail joined her at the bar, her Shih Tzu, Missy, wearing a tiara this evening. She grabbed Beepo out of Yolanda's hand. "Doesn't he look like a prince with this little beret? I love it. I'm going to make them dance together. Maybe we'll have a wedding soon!" she said over her shoulder to Yolanda as she strutted toward the stage and put the dogs down together.

To her credit, Missy appeared to move her tail to the music, but Beepo was only concerned with freeing himself from the beret.

"Is it always this wild?" I asked Max.

He grimaced. "No. I must have poured a little heavy."

"Should I pop some more snacks in the oven to sober them up?"

Shrugging, he said, "People usually go over to DelVecchio's to eat if they get too lit. But they're closed tonight, right?"

I looked out the window across the patio to the darkened restaurant. It felt so disrespectful to have a bar full of people who were happy and dancing while they were dark.

Max picked up our conversation where we'd left off. "So, you need a ride . . . ?"

Yolanda suddenly slammed a hand down on the bar. "Did you say you needed a ride somewhere?"

I hesitated. The last thing in the world I wanted was to drive out to the country with the town busybody herself.

"You've a car, right, Yo?" Max said.

I stepped on his shoe and dug my heel into his toe. His head jerked in my direction, then he burst out laughing as he realized my dilemma.

Brenda joined us at the bar. "Yolanda, are you okay?" she asked in hushed tone.

"Why wouldn't I be okay?" Yolanda fired back, her voice cracking.

Brenda motioned Max for another cocktail, which he whipped up in short order. "Well, because I just heard about Geraldine."

Yolanda's lips curled unnaturally into a snarl. "Oh that." She flicked imaginary lint off her leather pants. "I don't care about that."

"Who's Geraldine?" I asked.

"Shh," Max warned too late.

Yolanda's nostrils flared. "Don't even say her name!"

I glanced from Max to Brenda. Brenda put an arm around Yolanda. "It's okay, honey."

"I'm glad that her poodle is up for best in show," Yolanda said. "I'm glad about it, really," she insisted a little too loudly; only her expression, that of a crazy woman, gave her away.

Abigail, who couldn't see Yolanda's face, joined us from behind. "Oh me, too! I'm so excited about Geraldine. A group of us are going to Carmel in the morning to support her. You'll come, won't you, Yolanda?"

Yolanda suddenly developed an eye twitch.

An idea began to take shape. If I could convince Yolanda to take me to Stag's Leap, then I could grill her about Dan's murder. After all, she had been standing over poor Dan's dead body. Did she have a motive for wanting him dead?

"Actually, Yolanda, I have to run an important errand tomorrow . . . but I don't have a car . . . I was hoping you could give me a ride," I said.

Max flashed me an approving glance.

Yolanda twirled a strand of her blond hair in her hand.

"I'll take you wherever you want to go. It's the least thing I can do after all you've done for us. Please! I have to thank you for pulling this off." She gestured around the bar. "And I have to tell you about next weekend. I'm going to ask a videographer to join us and also a social media consultant. She'll be tweeting real time during the auction, and then we can post the videos on the web for donations afterward."

A videographer, social media consultant, and an auction?

Oh my lord. What had I gotten myself into?

I felt faint. Rachel had to be back for next weekend, there was no way I'd manage to pull it off by myself.

"Uh. I need to look for Rachel. My uncle mentioned she might be at his cabin—"

Yolanda's eyes grew wide. "Stag's Leap?"

I nodded.

She clapped her hands like a child. "Oh goodie! I've always wanted to go to Stag's Leap. Let's leave first thing in the morning!"

Chapter Twelve

Yolanda turned up at my apartment at 8:00 A.M. sharp. She drove a flashy red convertible and leaned on the horn until I came out, not caring if she disrupted the entire sleepy neighborhood. Beepo lounged in the passenger seat, a jaunty bandana tied around his neck. He growled when he saw me.

A strand of Yolanda's blond hair escaped from under a bright polka-dotted scarf that matched her skintight skirt. She wore large gold-rimmed sunglasses and aviator gloves. All that was missing to make it a complete Hollywood scene was to have Beepo in sunglasses.

I wore regular jeans and a navy tank top. Yolanda's lip curled up slightly to match Beepo's growl upon seeing me look so plainly boring.

She was sipping a coffee drink from a paper cup. She motioned to the cup holders and said, "I got a latte for you for the road."

"Thank you," I said, climbing into the passenger seat. Beepo barked madly at being upended.

"Hush, Beepo!" Yolanda scowled.

He stopped barking and scampered onto my lap.

"Uh . . . I don't think . . ."

Yolanda put the convertible in reverse and gunned it out of my apartment house driveway.

Wait!

Was I expected to ride the entire two hours with the dog in my lap?

Beepo dug his little talons into my leg and stuck his tongue out, wagging as the wind ruffled his fur.

Oh, whatever. I suppose it was going to be a choose-your-battles type of day. Now I was glad that I'd worn simple jeans.

"Should I take 101 or the Coast?" Yolanda asked.

"Either way, just head south for about an hour, then we'll head inland."

"I'll take the coast," she said. "Beepo loves looking at the ocean."

Really? How did she know?

"So, you've never been to Stag's Leap?" I asked.

"No," Yolanda said. "But Rachel's talked about it so many times, I feel like I have. High windows overlooking the lake, stone fireplace, huge canopy bed." She wiggled her eyebrows at me, which made me wonder just what type of encounters Rachel had had up at the lake house in recent history.

"I have to warn you, I have no idea what kind of condition it'll be in. My uncle's not the best housekeeper as is, and no one that I know of has been out there in ages. Has Rachel been up there recently, do you know?"

Yolanda shrugged a shoulder, then waved her hand around as if to dismiss the question. "Don't worry. I'm up for an adventure."

I studied her for a moment: her nose, straight and narrow; sunglasses perched covering her catlike eyes; more blond curly hair escaping the scarf and waving in the wind. "Not such a dramatic adventure as that other night, I hope."

She clasped a hand over her heart. "Goodness, no. That was truly awful. Poor Dan. I can't think the police would dare think Rachel has anything to do with it, though."

I took a deep breath. I certainly hoped that was the case.

"So who's this Geraldine and what's so bad about her dog winning best in show?"

Beepo howled as if possessed.

"Geraldine is a long story. But suffice it to say, thank you for getting me out of that one. I know you really didn't want to hang out with me today."

Guilt flashed through me, but before I could respond she grabbed her smartphone out of the middle console and handed it to me. "Here, see if you can find any good road trip tunes."

I scrolled through the music selection on the phone as best I could with Beepo jockeying for position on my lap.

"Just hit play when you find something you like; I have the stereo hooked up through Bluetooth."

I found some Diana Ross and hit PLAY. The music magically filled the car and Beepo howled alongside the tunes.

Yolanda began to warble and croon alongside them. I sipped my latte and prayed for no traffic on the expressway. The faster I got out of the car, the better.

After a while, we arrived at our exit. We left the freeway for a single-lane highway that meandered through the mountains. Being here brought back childhood memories of when my parents were still alive.

"You're quiet," Yolanda said.

"Lotta ghosts in these parts."

Yolanda sighed. "Well, I envy you that. Having the

memories. I don't have any fond memories of my childhood. It was always one ratty trailer park or another."

"You grew up in a trailer park?"

She gave me a sideways glance. "Why does that surprise you?"

"Because you're so refined and delicate."

She laughed. "Refined? Oh my momma would split a
stitch hearing that. But thank you. I do my best to leave
the past right where it is, thank you very much."

Beepo must have sensed her discomfort because he
hopped from my lap to hers. She stroked his triangle ears
as she drove, the large aviator gloves covering almost his
entire head. She slowed the car as we approached a fork
in the road.

"Go left here," I said. "It's a little farther."

We took the left turn onto a dirt road. The road was so
rugged with grooves and dips that I feared we'd get stuck.
Just what exactly would I do if I was stuck out in the middle of nowhere with Yolanda and Beepo?

I glanced nervously at my mobile to make sure I had
cell phone coverage.

"Are you checking messages?" Yolanda asked. "Any
news from Rach?"

I suddenly felt guilty that while I was planning my
escape from Yolanda, she was thinking about my harebrained sister.

"Unfortunately, no messages," I said.

"We need a Jeep to get through this muck," Yolanda
said. "I bet that sexy Officer Brooks drives a Jeep in his
downtime, whatdya think? Or is he a F-150 kind of guy?"
She glanced at me and I felt my cheeks grow hot.

She laughed. "Are you blushing?"

"No!" I said too quickly.

"He's a tall drink of water, ain't he?"

My throat went dry as I considered that Yolanda and I might be in competition for the same man.

"He's seems nice," I said nonchalantly. "Are you interested in him?"

"Interested in him?" Yolanda hooted. "Good heavens no! Besides, don't you have a date with him today?"

How did she know?

She giggled at my surprise. "Anyway, don't worry about it. I have my sights set on a bigger prize."

"Really?"

She sighed, and even though I couldn't see her eyes, I imagined she got a dreamy look in them from her tone. "I think Officer Gottlieb is the cat's meow."

Beepo snarled and jumped back into my lap.

Yolanda laughed. "I didn't mean anything by that, honey."

"Gottlieb, eh?" I asked.

She nodded. "I go right for the top. The man in charge. And he's bald. Isn't that so sexy?"

I laughed, and when she glared at me, I sat up straighter. For no reason other than to prove she could trust me with her crushes.

Yolanda was interested in Sergeant Gottlieb, eh?

I had a hard time imagining the two of them as a couple. From the limited impression I'd gotten from Gottlieb, he was a serious man. And Yolanda seemed so flighty. . . .

Could getting on the sergeant's good side influence an investigation? I suddenly questioned Yolanda's motivation. What kind of statement had she given him about finding Dan?

My fingers traced Beepo's paw; he yanked it out from under me and jumped to the backseat.

I worked my lip, wondered about the best way to broach the subject. Finally, I decided to just come right out and ask. "Yolanda, how did you get into The Wine and Bark on Friday?"

"What do you mean? I came in through the back."

"Was it unlocked? Or do you have a key?"

"Oh no. I don't have a key. I've been bugging Rachel for one for ages. I want to rent the storage space from her. I have a bag business. I design high-end purses and my business is growing so much I need a streetfront space. Window display, the works. I have some at Designer Duds . . . have you seen my handbags?"

"No, I don't think so." The only bag I remembered seeing was a ridiculous bright yellow and orange purse in the shape of a chicken.

"Well, Evie rents the side I'd like for storage," Yolanda continued. "I've been trying to convince her to switch to the other side, but that's where Rachel stores the bar stuff . . . inventory and things like that. Evie is totally stubborn and unreasonable. Anyway, the back door was unlocked on Friday. I didn't think anything of it, because it was almost time for Yappy Hour. I just figured Rachel had got there early to set up, like she always does."

We took a few more turns; the foliage became thick and deep, the scent of pines overwhelming.

Yolanda took a big sniff. "Smell that, Beepo honey? That's what I call gen-u-ine woody smell." She glanced at me. "Those fragrant candles just aren't the same!"

There was a clearing up ahead, where the road plateaued into a view of the lake. "Pull over up here and we can see the valley," I said.

Yolanda pulled to the side of the road, and we got out and stretched our legs. In the spring and winter the valley boasted green rolling hills, in the summer and fall we got treated to a view of the golden hills of California. My shoulders relaxed a notch to breathe in the fresh clean air and take in the view of the undulating landscape.

I fidgeted and paced back and forth along the side of the road. "It's only a few minutes' ride down the hill now," I said.

Yolanda studied me a moment. "Are you nervous about something?"

I shrugged. "I guess I'm nervous about finding Rachel and nervous about not finding her at the same time. Abigail told me she eloped."

"What?" Yolanda shrieked. "No way. She would have said something to me."

I laughed. Yolanda seemed more offended about being left out of the gossip than shocked about the fact that my sister might elope. "Abigail said Rachel was on a honeymoon cruise. I didn't believe it myself, but I'm afraid that could be the case."

Yolanda nodded sagely. "Okay, back in the car. The only way to beat fear is to outrun it."

◇◇◇

Shockingly, the cabin at Stag's Leap looked the same as I remembered it. Yes, the porch was sagging and the paint job was severely faded and chipped, but the beautiful exposed wooden logs that supported the structure were sound and the high glass windows still afforded the best view of the lake around.

No vehicle was parked in front; however, around the perimeter of the cabin, things looked freshly disturbed, as if someone had been here recently. My heart soared. Maybe Rachel was hiding out here after all.

We climbed out of the convertible, and Beepo scampered to the front door, his nose gyrating a million miles an hour. After sussing out the territory, he barked at the door as if announcing us.

"Hush now, Beepo!" Yolanda scowled. She turned to me. "If I'd known there was a lake, I would have brought my bikini."

I smiled. "Hopefully, we're not staying long. Just long enough to drag Rachel out of here by her hair."

Yolanda scoffed at me. "Jeez. Glad you're not my sister."

"Don't be mad at me. You can be mad at Rachel for putting us through finding Dan on Friday night."

"Well, it wasn't her fault, was it?"

I shrugged. It wasn't Rachel's fault we'd come across Dan murdered, that was true, but I still blamed her for disappearing and leaving me to deal with the mess.

Rapping sharply on the door, I said, "Well, if she's got a good explanation, I'm willing to listen."

Yolanda clicked over to the window in her high-heeled sandals. She perched her sunglasses on top of her head and cupped her hands around her eyes, then peered inside.

"Hello?" I called out.

"No lights on," she said.

I tried the handle on the door and it cracked open. Beepo shot through the opening like a cannonball.

"Wait!" I yelled at him.

Yolanda laughed. "Oh, that's what dogs do!"

The interior of the cabin had a strange vibe. The old couch was still there, but it seemed like newer throw pillows had been added, and the place reeked of bacon grease and cigarette smoke.

"Seems like someone's been here recently, right?" I asked Yolanda.

She nodded. She was looking at the stone fireplace. She took a few steps toward it and grabbed a fire poker from the tools next to the hearth. The poker was so heavy she had to use two hands to steady it as she jabbed at the fire pit. It was littered with cigarette butts.

"What?" I asked.

"Nothing. It looked like something was smoldering. But I was wrong. No telling how long these ashes have been here."

The cabin had two bedrooms that adjoined.

"Let's check the bedrooms for clues," she said.

"Or the fridge," I said.

She nodded at me and pointed toward the direction of the kitchen. I headed there while she walked in the opposite direction to one of the bedrooms.

The thought of Yolanda gripping the fire poker swirled in my head: her dainty hands with the pristine manicured fingernails. Was she really strong enough to kill a man? It seemed absurd. But if not her, then who was the murderer?

The refrigerator was empty except for a stick of butter and a jar of olives.

I was sure those hadn't been left behind by Grunkly all those years ago. Rachel must have been up here sometime in the past few years. Either that, or we had squatters.

Opening one of the overhead cabinets, I found a bottle of vodka, Stoli. It had to be Rachel's. She probably came up here every once in a while with friends or maybe a boyfriend . . . maybe even Dan. . . .

The smell of cigarettes and the butts in the fire reminded me of Grunkly, but the smell wouldn't have lingered all that time, and Rachel didn't smoke.

Had Dan?

A piercing scream echoed throughout the cabin. I dropped the bottle onto the tile floor and it shattered at my feet. Vodka and glass covered the floor.

"Shoot!" I yelled as I stepped over the mess and raced

toward the bedroom. "Yolanda! Are you all right? What it is?"

She was standing in the doorway of the second bedroom, her hand clamped over her mouth. She whipped around toward me. "Don't come in here!"

"What?" I froze.

Oh God, not another dead body. . . .

My throat went dry, and suddenly it felt like the temperature in the cabin was over a hundred degrees. "Why not?" I pressed. "What's in there?"

Yolanda chewed on her lower lip. "I think if you don't see it, then you can't say anything to the police. Especially, you know, you won't slip on your date with Officer Brooks." She thrust her arms out and blocked the entrance to the bedroom.

My blood pressure skyrocketed and sweat formed on my temple. "Yolanda, is there a . . . is there someone else in the house with us? Alive or . . ."

"No, no." She shook her head back and forth. "Nothing like that, it's just something . . ."

Beepo skidded out of the room and ran circles between my feet.

"What? What's in the room?"

She studied me a moment. "It's something that I think Rachel might have done when she was mad at Dan. It's something silly. Childish . . . but if the police saw it . . . well, maybe they wouldn't think it was a joke."

"A joke? You screamed your head off when you saw it."

"Did I?" A guilty expression crossed her face, then she quickly composed her features back to neutral. "No, Beepo got underfoot. I think I stepped on his tail."

Beepo looked up at us, his brown eyes full of mischief, his tail wagging back and forth.

"He doesn't particularly look hurt," I said.

Yolanda shrugged. "He doesn't hold a grudge—"

"Yolanda—"

"Okay, okay. I screamed when I saw it. It just surprised me."

"What is it? Let me I see it," I said firmly.

She waved me off. "Let's forget it."

"If it's something that could incriminate Rachel, I think I need to see it."

"Honestly, she's not here," Yolanda said. "And that's what we came for, right? Let's just turn around and go home."

"She's been here recently, though. There's some vodka in the kitchen and olives . . . the place isn't a mess, either, like I expected. It's not all dusty and moldy. Someone came here and cleaned. . . ."

Although Rachel cleaning sounded far-fetched. She wasn't the tidiest person in the world. Perhaps her guest had cleaned.

Yolanda's eyes lowered. "Okay, so what? We know Rachel's been here within the past month or so, but what does it prove? She's not here now. She's probably on that honeymoon cruise after all, just like Abigail said."

I felt like I was staging a battle with Yolanda that I wasn't likely to win. I wanted to get into that bedroom to see whatever she'd seen, but she was blocking the entryway like a linebacker.

"Okay, maybe you're right," I said, softly. "I need to clean up the broken glass in the kitchen and then we'll go."

Yolanda's eyes grew wide and a grin lit up her face. She couldn't believe I was going to drop the subject. She linked her arm through mine. "Now you're talking, honey, let's clean up the mess."

I walked with her three feet toward the kitchen, then dropped my arm and slipped behind her toward the bedroom. I raced into the room before she could stop me and flicked on the light switch.

I gasped in horror as I saw what Yolanda had been trying to hide.

Above the dresser was an oversized photo of Dan that someone had mounted onto a corkboard and had used for target practice. Worse, along the bottom someone had scrawled in red letters resembling blood, "Dead Meat!"

A hush descended upon us and I regretted not taking Yolanda's advice. I knew Rachel owned a gun. Grunkly had taught us both how to shoot when we were kids. We'd go into the woods, right around this very cabin, and set up cans to aim at. Rachel was a natural-born Annie Oakley. Filling my lungs with air, I turned to Yolanda. "You think this incriminates Rachel?"

She shrugged. "It doesn't look good."

"No," I agreed. "And it is childish. . . ."

She nodded. Beepo followed her into the room and the three of us stared at the corkboard in silence.

After a moment, I said, "You're right. It doesn't prove anything, but I certainly don't want the police to know about it."

Yolanda slipped her fingers over her mouth and made the universal "my lips are sealed" motion.

"I should have listened to you," I said.

"You'll just have to learn to trust me."

An unsettling feeling gripped me. Was someone setting up my sister? I needed to figure out who'd been in the cabin and I needed to figure it out fast.

Chapter Thirteen

Yolanda and Beepo dropped me back at my apartment at noon. I had time for a hot shower and a brief lie-down before dressing for my date with the hunky Officer Brooks. I'd wanted to nap, but the image of Dan on the corkboard haunted me. Was I obligated to tell Brooks what I'd found? Did it mean that Rachel really did have bad blood with Dan?

The thoughts plagued me as I slipped into a lavender scoop-necked dress that sported an above-the-knee A-line skirt. I figured the dress was the perfect compromise between afternoon and evening, just in case the date ran late.

Fingers crossed!

My doorbell rang and I took three deep breaths to calm the butterflies in my stomach.

When I opened the door, my heart fluttered to see Officer Brooks out of uniform. He wore dark blue pants and a light-colored windowpane button-down shirt. He smelled of aftershave and mint, and something in my belly danced when his low voice rumbled out a hello.

"Do you want to come inside?" I asked, suddenly feeling stupid.

Why had I invited him inside? Was that done? What would he think I was suggesting?

I hadn't been on a real date since I'd broken up my exboyfriend, Hank, last year. And even then, after a few months of seeing each other our dates had deteriorated into hang-out sessions at one or the other's apartment, where we ordered bad takeout and complained about our jobs.

Brooks smiled. "If you're ready, we can get going straight away."

"I'm ready. I'm ready," I said, sounding a little overanxious.

Geez. This isn't high school, Maggie!

We left my apartment and took the short walk on the cobblestone path toward the fountain in the main square.

"Are you hungry?" Brooks asked.

I realized with a start that I'd only had a latte that morning. No breakfast and no lunch. Certainly a far cry from the gourmet breakfast the other day that Gus had cooked me. Heat rose to my cheeks and inanely I felt guilty for thinking about Gus while on a date with Brooks.

"I am hungry. You?"

He laughed, his face lighting up. "I'm a guy. I'm pretty much always hungry. How about the Charcoal Corral?"

"I don't know it," I said. "But it sounds good."

We walked around the town fountain. The smell of homemade waffle cones coming from the Dreamery Creamery would have detoured me had Brooks not taken my elbow and gently steered me down a charming narrow alley with vintage lampposts and hitching posts.

"They have the best burgers in town," Brooks said. "My favorite."

We stopped in front of a circa-1956 pink neon sign that

read CHARCOAL CORRAL. He pushed open the door and we were immediately greeted by the rich smell of frying meat and grease. A cheerful hostess settled us into a wood-paneled booth with a mini jukebox hanging on the wall.

She placed two laminated menus in front of us and disappeared. Brooks was about to pick up the menu, and then looked as if he'd suddenly been electrocuted.

"What is it?" I asked, alarmed.

He composed his facial features and shook his head. "No, it's . . . uh . . . I hope . . . You do eat meat don't you?"

I laughed. "Oh, isn't there a vegetarian offering here at the corral?"

He relaxed to see me laughing. "'Fraid not. Well, actually, I really wouldn't know. All I ever get is the buffalo burger with pickle disks and hoops of onion, topped with homemade hot sauce."

"Wow, my mouth's watering," I said, fanning myself with the menu.

A waitress in a short white uniform and high-top tennis shoes appeared at our table. "Hi Brad, the regular?"

He nodded. "You better believe it, Betty."

Betty glanced in my direction. "What's it gonna be, hon?"

"Uh . . ." I flipped open my menu, and my eyes glazed over at the ten thousand options. "Uh . . ."

"Need a minute?" She glanced at Brooks. "How about I come back with a couple drafts?"

"Do you drink beer, Maggie?" he asked.

"Yes," I said. "Meat eating, beer drinking. I'm not making a very good impression, am I?"

He smiled, then said to Betty, "Two drafts, please."

The waitress nodded and spun off toward the back.

"What do you mean, you're not making a good impression?" he asked.

"Girls are supposed to eat salad and drink, I don't know, something froufrou or light anyway."

He chuckled. "Like a greyhound or mutt-tini?"

I smiled in response, but said nothing.

"Salad and froufrou are overrated," he said. "I like meat-eating, beer-drinking girls."

He snaked a hand closer to the menu and picked at it. "I want you to feel comfortable to be yourself," he said in a low voice. "I'm not judging you."

Heat surged through me as he leaned in closer.

"Do you like country music?"

"Of course; it goes with meat and beer."

He smiled, then turned to the mini-jukebox and selected some Johnny Cash while I perused the menu. I decided on the Knuckle Burger, which came topped with bacon and cheddar and a side of crispy fries. Betty returned and took my order, leaving two icy drafts in front of us.

Brooks took a sip of his beer. "So, Maggie, where you from?"

"Originally, from Santa Maria. It's about an hour southeast from here."

Brooks nodded, as if he was familiar with the area.

"My great-uncle Ernest always lived here," I continued. "So I spent a lot of time in Pacific Cove as a kid, but I hadn't been back in . . . ages. You?"

"I grew up here," he said. "Went to Pacific Cove High. I left after high school. Went to Los Angeles for college and then trained with L.A.P.D. But Los Angeles is so . . . so . . ."

"It's so L.A.," I said, with a smile. "The girls eat salads and drink froufrou drinks." I took a healthy sip of my beer.

He laughed. "Right, it's so fake. After a while, I wanted to come home. And my mother . . . well . . ." A sad look flashed through his eyes, but he averted his gaze.

So he didn't want to talk about his mother. Why was that? I wondered.

"Anyway," he said, "I heard about an opening at the P.C.P.D., and I went for it."

"How long have you been back?" I asked.

"Just over a year. It's funny, though, at this point it feels like I never left."

The waitress stopped at our table and placed two steaming burgers in front of us. Brooks got a tower of onion rings that smelled heavenly, but he still eyed my crispy fries.

"Trade you one?" he asked.

"I thought you'd never ask," I said, picking a warm ring off the tower. I bit into it and rolled my eyes. "Delish."

He laughed. "This is pretty much the point where I stop talking," he said, taking a huge bite out of his burger.

I winked at him. "I won't judge you." Biting into my Knuckle Burger, I savored the red meaty deliciousness of the prime aged corn-fed beef. "Oh my God," I murmured.

He smiled. "Right? If I wasn't a cop, I'd open a place just like this."

"Oh yeah?"

"Sure! I could eat onion ring hoops all day."

"'Til the cows come home," I joked, sipping on my draft.

"I'd call it Fat Patties."

I nearly spit out my beer. He laughed and we both chuckled for a moment.

"Fat Patties!" I repeated. "You'd alienate all the women."

He quirked an eyebrow. "All?"

"Most," I clarified.

He shrugged. "I could live with that. I only need one." His eyes stayed on mine and my breath caught.

Oh, this guy was smooth.

Was he for real?

I reminded myself that he'd said one woman, not *this* woman, and took another bite of my burger, then washed it down with some fries.

"Where did you come from most recently?" he asked.

"New York."

He let out a breath. "New York, wow. Pacific Cove is a change from that. You'll find we're a pretty sleepy little town. Not a lot goes on here. Are you . . . uh . . . do you miss it?"

I almost choked.

Not a lot goes on here?

"Well, let me just say, I've never tripped over a dead body in New York—a few homeless street people sleeping in the subway station maybe, but a dead guy, never!"

Brad studied me. "I suppose you've brought your own brand of excitement to the cove, though."

I held up a hand. "Don't blame that on me."

He took a slow bite of his burger, then a sip of his beer, all the time silently watching me and giving me the bad feeling he'd slipped back into officer mode. Well, if Brooks was up for talking about the investigation, then I might as well probe a bit.

"Do you have any idea what happened yet? Any suspects?"

He squinted at me, his electric-blue eyes penetrating the invisible wall around me that I pretended shielded my vulnerability. "Gus DelVecchio pretended he was shocked when I gave him the news, but I know for a fact he already knew."

A bubble of guilt crept into my throat and I tried to swallow past it. "That doesn't make him a suspect. I told him."

Brooks cocked his head to the side, frowning. "You did? Why?"

I couldn't very well confess that I was drunk—what kind of impression would that make? So I opted for stupid instead. "I wasn't thinking, I was upset."

"Finding a dead body is a very upsetting thing. But if finding the person responsible is important to you—"

"It is! It absolutely is."

He nodded. "Then I suggest you not compromise the—"

"I wasn't trying to compromise anything. I'm sorry. I . . . shouldn't have said anything to him."

Brooks's face softened, then after a moment he said, "I didn't realize you knew him."

"Gus?"

"Yeah."

"I don't really know him. I just met him recently. But he thought Dan was with Rachel and I couldn't let him think—"

"What?"

Uh-oh! Playing dumb wasn't working all that well. Now I'd really gone and said something stupid.

"Ummm . . ." I looked around the booth and feigned interest in the mini-jukebox.

"Why did he think Rachel was with Dan?"

I sipped my beer. I might as well come out with it. He'd find out sooner or later. "They used to date."

He nodded. "Right. But they broke up, correct? Why did Gus think they might be together?"

I shrugged. "I guess he thought they might have reconciled."

"Have you heard from her? Do you have any kind of update on her whereabouts?"

The image from the cabin of Dan's photo used as target

practice flashed before my eyes. I grabbed my draft beer and took a swig, buying time. Yolanda had been right. I'd have been better off not seeing the stupid thing.

"I haven't heard from Rachel. I tried contacting the cruise line office, but they were closed for the weekend. I was planning on going into the office tomorrow morning to see if they have a way to reach passengers on the cruise."

He chomped on an onion ring.

"I'm worried about her," I continued inanely. "What if . . . What if something's happened to her?"

Brooks put down his draft. "Like what?"

"Maybe she saw something . . . and the killer has kidnapped her. . . ." I swallowed back my fear. "Or worse . . ."

"Well, let's not get carried away with conjecture. Do you have any reason to believe she's been kidnapped?"

"No," I admitted.

Brooks nodded. "We didn't find anything at the scene of the crime to indicate a struggle like that. And you didn't find anything out of the ordinary at her apartment, right?"

"What do you mean, out of the ordinary?"

He shrugged. "No forced entry, broken doors, broken windows, not even anything to suggest she hadn't planned on leaving, like a plate of unfinished food." He bit into his hamburger to prove his point.

I smiled. "Right, I didn't find an abandoned hamburger, but . . ."

He looked into my eyes and my tummy gave a little quiver. "You're pretty worried about her, huh?"

I nodded.

"Do you want to file a missing persons report?"

Part of me knew Rachel was just being Rachel. She was unpredictable, a go-with-the-flow kind of gal. But I knew my sister could cause trouble without even trying to, like the time she told my ex-boyfriend off in the middle of a crowded store, or when she "accidently" set fire to my apartment. I had covered for her then, like I'd done a hundred times while we were growing up.

The thing was, if I asked Officer Brooks to look into her disappearance, I was certain he could come up with an entire dossier on how Rachel could have killed Dan.

I fidgeted with my beer mug. "I'm sure she's on the cruise," I lied. "I guess I hate to admit she'd elope without telling me."

Brooks's face relaxed and he reached his hand out across the table to lace his fingers through mine. His hands were strong, the nails cut square. "Don't worry," he reassured me. "I'm going to get to the bottom of everything."

That's exactly what had me worried.

Chapter Fourteen

An obnoxious, insistent ringing jarred me out of slumber on Monday morning. I'd been dreaming about Brooks and how sweet, honest, and reliable he was. In my dream we were on a cruise, destination unknown, and the only thing certain was that he looked hot in his swim trunks.

It took me a moment to realize the ringing was my phone.

I rubbed the sleep out of eyes, and my first thought was of Rachel. I jumped to answer it.

"Hello?'

"Hi, this is Jan, from Soleado Cruise Line. Is this Maggie Patterson?"

It was the call I'd been waiting for, and yet instead of being elated, I was strangely discombobulated and disappointed.

"Yes," I muttered.

"Oh, great! I've reviewed your résumé and application and was wondering if you had time to come in for an interview this morning, say around ten or eleven?"

I agreed quickly and we hung up. I'd have to get ready

in a hurry in order to make it on time. I scoured my closet for something appropriate to wear. After being in Pacific Cove a few days, I realized that everything I owned seemed so New York, type-A, financial advisor—bottom line, too conservative for a cruise operation.

Basically, my wardrobe was no fun at all.

I remembered the navy jacket with white anchors embroidered on it that I'd seen at Designer Duds. Would that be too presumptuous?

I glanced at my watch. I didn't have enough time to pop down there and buy it. I showered and shrugged into slacks and a burgundy silk top that I figured would look good without the jacket. It was bit on the conservative side, but that was okay for an interview. I rationalized that at least I'd feel businesslike.

My phone rang again. It was Grunkly. "Did you find Rachel at Stag's Leap?" he asked.

"No! She wasn't there. It does seem like she's been up there recently, though," I said.

Grunkly made a clucking sound. "I can't believe she'd disappear like this and not tell us where she was going."

"I know. Listen, I got a call for interview at the Soleado Cruise Line—"

"What? The cruise line? Would you have to travel a lot if you got the job? Why do you want to work there?"

It seemed I'd had this same conversation with Grunkly about five times. "Yes," I said. "I want to travel."

"Why? Don't you like it here in Pacific Cove?"

"I have to get a job, Grunkly. You know, in order to pay rent and buy groceries and stuff."

"Pfft. Don't worry about rent, Maggie. You can always come stay with me."

The thought of living at Grunkly's cluttered house almost sent me into a panic attack. "Uh . . ."

"And speaking of groceries . . . how about the filets you were going to pick up for us? Why don't you grab some for tonight and come over for dinner. I'll buy."

"Sound good. I'll see you tonight."

◇◇◇

The Soleado Cruise Line office was a few blocks from one of the piers. The office was pristine and smelled like the ocean, making me want to sail away, which I'm sure was the desired effect. A couple was looking at travel brochures, while an agent pointed out some attractions to them.

The agent looked up as I walked into the office. She was a pretty woman in her mid-forties with a mane of curly dark hair and a pair of pink half-glasses perched on her small nose. She smiled brightly and said, "I'll be right with you."

"No problem," I said.

There was a row of clear plastic holders that contained a supply of colorful brochures, each of an exotic location where Soleado cruised: Hawaii, French Polynesia, the Panama Canal, the Caribbean. I smiled, recalling my dream about Brooks in his swimsuit. What an absolute dream it would be to go on one of these foreign cruises with him. I tugged on one of the brochures for the Mexican Riviera Cruise to free it from the holder and accidently upended the entire display.

Oh no!

The holder crashed onto the tile, spinning and whirling like a top, spewing over fifty brochures out across the floor.

My face reddened and I immediately bent to pick up the brochures, saying, "I'm so sorry!"

The agent materialized beside me and gave me a stern, "I'll get that."

The couple turned on their heels and disappeared out the front door, singsonging a "Thank you!" that seemed more of a dismissal.

Shoot. I've likely just lost her a sale.

"How can I help you?" the agent asked, through clenched teeth. Trying hard, I'm sure, not to bite my head off.

"I'm here to see Jan. About the purser position."

The agent fixed her face in a disapproving look. It seemed Jan would get an earful about me before even meeting me.

"What's your name?" she asked, adjusting her glasses so I was in full magnification.

"Maggie Patterson."

The agent replaced the plastic holder with the brochures on the counter and said, "I'll let her know you're here."

I supposed it could have been worse. The agent could have been Jan; that definitely would have started us off on the wrong foot.

What was wrong with me?

Probably still nervous and stressed out about finding Dan. Not to mention Rachel still hadn't called me. How on earth was I supposed to concentrate on a job interview when I should be looking for my sister? Not to mention I'd promised Gus that I'd help him look into finding Dan's killer.

I wandered over to the watercooler. There were tiny paper cups in a tube alongside of the cooler. I pulled out a cup and pressed the blue button for cold water. Nothing happened, so I pressed the red button. Hot water poured out, scalding my hand.

Dropping the cup, I made a small spill on the floor.
Really?
What kind of a klutz was I today?
I stopped to pick up the cup, as voices neared. A woman called out, "Maggie?"

Bolting upright, I slammed my head on the cooler and toppled the entire five-gallon bottle. Water poured over my slacks, soaking me, then rushed across the tile floor right up to the woman's shoes.

The agent, the other woman, and I were frozen in place.
Oh God!
I wished I could disappear behind a magic vanishing cape.

"Are you all right?" the woman asked.

I looked at my wet slacks, then at the floor, now slick all the way to the doorway. "Uh . . . huh."

"I'm so sorry. That was my fault!" the woman said. "I shouldn't have frightened you that way." She turned to the agent. "Sue, can you please get a mop?"

The agent lowered her glasses and flashed me a red-hot look as if darts were coming out of her eyes, then she turned to the other woman and said sweetly, "Of course."

"Stay there," the woman said to me. "Have a seat. As soon as Sue mops up, she'll show you to my office."

I took a seat by the window and looked out at the beach. My slacks stuck to my legs and I felt trapped. The agent came back and cleaned the floor in short order, then motioned me down the hall. "First office on the right. And for God's sake don't touch anything else."

Finding Jan's office, I knocked on the door. Her voice rang out, welcoming me in. She was in her forties and looked the epitome of efficiency. Even though I was out of my element today, I could tell Jan was my kind of woman. She worked her way expertly through the interview questions: what was my past experience, easy; my greatest achievement, another easy one, graduating summa cum laude from Saint Mary's; my top strength—reliability. What was my greatest weakness . . . ?

Uh?

Clumsiness? Nosiness? But I couldn't say that in a job interview, so I confessed I was a workaholic: certified accountant and numbers extraordinaire, hadn't had a day off since I started babysitting at the ripe age of ten, which is why I applied for the Soleado Cruise Line's open position. A job whose office was a new port every day was just what I was looking for.

Perhaps then my pants could dry off.

Jan was all smiles when we finished the interview. She told me that they had a few more candidates to interview and that I'd hear by the end of the week.

When we finished with the interview questions, feeling like I'd already made a fool of myself and I really didn't have all that much left to lose, I asked, "Jan, I think my sister may be on the Mexican Riviera Cruise that left Pacific Cove on Friday. Is there a way to get a message to her? I'm afraid it's urgent."

"Oh certainly, just ask Sue at the front. She can pull up the itinerary for you and you can leave a message at the next port."

Sue again? She'd be as happy as a clam to help me, I was sure.

I left Jan's office and headed out to the front lobby. Sue was talking to two middle-aged women who were booking a cruise for their travel club. She seemed happy to be closing a big deal. I wondered if now was the time to push my luck?

The women chatted among themselves, frantically clicking on their smartphones looking up dates.

Sue fixed me with a glare, but her voice had a pleasant up lilt for the benefit of the women in earshot. "Yes, Maggie, is there anything else I can help you with?"

I cleared my throat, suddenly nervous. "I want to get a message to my sister. She's on the Mexican Riviera Cruise that left Pacific Cove on Friday. Jan said you could help me."

Sue glanced at the women, who were still absorbed in their phones, and seemed to decide it was a safe risk. She stepped around the counter to the computer console. "The seven day or ten day?"

"I . . . I don't know."

She rolled her eyes. "Name?"

"Rachel Patterson."

Her fingers flew across the keyboards. She bit her lip, then made me spell Rachel's name. Finally she looked up from the computer. "Are you sure she left on Friday?"

No, I'm not sure at all!

"Yes," I lied.

"That's strange. I don't see her. Any other name she could be listed under?"

If it was true that Rachel had eloped, could her reservation be under Chuck's name? My throat was dry and I longed for a cup of water. I glanced at the cooler and noticed that Sue had replaced the empty bottle with a brand new one.

Dare I help myself to some water?

Sue followed my eyes to the cooler. She gave a stern shake of her head. I was definitely not allowed near the watercooler again.

"Can you look up a Rachel Hazelton or maybe Chuck Hazelton?"

Sue's fingers clicked away at the keyboard; after a

moment she frowned and said, "Sorry. I don't show either Chuck or Rachel Hazelton as registered guests."

◇◇◇

I left the cruise line office feeling dejected. Not only would I probably not get the job, but Rachel wasn't on the cruise, either. I wandered through the town square, aimless, until I got to the Meat and Greet. As I stood at the threshold of the building, I recalled receiving the text from Rachel that was the start of all my troubles. I sighed and pushed open the door.

The overhead bell rang out as I stepped inside. "Hi, Norma. I'm here for steaks again," I said, thinking about how Beepo had been the one to enjoy the last round of steaks I'd purchased.

Norma rushed out from behind the counter and grabbed my hand. "Oh dear! I heard about Dan. It must have been awful for you. I'm so sorry."

"Thank you. It was awful."

We bowed our heads without another word, observing a moment of silence for Dan. When we looked up, Norma blurted, "I have to say, though. I never did like that man very much. Although I feel sinful saying it now that he's dead and gone. But really—"

I squeezed her hand. "What is it, Norma? Do you know who might have wanted Dan dead?"

Her eyes flicked toward the door, and then she said in a low voice, "You know, now that you mention it, I heard that Max had it out with him the day before Dan was found dead."

"Max?"

The bartender extraordinaire who'd literally saved my bacon behind the bar.

The door to the bar had been unlocked when I'd gotten there. Max had said he sometimes helped Rachel bartend. Did he have a key to the bar?

Norma studied my reaction. "Do you know him?"

Before I could reply, the bell above the door sounded, and I turned to see Gus. He stood in the doorway, tall and imposing. He wore dark pants and a white shirt open to the third button, his olive skin peeking out, exuding masculinity. Heat rushed through me from head to toe. I blushed. He smiled widely when he saw me, and something inside me fluttered.

What was wrong with me? Why was I getting so flustered to see him, especially since I'd just had a great date with Officer McHottie, aka Brad Brooks?

"Maggie!" Gus said. "What a surprise. Good to see you!"

Norma looked from Gus and then back to me. She hid a smile as she said, "Oh, I have to check on that order in the back. I'll just be a minute." She disappeared.

Gus rapped his fingers on the counter. "I'm glad I ran into you. Are you free for dinner tonight? The restaurant's closed and, I think, so is The Wine and Bark, right?"

"Oh, um . . ."

Disappointment flashed across his face. "Do you have other plans?"

"I'm picking up a few steaks for my dinner with my great-uncle," I said.

"Ah! Steaks huh? That's a little more complicated than a frozen meal." I must have blushed, because he hurried to say, "What I meant, was . . . maybe I can cook for both of you."

My mouth salivated at the thought. "I couldn't impose—"

"It's no imposition! I love to cook. It's what I do. I'd love to grill some steaks for you and your uncle."

It hardly seemed fair to prevent Grunkly from having the opportunity to savor the exquisite culinary talent of Gus DelVecchio.

"I'm sure Grunkly would love that," I said.

Gus studied me. "How about you, though, Maggie?" He stepped closer to me and I could feel the heat wafting off his body.

Good God, what was up with my hormones?

"Would you like if I cooked for you both tonight?" he asked.

"Yes," I admitted.

Even though I'm confused as hell about you and Officer Brooks. But how could I deny the rush that it gave me just to stand next to him?

Norma returned from the back room. "Gus, what can I do for you?"

"Hi, Norma, I came to review this week's order." He grew solemn, and I knew he was thinking of Dan.

I browsed the greeting cards while Norma and Gus sat down to review the order for DelVecchio's.

From the snippets of conversation I heard, it seemed Dan ordinarily put in the meat orders. What was it about him that Norma hadn't liked? I'd have to ask her later.

Chapter Fifteen

On the way to Grunkly's, Gus and I chatted about my interview at Soleado. He chuckled when I told him about the watercooler. "Don't worry about it. I'm sure they'll hire you. We don't get your kind of talent in the cove very often."

"My kind of talent?"

"New York! That's serious street cred."

I couldn't tell him I'd been an utter failure in New York. At least, it felt that way. After my breakup with Hank and the downturn in the economy, I'd slowly lost most of my clients, until I was forced out of business.

Gus maneuvered us around the town fountain. We took a small side alley I hadn't been down before. A delicious aroma of fresh baked goods wafted through the air.

"I figure we can stop by Piece of Cake and pick up a baguette to go with dinner," he said.

Oh man, I was getting weak-kneed just thinking about Gus in his element. Fresh steak, fresh bread. It was going to be one hell of a meal. We entered the bakery and I thought I'd died and gone to heaven. Tray after tray of

éclairs, cannoli, cream puffs, sugar-covered beignets, crois-
sants, and cupcakes lined the right side of the store, while
racks of homemade bread in every variety imaginable
lined the left side of the store. A heavily pregnant woman
wearing a mint green apron greeted us.

"Hi, Gus, are you here to put in your order?" she asked.

Gus shook his head. "DelVecchio's is closed for the
week . . ."

She glanced from him to me. "Oh . . . right. Of course
it is. I'm so sorry. I heard about Dan. I'm so sorry." She
nervously smoothed her hands around the front of her
apron, her palms coming to rest on her extended belly.

We selected a sourdough baguette, then a few small
tarts for dessert. Gus and I wound our way toward The
Wine and Bark to pick up a bottle of pinot for dinner.

"I'd take you to the farmers market to buy some fresh
vegetables, but they're closed today," he said.

I stopped walking and looked him square in the eye.
"Gus, I have to level with you about something."

His eyes darkened and he suddenly became serious.
"What is it, Maggie?"

"Grunkly's house is a mess. I'm nervous that you won't
be able to cook anything over there at all. . . ."

He waved a hand around. "Don't worry! The mark of a
good chef is to make a nice meal no matter the circumstances!"

I laughed. "Okay, you might be in for more than you
bargained for, but don't say I didn't warn you."

◇◇◇

Grunkly eyed Gus suspiciously. "A cook?" He didn't exactly say cooking was women's work, but his expression
more or less said it.

Gus chuckled. "I prefer the word *chef*."

Gus and I entered Grunkly's house. The scent of cigarette smoke lingered.

"Have you been smoking again?" I asked Grunkly.

"No, no. You know I'm not supposed to smoke, honey."

Gus hid a smirk, but I narrowed my eyes at Grunkly. "If I find a pack of Lucky Strikes here, you're not getting dessert."

"There's dessert?" Grunkly asked hopefully.

I showed Gus to the kitchen, maneuvering around the graveyard of electronics and stepping over three stacks of papers. Gus, to his credit, said nothing about the mess. If possible, the kitchen was even more of a disaster than the rest of the house. Grunkly normally ate off paper plates, so locating the real dishes along with utensils was a challenge.

Gus and I tackled the kitchen together. I found the glassware while he wiped the counters. I had a strange, comfortable, and homey feeling working next to him. He filled the sink with suds and sang in Italian while he rinsed dust off the dishes.

"I never wash them by hand anymore, with the dishwasher and all, but I love it. Isn't it a nice feeling to put in a dirty plate and see it come out clean from your own labor?"

I laughed. "I guess you can look at it that way. Or you can see it all as one messy, greasy operation."

He frowned, seemingly at a loss to understand how anyone could see washing dishes as a chore.

"Besides," I said, "Grunkly has a dishwasher. It's just on the back porch."

"What?"

I giggled. "You heard me." He followed me over to the back porch and I swung open the door for him. Outside was a dishwasher circa 1981. Gus laughed so hard tears sprang to his eyes.

"Why does he have it on the porch? Does it work?"

"Of course it works!" Grunkly said, peering at us from the kitchen door. "I don't keep anything around that doesn't work. The rinse cycle is just a little off, so I use it for other things."

Gus tried to keep a straight face. "Other things?"

"Well, I couldn't get the plumbing to work right out there, either. I didn't want Maggie or her sister tripping on any pipes, so I just store herbs in there."

A look of horror crossed Gus's face.

I wondered why I'd allowed him to talk me into his coming over here. Surely he'd see the ridiculousness of trying to cook at Grunkly's, and that would run him right out of the house and away from me.

I realized how much I was enjoying working in the kitchen with Gus; then a strange feeling swept through me, almost as if I felt guilty for feeling good. As if I was betraying Brad somehow by enjoying Gus's company. But that was silly. Brad and I had only shared a simple dinner date. Who knew if there was even any future for us? It wasn't as though I had promised either guy anything serious.

While Gus laid out the steaks and seasoned them, Grunkly leaned in to me and said, "Can I have a word with you, Maggie?"

Gus smiled at me as if to encourage us to have our conversation in private. He said, "I'll uncork the wine."

Grunkly and I left the kitchen to the relative privacy of his living room. Grunkly pressed a message into my hand. "Rachel called."

"She did!" A zip similar to that of an electrical current danced up my back. "Where is she?" I demanded.

A guilty expression crossed Grunkly's face and he admitted, "I forgot to ask her."

"What?" I stuttered.

Anger ripped through me and I fought the urge to throttle my dear, elderly great-uncle. After all, it wasn't his fault Rachel was so irresponsible.

He raised an eyebrow. "Is it important?"

"Of course it is! She's a lead suspect for Dan's murder!"

"That's ridiculous. That child couldn't hurt anyone!"

"What else did she say? When is she coming back? Has she eloped or what?"

Grunkly's eyes darted back and forth and I knew he'd not asked her any relevant questions. "Uh . . ." he said, "she said she didn't want to call you because she thought you were mad at her."

"Of course I'm mad at her. She's disappeared, off gallivanting somewhere, and I'm stuck here in the middle of a murder investigation."

Grunkly worked his lower lip. "Do you have any idea who could have killed him?"

I told Grunkly about my conversation with Norma and what she'd said about Dan and Max.

Grunkly grimaced. "Do you think Max could have bumped him off?"

"I don't know. He was very nice to me, helping me with the bar and all."

Grunkly gripped my arm. "Beware of Greeks bearing gifts, Maggie. It could all be a ploy to get your guard down."

A shiver danced up my spine. Was Gus also being nice to me to throw me off his trail?

"Who else are the police looking into?" Grunkly asked.

I motioned toward the kitchen with my chin.

"He can't hear us," Grunkly said.

"No—I mean him. They're looking into him."

Grunkly looked shocked. "You've brought a suspected murderer into my house!"

"Grunk—"

"And he's cooking for us! What if he poisons us?"

"He won't. He's already cooked for me and I'm still alive. Believe me, you would have killed me if I'd denied you what you're about to taste for dinner."

Grunkly looked unconvinced, but the smell of olive oil and garlic wafting in from the kitchen was enough for him to say, "Let's make him eat first."

Chapter Sixteen

Although Gus had prepared a spectacular dinner for me
and Grunkly, I had another fitful night and awoke yearn-
ing for the normalcy of a routine. Getting a job would help,
but at the moment the only normal felt like finding Rachel
and investigating the Dan mystery. I jumped out of bed and
decided on a trip to the coffee shop before returning to the
Meat and Greet. I wanted to talk to Norma without Gus
around, but first I needed some caffeine.

I walked the short distance to Magic Read, the book-
store/café in town that hosted a magic shop. The young
clerk had a spiked green Mohawk and a frightening snake
tattoo that covered the length of his arm. I could barely
understand him due to the piercing in his tongue, but somehow got a nod from him when my order was ready.

I handed him a five-dollar bill and he thrust a pen
through it. He held up the bill to show me the pen had
penetrated it, then immediately pulled out the pen and
showed me that the bill was intact.

I laughed. Suddenly, he coughed up my change in coins

and said, perfectly clearly, "Here you go!" I marveled that he had no piercing in his tongue at all.

"Nice trick," I said. "Keep the change."

He chuckled and placed the coins into an overflowing tip jar. "Works every time."

Walking across the cobblestone path, I could tell the day was setting out to be another scorcher. It was still early, but already the sun lasered onto the stone path, reflecting back an almost blinding light. I made it over to the Meat and Greet and pushed open the front door with my hip, juggling the two coffees in my hand. The bell tinkled overhead as I walked in, and Norma looked up from mopping the floor.

"Maggie, you're here early. Everything okay with the filets last night?"

"Oh, yes, delicious. It's just that I wanted to talk to you about something." I handed her one of the coffees.

She smiled and asked, "Are you a mind reader?" She took the lid off the coffee and let the steam release into the air. The smell of coffee alone seemed to wake her up.

"No, but maybe the clerk who made the coffee is; at the very least he's a magician."

"Did he cough up your change?"

"Yup."

"How does he do that?" she asked.

"I don't know, but I'd like to. I'd be coughing myself some rent money, a down payment for a car—"

Norma laughed. "Right. We could pay off all our bills."

I sipped my coffee as Norma put away her mop bucket. "So, I wanted to ask you about Dan. You said something yesterday about him being difficult to deal with. I was hoping you could tell me more about him."

"Ah. Poor Dan. Well, let's see. He was kind of a stick-in-the-mud. He wasn't from here, you know. He met Gus in San Francisco at the culinary academy. Gus was always a whiz at cooking, but Dan not so much. He sure understood the business matters though. He was always negotiating a tough margin. A few times, I lost money with him, and I was getting ready to cancel their account."

"Cancel the DelVecchio restaurant account?"

"Yeah, I told Dan I didn't want to do business with him anymore, but that I'd work with Gus. He's a sweetheart, huh? And what a hunk."

I looked away and felt myself blush. I didn't really want to get into a conversation about Gus, but it was difficult to avoid since he and Dan had been so close. I tried to focus on the question at hand, and not on what a hunk Gus was. I cleared my throat. "Did Gus know you were getting ready to cancel the account?"

Norma shrugged. "I don't know if Dan told him or not. I imagine he would have—or he should have, at any rate. But Gus hasn't said anything to me."

An unsettling feeling zinged across my scalp. If Gus knew Dan was endangering his business, was that motive for murder? I couldn't imagine Gus hurting anyone, but was I being naïve?

I wandered over to the small rack of greeting cards and spun the carousel. The artist Coral was so talented that I was drawn to the cards, wanting to study each and every one of them. A postcard of one of the cruise ships departing from the dock caught my eye. I fingered the card, thinking of Rachel.

"Norma, I wanted to ask you about Max."

Norma rearranged the collection of gourmet cheeses and chutneys in her front counter. "Oh? What about him?"

"Yesterday you said he had it out with Dan, but what did you mean? Like a fight?"

"Well, an argument or something," Norma said. "I saw them exchanging words right here in front of the store. It didn't come to blows, but Max sure was angry about something."

Well, that was something.

Maybe there was more motive in the town than met the eye.

After chatting with Norma, I decided it was time to pay Max a visit. I strolled down the Main Street, past the Soleado Cruise Line offices, moving as fast as I could, even holding my breath as I walked past. I didn't want to run into Jan, because I didn't want her to think I was stalking the place and, worse, I certainly didn't want to run into Sue, the agent, because she just might hex me.

I turned the corner in front of Designer Duds. The little chicken handbag was still in the window, along with the navy-blue jacket with white anchors embroidered on it. The store didn't open until the afternoon; at some point I'd have to come back and buy the jacket.

The sun was beginning to heat up and warm the air. It was still early, but the Dreamery Creamery was opening its doors. I stood behind a little girl with freckles and copper-colored hair. She wore a blue pinstriped dress and sandals. She smiled when I got behind her in line.

"The waffle cones are the best," she said.

"What's your favorite flavor?"

"Mint chocolate chip." She grinned and I could see that some of her teeth were missing.

The girl working behind the counter had dyed burgundy hair and a long severe face. She reminded me of Evie Xtreme, the singer in the Howling Hounds. The girl said, "Hi, Coral, let me guess: mint chip on a waffle cone."

"Mint chocolate chip," Coral corrected.

"That's right," the girl with the burgundy hair said.

Coral?

My heart stopped.

As in, the artist?

No, it couldn't be. She was just a child!

"Um, Coral, do you paint by any chance?" I asked.

Coral grinned at me. "Oh yeah! I paint the greeting cards and postcards that my mom sells at the Meat and Greet."

"Norma is your mom?"

Coral nodded happily. "We're business partners. She's the Meat, I'm the Greet!"

I laughed. "I love your cards, I bought some the other day. I'd love to learn to paint like you."

Coral's eyes grew wide, first at my compliment and next at the huge cone that the girl with burgundy hair was handing her.

"Make mine chocolate," I said to the girl.

"After my cone, I'm going down the coves, to paint some more." Coral indicated a small tote she was holding. "I usually like to go to the beach, but it's been too crowded since the cruise line came to town."

"Really? Why's that?"

"They converted that stretch of beach into a port," the cashier said. "So while the cruise line is great for business, it leaves us with less beach."

I paid for my ice cream, and Coral's, too.

"You don't have to pay for mine," Coral said. "I have my own money from my card sales."

"I want to pay for it! Maybe you can give me a few painting pointers," I said.

She smiled wide. "You like to paint?"

"More like I'd *like* to paint, but I don't. Math is my strong suit."

Coral giggled. "I'll trade you painting pointers for a few math tips. Mom says I have to do math exercises all summer, otherwise I'm going to end up with a tutor." She stuck her tongue out and made a face as if having a tutor stunk.

"Done," I said. "I got you covered on the math."

We sat at a small table near the front window and licked our ice cream. It was divine, creamy and rich, and felt like it was going straight to my hips.

"It's all in the eye," Coral said. "I think all good painters need a good eye."

"I've heard that before, but unless it's a slipped zero, I don't know that I have a good eye."

"I do," Coral said. "Like, even if my mom hadn't told me you were Rachel's sister, I'd know."

"Your mom told you I was Rachel's sister?"

"Well, she just said you were in town, but you look a lot like her. Is she having fun on the cruise?"

My jaw dropped. How could this little girl know about Rachel and the cruise? "What do you mean?" I stuttered. "Why do you think she's on the cruise?"

"I saw her get on." Coral dug into her tote. "Look, I even painted her." She pulled out a card and slid it across the table at me. It was a stunning depiction of the back of a woman walking hand-in-hand with a tall man. The woman had my sister's honey-blond hair.

"Who was she with?" I asked.

Coral shrugged. "Her boyfriend, I guess."

"Did you see him? Do you know who he is?"

Coral shook her head. "I don't know him."

So Rachel had gone on the cruise after all? Why hadn't she been on the registry?

In my distraction, a small bead of ice cream slipped

down my cone and landed directly on the postcard, right over Rachel's hair. "Oh, Coral, I'm so sorry!"

Coral laughed. "It's okay."

I wiped ineffectually at the card.

Coral looked on. "Now she has dark hair! It looks like you in the card."

"Let me buy it. How much for the postcard?"

Coral shrugged. "It's okay. You can buy me another ice cream tomorrow!"

I dropped the postcard into my bag. "It's a deal."

When Coral and I left the Dreamery Creamery, I tripped on something in the doorway. I bent to pick it up. It was Bowser's pink plush bunny. I pinched it between my pointer finger and thumb in the way a mom would pick up a dirty diaper.

Coral laughed. "It's not going to bite you."

"It's got beagle slobber on it. Gross factor to the max," I said, then laughed at my pun.

Coral didn't get it, her face crinkling up in confusion. "What?" she asked.

"Never mind. Do you know where Max, the guy with beagle, lives?"

She squinted at me. "Max, the guy that walks the beagle with the Roundup Crew?"

"Yeah," I said, plopping the sopping bunny into my bag. This would work perfectly. I'd return the bunny and grill him about his fight with Dan.

"He lives on the beach in the green house with the wraparound porch."

I laughed. Coral didn't know the address, that involved numbers, but she could describe the house to a tee.

She dug into her tote and pulled out another postcard. "It's one of my favorite houses. He lets me sit on the porch and paint. The light there is amazing." She fingered the card longingly as if she could pull the light right out of it through her fingertips.

"Thanks, Coral. I think *you* are amazing!"

Chapter Seventeen

The sun was high in the sky, casting a golden reflection off the Pacific, little rays of light shooting directly into my eyes. Why hadn't I brought my sunglasses? It had been early when I'd left the house this morning, but still, I should have known better. I squinted my way across the beach, shading my eyes with my hand. I was buffeted by the wind off the ocean. My hair swirling around whipped my cheeks. Sand kicked up and stung my eyes and stuck to my lips.

Ack.

Sometimes I hated the beach. It was days like that I missed the concrete jungle of New York. I felt, at times, that I enjoyed the beach more on an idyllic postcard, like the type painted by Coral, than the real thing.

The green house with the wraparound porch came into view. It seemed like a serene place, with a sprawling deck and a few Adirondack chairs. My sneakers were filling with the sand and it was getting hard to walk. I couldn't wait to reach the wooden deck. Once there, I immediately emptied my sneakers and dumped the sand back onto the beach.

I rang the front bell and waited. When no one answered, I walked across the back deck and knocked on the glass doors. I could see straight into the living room. Max was seated at a desk, engrossed in his computer. He startled at my knock. He wiggled his mouse and the computer screen went dark. He came to the back door, a smile lighting up his face when he saw me.

"Hi Maggie! You in the neighborhood?"

I dug out the pink plush bunny from my bag and handed it to Max. "This is getting to be a habit," I said.

He laughed. "Oh no! Where was it?"

"In front of the Dreamery Creamery," I said.

Max smiled. "Ah! That's where it went." He waved me into the house. "Come on in, it's about time I took a break, and it looks like it'll be a scorcher today. Want a cocktail?"

I shook my head. "Too early."

"No, it's not." He smiled. "I'll make Bloody Marys, they're practically a health food."

"They are?"

He gave me a mock frown. "Tomato juice? V8, I mean. Anything with vegetable juice is good for you, right?"

I laughed. "Well, when you put it that way, I can hardly argue."

Following him into the large kitchen, I took the place in. His beach house was almost as immaculate as Gus's apartment. There were black granite counters and a large commercial-size oven. Gus would approve of this kitchen. My mouth watered thinking about the kind of meal Gus could cook here. After all, he whipped up a gourmet offering in Grunkly's limited space.

"Nice place," I said.

Max smiled. "Thanks. It was a family vacation place, but I recently bought it from my folks and now it's global headquarters for my company."

"Global headquarters?"

He laughed. "Okay, it's my home office. I have a small start-up. Just myself and one other developer." He shifted uncomfortably as if he'd wanted to say more, but he didn't. He handed me a tall glass.

I sipped the cocktail.

"Delicious!" I said. "But I should have known."

He smiled. "Ice and spice. My key ingredients."

We marched out to the deck and sat in the pair of painted wooden Adirondack chairs. The sun was high over the Pacific and I thought jealously of Rachel. She was on a cruise, staring out at the azure water, while I was stuck here in Pacific Cove trying to unravel her mess. Okay, maybe it wasn't her mess, but I was definitely on the hook for watching her bar and her reputation.

Max looked out toward the water. "It's peaceful here, huh?"

I nodded. "Yeah, so peaceful it's shocking that a murderer is on the loose."

He sat straighter and nervously ran a hand through his hair. "I heard a rumor that Dan died when his head hit the floor."

"What do you mean?"

"Well, I don't know, really, just that maybe The Wine and Bark could be liable. I thought maybe that's why you came here. Maybe for an attorney referral."

"I need an attorney?"

He shrugged. "I thought maybe that's why Rachel took off. . . ."

I sipped the cocktail; the spiciness suddenly seemed overwhelming. "Who'd you hear the rumor from?"

Max bit his lip. "Oh, I can't seem to recall. Anyway, if you need an attorney, go to Bradford and Blahnik."

My heart plummeted at the thought of lawyers. Wasn't there a way I could get to the bottom of all this? I took a deep breath, then asked, "Did you know Dan very well?"

Max shifted uncomfortably. "Not really."

"I heard you two had a disagreement."

The Bloody Mary tumbler slipped between his fingers and splattered onto the deck. "Oh shoot! Sorry about that!"

We both stood, then Max scooted inside for a broom.

How strange. Had he dropped the glass on purpose? Instead of answering the question, created a diversion? I'd have to remember that tactic the next time Officer Brooks pinned me down on a topic. The thought of Brooks sent my mind spinning in another direction entirely. Where was he today?

Max returned with a broom, and he swept away the mess. When he finished, he asked, "Who did you hear that from?"

"Norma," I said.

Max nodded. "Right. I bumped into Dan outside of the Meat and Greet. He made a few unsavory cracks and we had a little bit of heated exchange. Norma must have overheard us. The truth is, I barely knew Dan. It's just that he was kind of a jerk."

I drained the rest of my cocktail and got up. "Thanks for the drink, Max. Are you going to be around tonight?"

He glanced at his watch. "Yes. I've got some work to finish up, and then I'll be around."

I leveled a gaze at him. "Do you happen to have a key to the bar?"

He frowned. "No. Why? Do you need me to open it up?"

I shook my head as I bussed my glass back to the kitchen. "No, just wondering." I noticed the plush bunny was still on the table where he left it. "Oh, where's your dog?" I asked, pointing to the bunny.

Max shuffled his feet and got an odd look on his face. "Uh . . . yeah . . . Bowser's asleep. He'll be happy to see the bunny when he wakes up. Thanks for coming by, Maggie."

I left the beach house with an odd feeling. Max was definitely hiding something . . . but what?

◇◇◇

The sun was getting higher in the sky, burning off the coastal fog that had tried to cool Pacific Cove. I figured now was as good a time as any to pay Officer Brooks a visit. The police station was on the east side of town, and by the time I arrived, my back was drenched with sweat.

Inside, the police station was institutional and sparse. Two uniformed officers sat at computer stations, one on the phone, the other surfing the net, no doubt. A woman officer glanced up when I came in and looked annoyed at being disturbed.

"Can I help you?" she asked.

"Is Officer Brooks in?" I asked.

Her faced twitched, clearly displeased with me. She indicated a hard plastic chair by the door. "Have a seat, please."

She turned on a heel and disappeared down a narrow corridor. She reappeared a few moments later trailed by Brooks. My breath caught as I watched his frame fill the doorway.

He didn't smile to see me, but his eyes lit up. I hoped that refraining from a smile was for the benefit of his colleague and not me.

"Maggie," he said. "Come on back to my office."

I followed him down the darkened corridor to a bright

room. On his desk was a framed photo of a woman on a beach. The woman was a few years older than me, and striking. She looked liked a swimsuit model, lean and tan with legs that went on forever. In the photo, she gripped the hand of a towheaded boy. A pang of jealousy twitched around my heart.

He caught me looking at the photo. "My mom."

I picked up the frame. "Is that you?"

"Yup." He took the frame out of my hand and replaced it on the desk. He was very serious; something was up.

"What can I do for you?"

"I have an eyewitness that Rachel is on a Soleado Cruise," I said, digging into my bag and pulling out the postcard. I handed it to him.

He squinted. "What is this?"

"It's a postcard Coral painted. She's Norma's daughter."

He dropped the postcard on the desk. "I know who Coral is. But this doesn't prove anything."

"What do you mean? She saw Rachel get on the boat." I gestured to the card. "She painted her."

He shook his head. "The painting is of the back of a dark-haired woman. It could be you. In fact, it could be you walking with Gus DelVecchio."

Ah! That's what this was about.

"The woman in the painting has light-colored hair. I dropped chocolate ice cream on the card."

He snorted.

"And it's not Gus. I don't know who the guy is. Maybe it's Chuck, the guy she eloped with."

"Look, I've already reviewed the ship's passenger list. Rachel Patterson isn't on it."

A muscle behind my eye throbbed, causing my left to twitch, and I swore it made me look like a madwoman; either that, or Brooks might think I was winking at him.

When I remained silent, Brooks said, "Look, I'm really sorry, Maggie, but we have to examine the facts here. Dan was found in Rachel's bar. He and Rachel used to date. No one can get ahold of her—"

"Rachel didn't kill Dan! Just because he was found at the bar . . . it doesn't mean anything. There're other people in town who could have done it. Did you know Dan and Max had an argument outside of the Meat and Greet? Talk to Norma—"

"Brooks," a voice barked from the down the hall.

Brooks straightened his shoulders and took in a deep breath.

By the way he'd steadied himself, I knew trouble was a brewing.

Sergeant Gottlieb stuck his bald head into the room, his dark bushy eyebrows furrowed. He started when he saw me. "Oh, excuse me. I didn't know you had company, Brooks." The way he spat it out made me feel like I'd over-stayed my welcome.

I picked up the card from the desk and stuffed it back into my bag. "Sorry to bother you," I muttered to Brooks.

He gave me a sharp nod, almost a dismissal, yet there was something else in his face. An apology?

I stormed out of the station more determined than ever to get to the bottom of things. The police were hell-bent on blaming this awful crime on Rachel, and I had to help her.

Chapter Eighteen

Down the street was the Bradford and Blahnik store. I entered and was startled to see Brenda there. She was holding a pair of chartreuse strappy sandals by Manolo Blahnik. She smiled when she saw me. "Oh, hi, Maggie! Are you here for a fitting?"

"A fitting?" I asked.

"Oh, or . . ." She put down the sandal and smoothed down her skirt. "Are you here for a consult?"

The chrome handle to the door was heating up in my hand and part of me wanted to turn tail and run.

"Uh. I . . . I don't know. I guess I'm here to see Bradford."

She grinned widely and stuck her hand out. "Welcome! I'm Brenda Bradford."

I tried to hide my surprise. "I didn't realize you were an attorney."

"Come on in," Brenda said, putting the Manolos back in the box. "I was admiring the new shipment."

"They're stunning," I said.

She wiggled her eyebrows at me. "I give a fifty percent discount on shoes to clients."

I glanced back at the strappy sandals. "Tempting."

But first I'd have to get a paycheck, and one thing about working at The Wine and Bark was that I wasn't actually getting paid.

Brenda walked me through a small adjoining room to her office. Her office was small and cramped, but immaculate. Her Chihuahua, Pee Wee, was nestled in a blue doggie bed in the corner of the office. He lifted his head and opened an eye upon hearing us enter, but must have considered me boring because he dropped his head and snuggled down to continue his nap.

"Do you want some coffee?" Brenda asked.

"No, thank you, I'm fine."

"What can I help you with?" she asked.

"Well, I guess I need to talk to you about Dan."

She held up a manicured hand. "Wait a second, Maggie. I have to tell you that I'm not a criminal lawyer."

I nodded. "I understand. There's a rumor The Wine and Bark could be held liable for Dan's death."

Brenda pressed her lips together and thought for a moment. "So, are you looking at a civil suit?"

"Oh God, I hope not. But I guess, I just wanted to see if that was even a possibility."

Brenda shrugged. "Perhaps."

The door to the main storefront jangled open and a familiar voice called out "Hello?"

Brenda sprang up. "Oh, Maggie, can you excuse me a minute?"

As Brenda made her way around her huge glass desk, the familiar voice, followed by an even more familiar and annoying bark, echoed throughout the store. Yolanda popped her head in the doorway. "Brenda. Oh! Oops. Sorry to disturb you. I didn't know you had a client."

I turned to face Yolanda. Her face was a mixture of surprise and delight at finding the next gossip item.

"Mags! What you doing here?" Yolanda shrilled.

Beepo yapped at my heel.

Brenda took Yolanda's elbow. "You know, whatever goes on in here is always confidential."

Yolanda pressed a hand over her heart. "Of course! I wouldn't dream of breaching any attorney-client confidences."

Brenda pressed her lips together and escorted Yolanda out of the office; Beepo remained at my feet and growled.

"Shoo," I said.

He bared his teeth and nipped at my ankle, his wet nose pressing up against my skin. I yelped.

"Beeeeeepooooo," Yolanda trilled. "Don't be naughty!"

I rose from the buttery leather chair and went out to the shoe area, Beepo following me yapping. Yolanda tsked at him and picked him up.

Two hideous bags were propped by the door. One was in the shape and likeness of a pig and the other in the shape of a frog.

I gasped. These bags were just like the chicken bag at Designer Duds.

Yolanda mistook my horror for some sort of appreciation, because she said, "Oh! You like them?" She thrust the frog purse at me. "Green goes with your eyes."

"I . . . uh . . ." I glanced at Brenda for help, but her look of horror caused me to erupt into a fit of giggles.

Brenda stepped forward and gently pushed the frog bag back toward Yolanda. "Maggie is under quite a bit of stress."

Yolanda clutched the frog bag to her chest, the bag and Beepo competing for space. Beepo growled at the frog. At least I had company thinking the thing was hideous. Maybe Beepo wasn't so bad, after all.

"Hush, now!" Yolanda said to the dog. "You know it took Momma hours to design this beauty." She turned to Brenda and me and said, "I call it Le Petit Frog Prince."

Laughter overtook me, and in trying to repress it, I snorted and choked. Brenda thumped me on the back. "Yes, well, Yolanda. What can I do for you?"

Yolanda scanned the shelves: leather boots, designer sandals, and colorful pumps littered the store. "Any new deliveries?"

Brenda marched over to the Manolos she'd promised me 50 percent off of. "These strappy Blahniks came in."

Yolanda dropped Beepo and shoved Le Petite Frog Prince at me again. Her arms free, she half squealed and gasped as she stretched her hands toward the Manolos. "Oh my! Those are out of this world!"

I tried not to feel offended. After all, even if she bought them there'd be other shoes I could indulge in. A pair of mulberry-colored pumps caught my eye.

Yolanda flung her heels off and shoved her foot into the strappy sandals. "What size are they?" She reminded me of one of Cinderella's stepsisters trying to squish her foot into the glass slipper. She extended her leg out gracefully. "What do you think, Maggie?"

"I think it matches Le Petit Frog Prince beautifully," I said, holding the frog purse next to the shoe.

Yolanda's foot recoiled, just as Beepo launched toward the purse. I suddenly felt like a matador flinging a cape outside of the bull's reach.

Yolanda stood and collected Beepo in her arms. "I'll

take the shoes, Brenda. Can we make room for some of my bags in your window?"

Brenda looked as if she had sucked on a sour lemon. "Oh, darling. You know I'm waiting on a shipment from—"

Yolanda waved a hand around madly. "I won't take no for an answer." She pushed aside some shoes in the window display. "There, I found room. You know these are handcrafted and go for five hundred dollars. And yes, even though they are displayed at Designer Duds, they aren't moving very fast—because, well, have you seen the awful things they have at that store? My bag is right next to an awful captain's jacket with anchors. I mean, pul-ease!"

Yolanda turned from the window and squinted at me, the frog purse still in my hands. "You know, Maggie, you should keep the purse. It goes with your eyes."

"My eyes are brown."

"Well, that's what I mean!" Yolanda shrieked. "Brown and green camo—it's the latest fad."

I looked at Brenda for help, but she was snickering as she put her window display back in order. "I'll ring you up for those shoes now, Yolanda."

Yolanda sashayed over to the cash register and pulled out a credit card. "Maggie, have you given any thought to the rental space at the bar? Can I please have Evie's side?"

"Who owns the building?" Brenda asked.

"My great-uncle. He rents the space to Rachel for The Wine and Bark."

Yolanda's eyes grew wide. "What?"

I looked from Brenda to Yolanda then back to Brenda. Brenda grimaced. "What?" I asked.

"Can you talk to him for me? I've been begging Rachel to let me lease that part of The Wine and Bark for my bags for so long, but you know, maybe you can convince your uncle to lease the entire space out to me. I'll pay good rent.

And after all, who knows how long the bar can stay open with the money it's losing."

I froze.

The bar was losing money?

"What do you mean? The bar is losing money?" I managed to choke out.

"Well, sure, everyone knows that. It's closed every day until Yappy Hour. I could make a storefront out of the storage room. There's two big rooms. Rachel only uses one."

"Evie uses the space Yolanda wants, though," Brenda said.

Yolanda flashed her a look that would quiet a storm. Brenda's lips thinned.

"It wouldn't be a big deal to move the inventory. The only thing in the other space is the band equipment," Yolanda said.

Yolanda looked at Brenda. "Do you have any coffee made, honey? I need a lift."

Brenda glanced at me. I think she was calculating the odds of me evaporating out the door if she left the room.

I nodded to her, trying to reassure her that I'd wait for her return.

"I'll get you a cup," she said to Yolanda as she left the room.

Yolanda lunged at me. "How was your date with Officer Hot?"

"The date was fine, I think. But since then . . ."

"What?" Yolanda probed.

"I told him I was worried about Rachel and he promised he'd get to the bottom of everything. But I just saw him and he's thinking Rachel—"

"You didn't tell him about the target—"

"No!" I said sharply.

Yolanda's eyes grew wide, and she said, "Me, either."

Only I wasn't sure if I could believe her.

"Rachel's not on that cruise, by the way. I checked in with them when I had my interview."

Yolanda looked offended. "What interview?"

"For purser."

"Purser? What about The Wine and Bark?" she asked.

"What about it?"

"You can't go work for the cruise line when we need you."

Beepo sniffed at my feet, I took a step back.

"Please. You don't need me. Rachel will be back soon. You'll see—"

"But we like you now, you can't leave," Yolanda said.

I laughed. "Well, I'm not even sure I'll get the job. I knocked over a display rack and a watercooler while I was in there."

Yolanda smiled. "That was your subconscious sabotaging you. You know you want to stay here."

"Don't be silly. I was clumsy, that's all."

Brenda returned with a paper cup of hot coffee for Yolanda. Yolanda sipped her coffee as Brenda bagged the new shoes for her. Once she was done shopping she wiggled her fingers at us and left with Beepo yapping at her heels.

Brenda and I returned to her office. Brenda resumed her position behind the desk. "Do you have insurance for the building?" Brenda asked.

"Yes, of course." Although now I was getting a bad feeling about something . . . as if my memory was trying to drag up something important that I'd forgotten. What was it?

"All right," Brenda stated matter-of-factly. "Get me a copy of the insurance declarations and I'll take a look. We'll have to wait and see if Dan's folks want to file a suit, which I have to say, I'd find highly unlikely. But in the meantime, I'll study your policy and see if there's anything to worry about."

And then I remembered . . . the insurance bill at Grunkly's house . . . it had gone unpaid. . . . Oh no.

Chapter Nineteen

I arrived at The Wine and Bark early enough to set up and, frankly, to think. I paced around in the darkness of the bar and thought about Dan. To think Rachel was somehow involved now seemed ludicrous, but was she really on that cruise? Through the window I could see the Howling Hounds lead singer, Evie Xtreme, approach. She had a serious expression on her face. She seemed guarded and her eyes darted around the courtyard. Flicking on the lights, I moved to the front door to let her in.

"Hi Evie, what's up?" I said.

"Oh, hi, Maggie. How are you? I'm glad you're here. I just came to pick up one of my guitars. I rent the back storage area."

"Right, right," I said, stepping aside to let her pass. She smelled of tobacco, and her hair was windblown like she had just come from the beach.

I followed her to the back storage room. It was a small cramped room, but it did have huge storefront windows. Right now the windows were painted over with dark paint that included small doggie etchings and little dancing wineglasses.

"Evie, I wanted to talk to you about the storage area . . . I spoke to Yolanda and it seems that she might want to rent this place."

Evie turned sharply toward me. "Ugh, her again. She keeps nagging me about it, but Rachel said she'd rent it to us for a year and I'm only onto my sixth month of the lease."

"Right," I said. "I don't want to alienate anybody. I was just thinking if we cleaned up the other room without the storefront window, maybe you could use that as storage?"

Evie shrugged. "Yeah, Yolanda always gets what she wants, doesn't she? Everybody else has to be inconvenienced in order for her to figure her problems out."

I studied Evie a moment: her face was suddenly red and she looked angry. "Oh, you don't get along too well with Yolanda?" I asked.

Evie shrugged as she rummaged through some boxes that were pushed up against the back wall. "Well, it just seems that everybody needs to bend over backward to help out Yolanda, that's all."

I knew the feeling. Yolanda did seem very domineering. The way she pushed her bags on people. And yet, I was beginning to soften toward her. After all, she'd gotten me out of a pinch with a ride to Stag's Leap and, if she could be believed, was keeping the secret about the creepy target there.

"And another thing," Evie continued. "Yolanda made us rearrange our whole schedule just so we could perform on Friday for that silly fund-raiser. I had some other gigs in town lined up, but she has a way of coercing people."

"She coerced you?" I asked.

"Well, one of my band members, Smasher, has got a

mad crush on her. He'd follow her to the ends of the earth. Not that she'd ever give him the time of day, but she asked him, he said yes, and without him I can't do my other gig."

"I guess that fund-raiser is a pretty big deal."

I absently wondered if Rachel would resurface for it, or if I'd be on the hook to manage it by myself.

"Oh, yeah," Evie said. "I know the guy who died. He was against it. Of course, he was against anything to do with dogs."

Goosebumps covered my arms.

Yes, Yolanda had been the one to find Dan. Had they been fighting?

I took a chance that Evie might have some useful gossip. "Do you know if Yolanda locked horns with Dan?"

Evie laughed. "Well, who doesn't she lock horns with?"

"Oh . . ." I said, at a loss for words. I shrugged. "I guess, I don't know her that well . . ."

"She's just kind of pushy," Evie said, pulling a guitar case from one of the boxes and slinging the strap around a shoulder. "Have you seen those stupid bags she designs?"

I had to stifle a laugh. "I've seen the bags," I said.

"That's what she wants to put in here in my storage space. She wants to open up a stupid animal bag collection, like anybody wants to carry around a handbag in the shape of a chicken."

"She's got a frog one and a pig one now, too," I said. "In fact, she was trying to push her frog one on me just today."

Evie laughed, her face suddenly lighting up. "Did she tell you it goes with your eyes or something?"

We laughed together.

"Yeah," I said.

"She told me the chicken went with mine, like my eyes are yellow. Give me a break."

I looked at Evie's eyes. She had beautiful green eyes. Probably the frog would have better suited her. Although I had to admit that her eyes had a hint of yellow that was almost catlike.

We left the storage area. Evie pulled out a ring of keys and locked the door, then we walked together out to the front part of the bar.

"Would you like something to drink? I can mix you up a greyhound or a martini."

"Do you mean a mutt-tini?"

I glanced at my watch; still an hour to opening. "Well, since it's not Yappy Hour yet, I feel like it's okay to say plain martini."

She laughed. "How about just a beer?"

I served her some peanuts and a beer and we sat at one of the cocktail tables near the window watching the courtyard. Across the patio, Gus made his way toward the front door of DelVecchio's. Alongside him was the waiter from the other night, the one who usually worked the patio tables. Gus squinted over toward us, one hand shading his eyes from the sun as he glanced in our direction.

My understanding had been that DelVecchio's would be closed for the week. I wondered what they were doing at the restaurant.

Evie's eyes followed mine, but she said nothing, only sipped her draft beer.

"They really have it out for the bar don't they?" Evie asked. "What with the no-dogs sign and everything . . . Dan hated the dogs on the patio. . . ."

"Gus, too, right?" I asked.

She shrugged. "Oh, I don't know him very well. Everyone says he's a temperamental chef. I try to stay away from temperamental people."

Gus hadn't struck me as temperamental, and I wondered if I was missing something about him.

*You're probably blinded by his red-hot sex appeal,
Maggie,* I thought to myself.

"I can understand that people wouldn't want dogs
around their food, though," Evie said. "But these doggie
people, they want to share their lives with their dogs and
bring them to the spa or make them happy or whatever."
She rolled her eyes and polished off her beer.

"You don't like dogs?" I asked.

She shrugged. "I like dogs. I'm just not a fanatic."

"Your band is the Howling Hounds."

She giggled. "That's a marketing gimmick Smasher
came up with. It keeps the gigs steady."

"How well do you know my sister?" I asked.

She shrugged. "Oh Rachel? Well, we're pretty friendly.
Why?"

"Any idea where she is? Abigail told me that Rachel
had gone and eloped . . . and, well, I haven't been able to
locate her. . . ."

"Eloped?" A strange expression crossed Evie's face.
"With who? I thought she was dating Dan. What happened?"

I shrugged. How could I explain Rachel's erratic
behavior? She'd been that way her entire life and people
always looked to me to rationalize it.

Evie leaned in. "I know she's your sister and all, but it
was rumored that things went down pretty bad between
Dan and Rachel and now that she's missing, it's sort of . . ."

"She's not missing," I said. "Apparently, she's eloped."
I said it firmly, even though I had trouble believing it myself.

Evie played with her empty beer mug. "Don't get mad.

I didn't mean anything by it. You just showed up out of nowhere to take over the bar."

"I'm not taking over the bar," I said. "I'm just running it while Rachel is away." I stuttered through it feeling like an idiot.

Evie held up her hands to me to stop me in my tracks. "I didn't mean anything by it," she repeated. "No offense. The band likes playing here. I like renting out the storage room. I hope we can do business together just like I did with Rachel."

"Right, of course."

She leveled a gaze at me. I understood she didn't want to offend me, she wanted to continue business with The Wine and Bark. She bussed the empty beer mug to the bar.

"Do you want another?" I asked.

"No," she said. "I have to go, and we're performing tonight at the Magic Read."

There was a strange energy between us now. How had I gotten at loggerheads with Evie? Now she must think I'm a lunatic.

With a hand on the door, she asked, "Who's the lucky guy?"

"I think his name is Chuck Hazelton. Computer guy. . . ."

"Oh well, congratulations! Chuck is Max's business partner. Techie guy. They're going to cash in some day with some major stock, I'm sure."

Chuck was Max's partner? I couldn't believe Max hadn't said anything to me. I suddenly felt disoriented. It seemed everyone in this town had secrets they were keeping from each other. Why hadn't Max told me? What else was he hiding?

She left and I cleared our table. Soon the crew would

be arriving, and I needed to get things in order before the bar was ready to open.

◇◇◇

A few minutes to five and I began to organize the bar. Since it was only a Tuesday night, I didn't expect it to be crowded, but still, my chance to think things through would evaporate as soon as I had company. Why hadn't Max told me about his partner? And what exactly was I going to do about the possibility of Dan's parents suing?

The first person to arrive was Abigail with her white Shih Tzu, Missy.

She was in the mood for a chardonnay, which I happily uncorked and poured. At least I didn't have to get jiggy with the shaker without Max to pick up the pieces. I gave Missy a Bark Bite and asked Abigail, "So, what can you tell me about the guy Rachel eloped with? Is he really a partner of Max's?"

Abigail munched on some bar peanuts. "Oh yeah. I was surprised to hear it, too, believe me, but Max and Chuck will make out in the long run. They're working on some robotic app. Did you know? Anyway, so even though I wouldn't have picked Chuck as a good match for Rachel, he is a good catch. They'll be rich in just a few years."

It wasn't so much the financial picture I was concerned about, it was feeling betrayed by Max.

Through the window I could see Max approaching. He had Bowser with him. The dog dropped his pink plush bunny at the door of The Wine and Bark, ready for Max to play with him. Instead, Max picked up the bunny and sauntered inside, Bowser trailing along.

"Howdy? Just you two so far?" Max sang out.

I bristled at the confrontation I knew was brewing.

Abigail must have sensed something, because she excused herself to the restroom.

"Why didn't you tell me Rachel had eloped with your business partner?" I challenged.

Max stiffened and automatically looked down the corridor to the ladies' room. "Oh, did Abigail tell you that?"

"More or less," I said.

He nodded sagely. "I'm sorry. Chuck and Rachel swore me to secrecy."

"But why?"

He shrugged. "She didn't think you'd understand. Said you were so cynical about men and that you'd never believe in love at first sight."

I felt like I'd just been punched in the gut.

Me? Cynical about love?

Okay, maybe there was some truth to that. I definitely wouldn't have advised my sister to elope. Especially not with a guy she'd been dating only recently.

"Do you know where they are?"

"I thought they were going on a cruise to the Mexican Riviera."

I poured myself a glass of wine from the open bottle of chardonnay, then poured a glass for Max. He accepted without hesitation. "I can't locate them on that cruise and neither can the police."

Max twirled the wineglass stem in his fingers. "I really don't know. They told me they were booked for the cruise, but maybe Chuck thought I'd slip up and covered his tracks?"

Abigail returned from the restroom to overhear the end of our conversation. "Rachel told me the same thing. Mexican Riviera cruise."

Out the window, I saw an older couple approach DelVecchio's. They peered around the darkened windows,

then crossed the patio over to The Wine and Bark.
They stood outside the door for a moment, their heads
leaned in toward each other, having a serious discussion.
After a moment, the door opened and the couple stepped
inside.

Some kind of internal alarm went off in my head. It
must have for Abigail and Max as well, because they suddenly cleared out from their seats at the bar and retreated
together to a corner table.

The couple approached the bar. The woman looked
anxious, the man protective as he guided his wife by plac-
ing a hand on the small of her back.

"May I help you?" I asked.

Part of me hoped they were tourists. Lost and hungry,
looking for a place to eat after finding DelVecchio's closed.

"Are you the proprietor of this establishment, Rachel
Peterson?" the man asked.

"No, I'm her sister, Maggie Peterson. What can I do for
you?"

The woman looked despondent as she sunk onto the
barstool. Her red-rimmed eyes nervously darted about.
The man remained standing, his eyes on me as his wife
nervously fiddled with her dress.

She was painfully thin and had sunken cheeks. Her
hands twisted endlessly as she searched the room. She
looked like a woman desperately in need of answers.

"We're Mr. and Mrs. Walters. Dan was our son," the
man said. "We wanted to come here, because the police told
us this is where he died."

"I'm so sorry for your loss, Mr. and Mrs. Walters. I'm
the one who found Dan. . . ." I didn't actually know what
to say next. I couldn't imagine a pain greater than the one
I saw etched across Mrs. Walters' face.

"Thank you," Mr. Walters choked out. He squared his

shoulders, but his face betrayed the raw emotion he was fighting.

Mrs. Walters dove into her handbag and dug out a white linen handkerchief. She dabbed at the corners of her eyes, and Mr. Walters squeezed her elbow.

"You found him?" Mrs. Walters asked. "Did it look like he suffered?"

"No," I lied.

Actually, I had no idea. How would I know? But it seemed the humane thing to say.

"The police told us it's an ongoing investigation," Mr. Walters said. "They'll have the autopsy reports soon. Although they said it's likely that Dan died from trauma to the head."

I knew this couple was in the midst of a deep grief, so I bit my back my desire to question them on the rumor circulating about suing The Wine and Bark.

"Can I offer you a glass of wine? Mr. Walters?"

Mrs. Walters bristled. "Definitely not." She tugged on Mr. Walters's sleeve. "Let's go, Donald!"

Together they made their way toward the front door of the bar. Missy let out a little farewell bark, which seemed to annoy them further. They exited the building, and I felt like I'd missed an opportunity.

They were determined to get justice for their son and I didn't blame them, I just hoped that they wouldn't take The Wine and Bark down with them.

Chapter Twenty

As I was closing the bar, I heard a loud crashing sound out on the back patio. Who was out on the patio in the dark? And at this hour?

I searched the counter for a weapon. At one end was a small nail hammer, presumably used to hang the autographed framed photos of dogs in the restroom corridor. As I gripped the hammer, I noticed one of the bar windows was still open. I rushed to close it. Another sound, closer this time. My pulse quickened as I glanced around. Was I alone inside the bar?

Nothing looked displaced.

But what if someone had gotten in here without my tracking them? What if they'd hidden in the bathroom and not left with the others?

After all, Dan was dead, and Rachel was AWOL!

The logical part of my brain surged with a message, *"Calm down!"* but I gripped the hammer furiously over my head anyway.

Then I heard the footsteps.

Someone was in the bar!

Suppressing the scream rising in my throat, I ran behind the bar and grabbed the cordless phone. My heart racing, I punched in 9-1-1.

The operator said, "What is the nature of your emergency?"

I ran toward the front door. I had to get out of the bar. Inside I was a sitting duck.

"Someone's broken into my business. Please send the police. Hurry!" I fumbled with the locks on the door, but couldn't manage with the phone and hammer still in my hand, so I dropped the phone.

That was stupid!

I hadn't even given the operator my address! Could they trace my call and get my address?

Yanking open the door, I raced right into a dark mass. A man. He grabbed at my arms, but I was ready for the fight of my life.

I clenched my small hammer. I estimated the man was too tall for a successful blow on the head, so I brought it down onto his shoulder. I yelled out my best self-defense karate scream—"Hi ya-ah!"—and kicked at him and punched with blind fury. The heel of my foot caught the man on the inside of his thigh, missing his groin by an inch. What poor aim I had!

Thankfully, it still doubled him over, but he yelled, "Wait, Maggie. It's me."

I stopped suddenly at the familiar, kind voice.

I'd just beaten up Gus!

"Oh my God! Gus! I'm so sorry. I didn't know it was you! I thought you were a criminal!"

He limped over to one of the patio tables and took a seat. He rubbed at his shoulder with his hand. "No, I came over to see if you were hungry. I figured you were closing around now and thought maybe you hadn't eaten yet."

My heart softened. "You're so sweet!"

"Forget it now," he joked. "If I feed you'll just get stronger." He rubbed at his shoulder. "What did you hit me with?"

My face burned with embarrassment. "A hammer," I confessed, looking down at it still clenched in my hand.

He chuckled, a low rumble of warmth and relief vibrating out of him. "Oh my God! I'm glad you didn't get my head. Might have knocked me out cold."

Or worse . . . I shuddered at the thought.

Is that what had happened with Dan? Had he surprised someone and they'd struck out at him, thinking they were in danger? If that was the case, the killer really could be anyone. "Are you okay?" I asked. "Do you want me to get you some ice?"

"Nah, just need to catch my breath." He alternated rubbing his shoulder and rubbing the inside of his thigh. He turned around to look at the dark bar. "Are you all done for the night here? Want a snack at DelVecchio's?"

"Yes and yes. I just need to take the trash outside."

"I'll help you with that," he said, standing up.

He followed me inside and grabbed the black trash bags I'd tied up. I was happy to see that he was no longer limping.

I returned the nail hammer to behind the counter where it lived, then gave a final look around. All was quiet. We left the bar and I made sure to lock the door. No more boogeymen tonight!

I felt so relieved and secure now with Gus by my side. We rounded the buildings and entered the alley where DelVecchio's and The Wine and Bark shared a Dumpster. Alongside the Dumpster were smaller cans: a black one for refuse, a green one for compost, and a blue bin for recycling. All the bins were stationed along the alley, the stench overwhelming after the hot day.

"Yuk. Smells like rotting fish back here."

Gus shrugged. "I guess I'm used to it. I don't even smell it anymore. Do you like fish? I have some fresh halibut. I can make you pesce alla stemperata."

"What's that?"

"Garlic, pine nuts, raisins, capers, and olives. Tomatoes, if you like them," he said.

Despite the odor of refuse, my mouth watered. "I love halibut and tomatoes."

He lifted the trash bag over his shoulder and easily threw it in the oversized garbage bin.

Grabbing his hand, I said, "Thank you, Gus."

Sirens sounded in the background and something tickled at the back of my mind, as if I'd forgotten something.

Gus stepped closer to me, electricity sparking between our bodies. "I'm happy to help you, Maggie."

The sirens were fast approaching, growing louder.

He began to lower his face to mine, and then it suddenly hit me. I jolted away from him. "Gus! I called 9-1-1."

"What?" He had a dreamy intense look in his eyes, and he wrapped an arm around my waist, pulling me closer.

"The police. They're coming here."

"Police? Why?"

"I called 9-1-1," I repeated. "I thought I was in danger."

He pressed the lower half of his body against mine. "You're in danger, all right." His voice purred in my ear.

Another voice called out: "Freeze!"

Gus and I turned to find Officer Brooks with his gun drawn and pointing straight at us.

Whatever relief I'd been feeling earlier completely evaporated. Right now, panic threatened to overwhelm me.

Gus and I both managed to raise our hands in surrender.

Brooks swore under his breath and lowered his weapon.

Another uniformed officer joined his side. "What's going on? We got a call about an active burglary."

My cheeks reddened. "I . . . I made a mistake."

How had everything in my life gone so wrong?

Brooks groaned. "Crap!" He yanked on the radio attached to his shoulder and barked an order to dispatch.

The other officer remained tense. "No burglary?" he asked.

Brooks didn't holster his weapon. "What made you call?"

"I thought I heard some strange sounds in the bar. I felt like I wasn't alone, like someone had broken in, but I was wrong."

Brooks squinted at Gus. "Did you hear anything?"

Gus shook his head. "No. I didn't hear anything unusual."

"Let's check the premises anyway," Brooks said to the other officer, "just in case."

The other officer nodded and stepped down the alley in the opposite direction from us. Gus separated himself from me and I flashed him an apologetic look.

Brooks walked between Gus and me purposely. I shuddered. It was never my intention to set these two men against each other, but now it looked like I'd done just that.

Gus moved toward one end of the alley and Brooks the other. I stood still, not knowing in which direction to turn; if I moved toward either one of them, I was taking sides. My gaze dropped to the cobblestones and I aimlessly looked around the Dumpster area. There were dark marks on the stone by the trash bin. As if the bin had recently been moved.

Then I saw it.

Behind the bin, what looked like a white tennis shoe peeked out. The shoe looked like it was attached to a foot.

Unable to control myself, I screamed a long, piercing, high-pitched wail.

Brooks and Gus dashed over to me.

Still screaming, I pointed at the foot. The other uniformed officer raced toward us.

I stepped away from the trash bin as the men together moved it to reveal the waiter from DelVecchio's.

Gus gasped and cried out, "No! Oscar! No!"

Chapter Twenty-one

"Oh my God! Is he dead?" I shrieked.

Brooks leaned over the man, while the other officer shouted an order into his radio.

Gus's arms were suddenly around me and I found myself sobbing into his shoulder.

Again?

It had happened again.

"He's dead," Brooks announced. "Gunshot to the back."

Why? Why had someone shot and killed the waiter, Oscar? They'd left him by the Dumpster in the alley, and it seemed so cruel and disrespectful, to be left dead beside a can full of garbage as if his life had had no meaning. I held back my tears.

Gus held me firmly and I realized I was shaking. What had happened? Who had killed the poor waiter and Dan? Had it been the same killer?

The other officer ushered Gus and me out of the alley. "We're going to need to take you in to the station. Strictly procedure, you understand. Just need a few questions answered."

"Do I need an attorney?" Gus asked.

The officer answered, "For what? Mr. DelVecchio, you're not under arrest. We just need a statement from you."

"I can give you my statement now, Ellington. I was in the restaurant all night. Oscar was here around four thirty or so. We walked in together. He'd come to pick up his paycheck."

"I saw him arrive," I said, then regretted it. Anxiety rippled through me. I'd seen Oscar arrive at the restaurant, but I hadn't seen him leave.

Officer Ellington squinted accusingly at Gus. "What were you doing at the restaurant all night? You guys were closed, right?"

"There was still work to do. I can show you." Gus stuck a hand inside his pocket, but the officers immediately held out their hands and yelled, "Whoa, whoa!"

Gus looked surprised. "Come on, Brooks. I was going to show my meal plan. I'm not reaching for a gun or a knife or something. You think I'm some hood kid that packs heat?"

Officer Ellington jumped to Gus and pushed him against the wall, frisking him.

"Is that necessary?" I demanded.

"We have a homicide on our hands, lady," he spat at me. "Are you a registered gun owner, DelVecchio?"

Brooks stepped up to me and said, "Come with me, Maggie. I'll see that you get to the cruiser all right."

"I'm not leaving him here," I said.

"I'm not asking you to leave him," Brooks said. "He'll be right behind you."

I turned to see the other officer getting in Gus's face and yelling, "Answer the question! You a registered gun owner or not?"

"Yes," Gus said. "Of course I am. I own a restaurant. Lots of cash trades hands."

Oh God, if the gun matched . . . I couldn't even think it.

Ellington finished frisking Gus, then together we all headed in silence to the police cruiser.

◇◇◇

At the station, Officer Ellington escorted me to a small stark room. In the middle of the room was a table with a box of tissues, a couple of notepads, and a small recorder. There was also a dark mirror on the wall, which I absently wondered about. Was it a two-way mirror? Was someone watching on the other side? Perhaps Brooks? Or Sergeant Gottlieb?

I sat in a hard orange plastic chair and Ellington sat across from me. He hooked a microphone into the recorder and said, "I tend to forget things, so I'm going to record it so I don't mess up."

Hmmm. Felt sort of like he was playing dumb. I had a nervous energy zinging through my body. I hadn't inquired about an attorney, but now felt the need to ask. "Do *I* need a lawyer, Officer Ellington?"

Not that I had one. Who would I call? Brenda was an attorney, albeit not criminal law. Could she help me out in a pinch?

The door to the room opened and Sergeant Gottlieb entered, scowling. Apparently he wouldn't be observing me from behind the two-way glass. Gottlieb and Ellington exchanged looks, then Ellington leaned forward and said all our names, the date, and the time into the microphone. When he finished he looked at me. "Ms. Patterson, can you tell us exactly what happened this evening, beginning from when you arrived at the bar, then when you called

9-1-1, and up to when Officer Brooks and I arrived on the scene?"

I took a big inhale, ready to launch into my story, but instead the mixture of dread and nausea that'd been building inside me dissolved into tears and I found myself sobbing.

◇◇◇

"My client has told you all she needs to tell you at this time," Brenda insisted, ushering me out of the small interrogation room.

I gripped Brenda's arm as if my life depended on it. She walked me through the police station, past the deserted front desk and out to the street.

"Brenda, you're a lifesaver," I said, wrapping my arms around her neck and squeezing.

"I don't know how I did it. It's a good thing I remembered enough from law school—"

"Now you have to go get Gus," I said.

She bit her lip and screwed up her face. "Oh Maggie, don't you think we should let him work it out?"

"No, go get him," I said, pushing her toward the police station door.

I stood at the doors, looking out at the industrial parking lot of police black-and-whites. It was so dark out that only the immediate area was illuminated by the streetlamps. Brenda followed my gaze out into the parking lot, her small blue Honda parked nearby. She looked at it longingly.

"But, what if . . . you know," she said. "Poor Dan and Oscar—"

"Innocent until proven guilty, Brenda, come on. Everyone has a right to get help and all that stuff, I mean, Hippocratic Oath and all."

"That's for doctors."

"Right to counsel, or whatever it is! Don't get technical on me." I sighed. "It's been a long night."

"He does have a right to counsel. That doesn't mean it has to be me!"

"Please, Brenda."

"I have a large shipment of Ivanka Trump's pumps coming in the morning, beautiful blend of suede and snake—"

"I'll never serve you another greyhound if you don't—"

"Don't say it." She turned on a heel. "Get in the car. I'll go get your boyfriend."

"He's not my boyfriend," I called after her.

I'd have to try to explain that to Brooks later.

<><><>

Unfortunately, Brenda hadn't been able to get Gus out of the police station. The police were detaining him until further notice. My suspicion was that Gus would likely have to produce his registered gun and/or a criminal attorney.

I tossed and turned all night dreaming about poor Oscar, Dan, and Rachel. In my dreams, Rachel was chasing me down a long dock toward a cruise ship. She had a butcher knife in her hand, screaming at me to give her a chance to cook some halibut, only the fish that jumped around me out of the ocean reeked like garbage. The ship's foghorn blasted through the fog, until I realized the noise wasn't in my dream at all, but rather a loud pounding on my front door.

Leaping out of bed, I slipped into a robe and dashed down the hall, hoping like hell it was my sister.

I pulled open the door to find Yolanda and Beepo. "Guess what!" she trilled. "My exhibitor application got accepted for Accessories The Show."

Yolanda sauntered into my apartment with Beepo scratching along behind her. Her arms were full of gear, which she dumped on my couch. She was dressed in a mauve top, complete with ruffles, and a skintight black leather skirt.

"What? What show? What are you doing?" I rubbed at my eyes, willing my brain to click in.

"The Show—Las Vegas!" She said it like I was an idiot. She pulled out a doggie bed from the duffel bag on the couch, then marched over to a corner of my living room and set it on the floor. "Here or in the bedroom?" she asked.

"I don't know what that is, Yolanda, but I—"

Yolanda stared at me, mouth agape. "It's the world's largest and longest-running all-accessory trade event!" she said.

"Oh, uh . . . congratulations. But I got sort of an emergency on my hands—"

"I can't believe you've never heard of it. It's where you go to see all the latest accessories from up-and-coming designers. From fashion jewelry to eyewear to footwear to hair ornaments and, of course, the latest in bags. Everything in bags! I'm telling you, evening, briefcases, daywear, and chickens! My chicken and frog bags are the latest, *hottest,* hot item! I'm talking red hot!" She grabbed my hands and spun me around. *"Uber fantastique!"*

"Yeah—"

"The thing is, I have to go to down there and check out the space. It's very last-minute and I need to be back Friday for Yappy Hour and the Tails and Tiaras fund-raiser, so I'm not going to take Beepo." She pulled out a tattered multicolored blanket from her duffel and handed it to me. "I need you to watch him while I'm gone—"

"What? No. Yolanda. I got my own problems right now—"

"Maggie! You have to. This is the opportunity of a life-time."

"You'll have other opportunities."

She balled up her fist and stomped her foot like a pee-vish child. Beepo began to bark repeatedly at my feet.

"Hush," I said, pointing a finger at him. He growled at me, then barked louder, finishing with an elongated growl. I ignored the dog and said, "Yolanda, last night Gus and I found one of the DelVecchio waiters dead. Oscar Ruiz. Do you know him? He worked the same shift as Yappy Hour on the patio."

Yolanda face was curiously blank.

"Anyway . . ." I shoved the doggie blanket back into her duffel. "We found him dead behind the shared Dumpster last night. Shot in the back. Officer Brooks brought us in for questioning. He released me, but not Gus. I have to fig-ure out what happened—"

Yolanda began to pad around my kitchen, Beepo cir-cling her legs. "Don't you have any coffee?" she asked.

I shrugged. "I guess I forgot to pick some up."

Her hand fluttered over her heart and the look on her face said I'd just committed a mortal sin. Without saying a word, she rummaged in her bag again, pulling up the doggie bed and tossing it onto my couch. Next she yanked out her phone and clicked on the screen.

"What are you doing?" I asked.

"Making a note to bring you some coffee."

"I'm telling you about finding Oscar dead behind the Dumpster and all you care about is coffee?"

She looked offended. "Of course I care about Oscar. I care so much that I know I can't listen properly until I've had more caffeine."

I picked up the doggie bed and shoved it back into her duffel bag, exasperated.

"At least we know they got the guy responsible," Yolanda shrieked. "I can't wait to talk to Sergeant—"

"What do you mean? The guy responsible! Gus didn't kill Oscar or Dan."

"You don't know that! He had plenty of reason to kill Dan. Those two always fought like cats and dogs!"

Beepo let out a howl and jumped into the duffel bag.

Yolanda scooped him out of the duffel and returned the bed to the corner of my living room. Beepo followed her and nosed his way into the bed. She crooned at him.

I retreated to my kitchen and dug out some tea bags. "I have black tea. That's got caffeine, right?"

Yolanda made a face but said, "Fine."

Putting on the kettle to boil, I asked, "What did Gus and Dan fight about?"

Yolanda sat on my kitchen stool and looked out the sliding glass patio doors to the ocean, as if the answer to my question was rolling out there under the powerful dark caps of the Pacific. She sighed. "Dan dated a lot of girls, you know. A playboy. I've never seen Gus on a date, not once. A guy that good looking . . ." She shrugged. "He's gotta be gay."

My heart lurched into my throat. "He isn't gay!" I shrieked.

She raised a perfectly waxed eyebrow at me. "R-e-a-lly?" she asked slowly, stretching out the word. "And you know this . . . how? I thought you were dating Officer Brooks."

My face turned hot, and when the teakettle began to steam and screech, it felt like a kindred spirit. "Never mind about that. Brooks and I aren't *dating*. We went on a date. *One* date. But even if you think Gus is gay, which he's *not*, I don't see what that has to with—"

"What makes you so sure?" Beepo jumped onto Yolanda's lap. She narrowed her eyes at me, and Beepo's ears quirked toward me.

"What?" I asked.

"What makes you so sure Gus DelVecchio isn't gay?"

I pulled out my favorite mugs; they were white with the face of an owl lacquered on the front. I'd always considered them good luck. Hadn't someone once told me owls were lucky? Well, at the very least they were wise, and I felt the need for wisdom at the moment. I popped in small bags of black tea and then poured the boiling water in. I handed a steaming mug to Yolanda.

Yolanda studied the owl. "These are great, by the way. Would you like a matching purse?"

I covered my face and laughed a hearty, big, stress-relieving laugh. "No! Who wants an owl purse?"

"Who, who," Yolanda hooted.

We both began to laugh uncontrollably while Beepo growled.

"He doesn't like my animal purses," Yolanda confessed.

"Really? He's jealous?" I looked at Beepo, who returned my stare with his own watery eyes. I suddenly felt a tug of affection for him.

"Jealous? Do you think that's what it is?" Yolanda stroked his head, and he turned his attention to her. She looked back at me and whispered, "Anytime he sees one of my bags, he pees on it. That's why I can't carry one around myself."

"Why are we whispering?" I whispered back to her.

Her eyes moved suggestively toward Beepo, and she continued on in a dramatic whisper. "I don't want to hurt his feelings."

Beepo barked at us.

"See?" Yolanda said. "He knows what we're saying!"

"Well, if he knows, then what difference does whispering make? He's got the best hearing out of all of us."

Beepo lost interest in our conversation and scratched his way over to his bed. He tucked himself in and looked out over the Pacific.

Yolanda and I sipped our tea in silence.

After a moment, I said, "Okay, tell me about Gus and Dan."

"They fought about everything. Gus wanted Dan to put an end to Yappy Hour, said the dogs were killing his business."

An unsettling feeling churned my stomach.

Was Gus the force behind the letter to Rachel citing ABC and health violations?

Yolanda twirled her hair as she sipped her tea. "Dan told me that he was trying to sell his piece of the business."

"He did? He wanted to sell his half of DelVecchio's?"

She nodded. "Yeah. Said he was tired of constantly fighting with Gus. They used to be such good friends, and then they went into business together and it sort of killed the friendship. Especially when the business started to fail. They weren't even able to make the payments to the Meat and Greet. Restaurants are so tough . . . low margins . . ."

"Who knew about Dan wanting to sell out?"

Yolanda shrugged. "I don't know. Probably everybody. This a small town."

Dread began to build inside me, a question forming that I didn't want to ask. Yolanda's eyes were on mine, almost warning me off. Then, as if I were watching a gruesome accident on the side of the road, one that's so hard to turn away from, I faced the question between us.

"Who did Dan want to sell to?"

Yolanda cringed and shook her head.

The dread inside me grew to the point that my heart felt compressed in the process. I fingered the owl on my mug . . . not so lucky today . . . and its hooting echoed in my ears, the question of the day: who, who?

"Who?" I asked.

Yolanda grimaced. "Rachel. She wanted to buy Dan's share of DelVecchio's."

Chapter Twenty-two

"Rachel wanted to buy out Dan's share of DelVecchio's?" The shock reverberated throughout my body as if I'd been hit by a semitrailer. First, the internal organs feel the hit, blood rushing to your heart and head, leaving the limbs feeling numb and deadened. How much of what Rachel had really been up to did I know?

Yolanda pursed her lips. "Well, it was a good idea, right? She'd have a share in the business and then—"

"And then what? Force Gus out? Make it a doggie diner?"

Beepo yelped his protest from his little bed nestled against my window.

I buried my head in my hands. "This is awful, Yolanda. It gives Rachel even more motive to kill Dan."

"No, it doesn't!" Yolanda slammed her fist on my kitchen counter, and Beepo's ears flapped up. "It gives Gus motive! He didn't want Rachel ending up with half his business!"

"Well, the way she runs her life, I don't blame him!" I said.

"So when Dan went into the bar to get Rachel to sign the paperwork, Gus followed him and thumped him on the head with the magnum bottle."

I stared at Yolanda. "What paperwork?"

"The contract selling his share of the business to Rachel."

"There was a contract?"

Yolanda worked her lip and shrugged.

"Was there a contract, Yolanda? Tell me what you know."

She leveled a gaze at me, and Beepo came over as if sensing she needed his support. The bad feeling rumbling around my gut started to churn into determination. Had Yolanda shared her suspicions with Sergeant Gottlieb?

Is that why Gus was being held by the police?

So far nothing she'd said was conclusive, it was all hearsay, and certainly my type-A analytical personality needed more information. I was a by-the-numbers kind of gal. Things had to add up for me.

"I don't actually know if there was a contract." She scooped Beepo back into her lap and made a big show of kissing him. He licked at her lips. Finally, when she realized I'd wait out her dog-and-Yolanda show, she said, "It's just stuff I heard. . . ."

"From who?" I asked.

Her eyes grew wide. A shot to the heart of every gossip is to ask them to reveal their source. She leaned in close, as if she expected the person she was about to throw under the bus might manifest themselves out of thin air.

"Well, I'm not supposed to say. I was sworn to secrecy."

"I know." I refilled her tea mug. "But you have to realize that two people have died and my sister—"

"I'll tell you on one condition." She fidgeted in her chair, then lifted Beepo up and held him out toward me. He snarled. "I need to leave him with you."

"Yolanda, come on. Isn't there doggie day care or whatever, I'm not a dog—"

"Don't say it," she warned. "I'm only going to be overnight. My flight leaves in a couple hours. Pleeeeaaaaase."

"What . . ." I rolled my eyes to the ceiling as if patience was stored up there among my recessed lights. I sighed. "What do I have to do?"

She quirked her head to the side. "What do you mean, what do you have to do? Nothing. Feed him, walk him, love him."

"That's not nothing."

She stood abruptly. "Come on, Beep! We know when we're not wanted. Someone claims to want to help her sister. Someone claims to want to help Gus . . . and yet, when it come to a little quid pro quo, *someone* acts stupid."

"Don't call me stupid!"

"I'm not calling *you* stupid. I just said *someone*—"

"Come on, don't manipulate me. What do you know about Rachel!"

Yolanda bent over to put Beepo on the ground; he tore off out of sight. When she straightened she said, "She's in Vegas."

"What!"

"She's not on the cruise. She went to Vegas to elope."

"Was the whole accessory show a lie? Something you made up to go to Vegas?"

"No," Yolanda said adamantly. "The show is true." She thumped a hand over her heart. "You have to help me. Do you know how hard it is to get into that show?"

I turned my back on her and topped off my mug with hot water. I was getting to know her rhythm: If I showed a lack of concern, she'd come to me. If I pressed, she'd walk out in a huff. I rummaged through my cupboard. "I wish I had some little cookies to go with the tea. . . ."

"The show is absolutely true," Yolanda shrilled, unable to stand my disinterest a second longer. "But you're right, I was going to try and find Rachel, too."

"Do you know where she's staying in Vegas?"

Yolanda's head flipped to the right as if she found something else infinitely more interesting. *Ah, avoidance in its true glory.*

"Spit it out!" I said.

"She's staying at The Mirage."

The Mirage. How apropos. Everything felt like a mirage recently.

"Have you told your Sergeant Gottlieb this?"

She smoothed down her skirt. "Of course not! I wouldn't throw Rachel under the bus. I know Gus is the killer! Absolutely without a doubt!"

Suddenly Beepo tore down my hallway, yapping at the front door. Yolanda and I fell silent as my doorbell rang. We stared at each other in a game of chicken. The doorbell rang again.

Slipping out of the kitchen, I went to answer the door, but out of the corner of my eye, I was aware of Yolanda glancing at the slim gold bracelet watch on her wrist.

I swung open the door, hoping to see Rachel's bright face and give her a piece of my mind, but instead Officer Brooks was leaning into the door frame.

I jumped back, deadly embarrassed at my appearance. I was still in my rumpled robe, with no makeup on and my hair frizzed with bed head.

"Oh, hi!" I tightened the belt on my robe. "I wasn't expecting you."

He nodded, a serious expression on his face. "I'm sorry to barge in on you. Do you want to get dressed?"

"Oh, yeah. I . . . come in." I gestured toward the couch as he stepped toward my living room. Yolanda wiggled her fingers at him. He greeted her warmly and then bent to pick up Beepo, who was sniffing around his boots.

"Hey little fellow."

Beepo shook his Yorkie tail so hard in response to the attention, it seemed his little bottom would wiggle straight off.

I beelined toward my bedroom to get dressed. I slipped into a pair of tan capris and a peach-colored blouse, hoping it showed off my rosy complexion. I applied the bare minimum of makeup—a touch of lip gloss and a wave of the mascara wand—so Brooks wouldn't get the impression that I'd suddenly gone into a tizzy over him.

My hair was a different matter altogether. I wished I had time for a proper shower, complete with shampoo and blow-dry, but as it was, I couldn't afford to leave Yolanda unsupervised with Brooks too long. Who knew what gossip would be exchanged! I settled for spritzing my hair with a scented styling lotion, dragging a brush through it, and promising myself a trip to the beauty parlor soon.

I was half certain even Yolanda, Ms. Never-leave-the-house-unless-you-look-your-best, might approve my appearance, but even if she didn't, I didn't have thirty minutes to do a full coif.

What the heck was Officer Brooks doing here anyway?

Had he come to bring me news? Or to interrogate me about Rachel again? He certainly had a serious vibe going on, and that didn't bode well. I gave myself a final glance in the mirror.

There, much better!

I emerged into the living room and found it empty. Where was Yolanda? A shadow moved across my deck, and I realized that Officer Brooks was standing on my patio, which overlooked the beach.

I slid open the glass patio doors and stepped out onto the small deck with him. He was holding Beepo in his arm and squinting out toward the ocean, the sun beginning to bloom into full force over the water.

"Nice view," he said.

"Thank you," I muttered.

"I'm sorry about last night, Maggie," he said. Before I could reply, he continued. "I've got bad news. I wanted you to hear it from me. Gottlieb has put an all-call out on Rachel. We got confirmation from the forensic team: Rachel's prints were on the bottle that killed Dan."

I was stunned. I hadn't had a moment to process his apology before making out what he'd just said about Rachel.

"Of course her prints are on it!" I said a little too loudly. "It's her bar, her prints are on everything!"

"I know. I'm sorry. I tried to talk to Gottlieb, but he's suspicious about her disappearance. It doesn't look good and—"

"She hasn't disappeared. She's . . . she's . . . Where's Yolanda? She'll tell you."

Brooks tilted his head to the side, and he studied me a moment, a puzzled expression on his face. "Yolanda took off. She said you were watching Beepo for the day. Said she'd be back tomorrow."

He handed the dog to me. Beepo curiously refrained from snapping at me. It was as if he knew he had to be on good behavior now. I took the dog from Brooks and settled him against my chest. He let out a whimper to let me know he'd been abandoned by Yolanda, too. I stroked his head.

Brooks watched me with Beepo, giving me the impression he was evaluating me. What did it mean if I was good with a dog? Did it mean I was loving, kind, nurturing?

I set Beepo down on one of my deck chairs.

"Rachel didn't kill Dan," I said.

Brooks let out a sigh. "I believe you, Maggie. I don't think she did, either, but her disappearance and now . . . well . . . we've uncovered a few things in her background," Brooks continued, "that don't look . . . well, I can't say much right now. I hope you understand."

"I don't understand! What things?" Even as I asked, I knew I didn't really want the answer. My voice must have sounded shrill, because Beepo leapt off the chair and scurried to my defense, growling and yapping at Brooks.

Doggie homeland security at its finest.

"Maggie, I can't share all the details of the investigation. . . ." He reached out for my arm.

I shrugged him off. "Whose side are you on?"

He scowled. "I'm on Dan's side and Oscar's side. The side of justice!" His expression returned to solemn, reminding me this wasn't a social call.

Why couldn't he just be here asking me out on a date? What did I have to do with all these troubles?

It had been a stupid question. What could he have said?

Still, I was on Rachel's side, that was for sure. I knew my sister and, yes, even though she was harebrained and impulsive and didn't think things through, she wasn't a murderer.

"If you find that Rachel did anything, I'm sure it was in self defense."

Was that the right thing to say?

I probably should have argued that Rachel wasn't a killer. Anxiety rippled across my chest. It seemed like there was no winning here.

Brooks pressed his lips together and looked out toward the ocean. The sun was getting higher, the heat wave in Pacific Cove would live another day. I tried to find hope in that. If the sun shone brightly that day, then everything would turn out all right . . . right?

"Rachel didn't kill Dan or Oscar," I insisted. "We know she's not even in Pacific Cove . . . how could she have killed Oscar?"

Brooks sighed. "I want to believe that, too," he said in a low voice. "But I can't take sides like that. I have to follow all the leads."

"Are there more leads? Who else are you looking into?" He was quiet, and I said in a mocking voice, "I'm not at liberty to say."

He squared his shoulders toward me and narrowed his eyes. "Gus DelVecchio."

I tried to repress the shudder that surged through me, but Brooks saw it anyway.

"Are you going to argue his innocence as well?"

I shook my head, feeling a bit defeated. I looked out at the Pacific for strength, and then asked the question I really didn't want to know the answer to: "Was it his gun that killed Oscar?"

Instead of answering, Brooks countered, "Do you know if Rachel owns a gun?"

Nausea threatened, and I squeezed my eyes shut to ward off the sensation. This was a turning point, I knew. If I sided with my sister, I'd likely alienate Brooks, who I so desperately wanted to get to know better, and yet . . . she was my sister, protecting her was second nature to me. Even as I told the lie, I knew Brooks saw through me. "I don't know."

"Um hum, that's what I thought," he said, keeping his eyes on mine, as if to give me another opportunity to answer.

Instead, I asked, "What about Yolanda?"

Beepo barked sharply at me, sensing my betrayal of his lovely owner. Guilt hammered at my temples. How could I throw Yolanda under the bus after she had been so nice to me? But the instinct to protect Rachel was overwhelming.

"What about her?" Brooks asked.

"Yolanda was standing over Dan when I walked into The Wine and Bark on Friday night. She could have easily cracked him on the head—"

"Finding a body is not a crime," he said.

"I heard from the singer of the Howling Hounds that Yolanda and Dan were fighting over the fund-raiser."

Brooks said in a low patient voice, "Yolanda's prints were not on the bottle. . . ."

"She could have worn gloves! She's got thick leather driving gloves. She wore them the day we drove to . . ." I stopped myself short. I couldn't complete my sentence without admitting I'd gone to Stag's Leap looking for Rachel and found a semi-death threat to Dan instead. "And she just left town! She could be fleeing the scene—"

I knew I was grasping at straws, but couldn't stop myself. Brooks leveled a gaze at me, a cross between pity and frustration. "I don't think she'd leave Beepo with you if she was fleeing the scene."

"Oh sure," I said. "Defend her!"

"I'm sorry, Maggie. I just came over so you could hear

it from me." He turned and walked back through my living room, toward the door. He left without another word, the door to my apartment slamming alongside the one to my heart.

Chapter Twenty-three

Well, this was a fine how-do-you-do; now I was stuck with Beepo while I tried to figure out what in the world had happened to Dan and Oscar.

Their deaths had to be connected. Was Oscar killed because he'd seen something tied to Dan's murder? When Brooks asked me about Rachel owning a gun, was it because Gus's gun maybe wasn't a forensic match to Oscar's wound? Was Rachel's? I hadn't see her gun when I searched her apartment, but that didn't mean anything. Maybe she kept it locked up at the bar. I racked my brain to think of where she would keep it.

Beepo howled up at me and pushed his bowl over to me with his nose. I rummaged through the duffle Yolanda had left and dug out a bag of kibbles.

I poured a cup of kibbles into Beepo's bowl. The sound of the kibbles knocking together drove him insane. He inhaled his meal and then, five seconds later, he looked up at me with pleading brown eyes. Just what was he thinking?

Please, give me another helping of food, I promise I won't burst.

Ignoring him, I picked up my cell phone and scrolled through the virtual yellow pages, looking for the number to The Mirage in Vegas. How dare Yolanda tell me Rachel was there, then take off to Vegas without me, leaving me in charge of doggie day care!

While I was holding the phone, it rang in my hand, and I instantly thought Rachel was calling. We usually had a case of sister ESP. I clicked over and answered the call on the second ring.

"Is this Maggie?" an unfamiliar voice asked.

The gravity in the man's voice unsettled me. Who was this calling and why? "Yes," I said. "Who's calling?"

"This is Benny." Benny was my great-uncle's horse bookie. If he was calling, the news couldn't be good.

"What is it, Benny? Is my Uncle Ernest all right?"

"Sorry to have to tell you this, honey, but he's in the hospital."

"Oh my gosh, no." My stomach cramped with worry. "What happened? Is he okay? Not another heart attack?" Beepo came to rest by my feet.

Did he sense my agitation?

"No, no, nothing like that," said Benny. "He was dragged by one of the horses."

"What? Dragged by a horse?"

"Yeah, I told him not to do it, but he was walking around the track—well, that's probably no big deal. He's done it a million times. I got a call on my cell phone, and I shouldn't have been distracted like that, but I left him. Now I feel horrible. Something must have spooked the horse, because he took off running and your uncle got caught in the lead. Tangled up really bad and dragged a few yards."

"Oh my Lord," I said.

"Yeah. His shoulder's pulled out of whack and he's bruised up around the hip. I'm surprised he didn't break a bone because, you know, at his age it doesn't take much. I got to him fast, thankfully. Called an ambulance and now he's in the hospital. He's not hurt so bad, though, so I think they'll release him soon, but probably not for a few days yet."

Relief flooded me. Thank God that it sounded like Grunkly would recover.

"I'm on my way," I said, hanging up. As I grabbed my bag, Beepo followed me around. "Not you, Beepo. I can't take you a hospital."

He yowled his complaint at me.

I pointed to his bed by the window. "Come on, I just fed you. By a dear and have a nap, I'll be back before you wake up."

Oh my God, I was talking to the dog now!

He looked at me unconvinced, but padded over to his bed and climbed in.

"That's a good boy," I said as I rushed out of my apartment. In fact, I stormed out so quickly I collided straight into a man. The man's hands grabbed my arms and I screamed.

"Maggie, it's me! Gus," he said. "Don't hit me again!"

Beepo barked from the inside of my apartment. Ah, he wanted to help me!

"Oh, Gus, you scared me. You have to stop sneaking up on me like that!"

"I wasn't sneaking up on you, I was about to knock."

He squeezed my arms and warmth zagged through my body. It seemed like we both noticed it at the same time because he suddenly let go and stuck his right hand into his jacket pocket.

"Um, the police released you?" I asked stupidly.

He nodded. "Yeah. They don't have any evidence to charge me. I told them they weren't going to find any, because I didn't do it, but they made it clear they were still going to try to get something. Dan's folks are in town; they went down to the station and spoke on my behalf. They told me they want to hire a lawyer for me. . . ." He sighed. "Let's hope it doesn't come to that."

"I just got a call from my uncle's friend, Benny. Grunkly's in the hospital," I said.

A worried look crossed Gus's face. "The hospital? Is he all right?"

"I think so. Pulled his shoulder out and he's bruised up his hips. I'm on my way to see him now."

"Do you need a ride? I can take you," he asked.

"That would be great." I didn't yet have a car in Pacific Cove and would otherwise have had to call a cab.

We exited my building through the front doors while I brought him up to speed on Grunkly's accident. He gasped.

"He got dragged by a horse? That's crazy!"

"I know, it's scary. I've tried to talk him into letting Benny and his horse trainer, Aaron, take care of that stuff, but Grunkly is stubborn as a mule. Always has been."

Gus and I walked toward a black BMW and he pressed the key fob in his hand. The car chirped in response and we climbed in. We drove the distance to Pacific Cove General Hospital. The day was warm, and for a brief moment I was able to put aside my worries about Rachel, Dan, and Oscar and actually enjoy the drive. But after a moment I began to feel guilty that I wasn't fretting about Grunkly.

What would I do without him? Grunkly had always been a steady influence in my life.

I felt responsible for his accident, like it was my fault. I'd been so caught up in figuring out where Rachel was and running the bar that I hadn't paid sufficient enough attention to Grunkly. I should have insisted he hire a new nurse and forbade him to go down to the track.

Gus glanced over at me.

A flush spread across my cheeks. Not to mention I'd been distracted by Gus. What was going on between us?

"Don't worry too much, Maggie," Gus said. "I'm sure your uncle will be fine."

"Thank you. I'm worried about you, too," I said.

He pulled into a parking spot and glanced at me. "Me? Why?"

"Because I think you're right—the cops like you as a suspect. They like my sister as one, too, for that matter, which also worries me."

He turned off the engine. "Do you know something I don't?"

I shrugged. "I'm not sure, Gus. I know Rachel didn't kill Dan or Oscar."

"Me too," he said, getting out of the car and coming over to my side to open my door.

"But I have a bad feeling about the gun that was used," I confided.

Gus held the door open for me and took my elbow. "Did Rachel own a gun?" he asked.

I grimaced. He sighed and walked me over toward the main hospital doors. Upon entering, we passed by a vacant nurses' station and ducked into a hospital corridor toward Grunkly's room. In the narrow passageway we intersected with Officer Brooks. Gus's grip tightened around my elbow.

"Brooks, what are you doing here?" I asked. My voice suddenly sounded shrill in my ears. I flushed, feeling embarrassed, as if I'd been caught red-handed doing something naughty.

What did I care if Gus's hand was on my arm?

It didn't mean anything. I was simply taking solace in a friend.

"I came to talk to your uncle," Brooks said. "He wanted to give a statement."

"A statement?" I asked.

"Yeah, he said someone was on the track and they spooked the horse intentionally."

A shiver raced up my spine. Someone intentionally scared the horse? "Who? Do you know who?" I asked.

Brooks shook his head. "He didn't know. Didn't really get a good look."

"Was it a man or woman?" I asked.

Brooks pressed his lips together and glanced at Gus. I followed his glare. Gus released my elbow and quirked an eyebrow at Brooks.

"Well, I won't keep you," Brooks said, passing by Gus and me in the corridor.

I wanted to call after him, but I didn't know what to say. Instead, I pushed open the door to Grunkly's hospital room. My great-uncle was seated in bed, his arm in a sling and eyes glued to the screen mounted overhead. He was watching racehorses on TV.

"Mags, this horse has thirty-to-one odds to place." There was a gray tray table in front of him with several packets of saltine crackers and a pitcher of ice water on it.

"How are you, Grunkly? You gave me quite a scare," I said.

"Did Benny tell you? The horse dragged me. Pulled my arm right out of its socket. Doc says I'm going to need to go to physical therapy." The way he said it made me certain he'd do anything but go to physical therapy. "But I'm fine, really. I'll be ready to go home after this." He indicated the TV.

Gus chuckled. I poked him in the ribs.

"Grunkly, I don't think you're going to be released today. Benny said you need to be observed overnight."

Grunkly waved a hand at me, indicating he thought the prognosis was nonsense.

"Don't listen to him, Maggie. I'm fine. Did you bring me some Lucky Strikes?"

Gus laughed again, and this time I turned to him and said, "You're not helping."

Grunkly saw Gus as his ally and smiled immediately.

"You got a car?" he asked. Without waiting for an answer, he moved aside the tray table. "I'm sprung!"

I pushed the tray table back into place. "What do you think you're doing? You're not sprung. You're not in jail, you know, this is a hospital." I suddenly remembered that Gus had likely spent the larger part of last night in a jail cell. Cringingly, I looked over at him and whispered, "Sorry."

Gus gave me a little wink, letting me know I hadn't offended him.

My great-uncle stared at us, his eyes wide. "I'm fine, Maggie. I'm telling you, I don't need to be in here." He patted his flat stomach. "I just need to get a little something to eat."

Gus smiled. "Now you're talking my language. I can bring you a special delivery later. Maybe a some chicken parmagiana or five-cheese ziti al forno? You tell me. What do you want?"

Grunkly's jaw dropped, and I noticed the food talk was the only thing that drew his eyes away from the TV. "Now that sounds real good."

Opening one of the saltine packages, I handed Grunkly a cracker. He made a face. "Let's talk to the doctor first before we make any exit or dining plans," I said. "Now tell us what happened."

He recounted walking on the racetrack, training the horse, and seeing somebody spook the horse.

"Who do you think it was?" I asked.

He shrugged. "I really don't know, Maggie. We should ask Benny."

"Where is he?" I asked.

As if on cue, Benny pushed open the door, holding a bag of Chinese takeout. Alongside the steaming white boxes was a small package wrapped in a brown paper bag. Benny shuffled the brown bag around while trying to distract me by pouring Grunkly a glass of water.

I narrowed my eyes at him. "What's in the package, Benny?"

Grunkly and Benny exchanged looks. "It's nothing, Maggie," he said, shoving the package inside his jacket pocket.

"Hand it over," I demanded, laying my hand out palm-side up.

Benny made a face but gave me the bag nonetheless.

I peeked inside the brown paper bag and found cigarettes. "I can't believe you!" I scolded. "You know Grunkly isn't supposed to smoke."

Benny looked properly chastened, but Grunkly ignored me completely. "Two minutes to post."

I glanced at the TV. I knew I was about to lose their attention.

"Benny, who spooked the horse? Did you get a look at them? Was it a man or a woman?"

He said, "I'm sorry, Maggie, I didn't really get a good look. I was on the phone." He pressed his lips together in a semi-apology as he tore open one of the Chinese food boxes.

The bugle sounded and the horses were off.

"Go, baby, go!" Grunkly yelled.

And I knew I'd lost my audience.

Chapter Twenty-four

Gus sat on my couch while I fussed in the kitchen scrounging around for lunch. Beepo buzzed around my feet, presumably hoping for a treat. My fridge was stocked with frozen pizzas, carrot sticks, and ranch dressing. I couldn't very well offer the premier chef of Pacific Cove anything frozen. I fought back the heartburn bubbling up that erupted just from thinking about cooking for Gus.

"I really don't know what to offer you. Should I order takeout?"

He shrugged, listless. "Don't worry about it, Maggie. I'm not hungry." He dragged a hand through his hair. "Do you have any beer?"

I pulled out a bottle of pilsner from my fridge and poured it into a tall glass for Gus. "Did Oscar say anything to you? Was he scared of anything or anyone?"

Gus accepted the glass. "No. I wasn't really close with Oscar. Our hostess, Melanie, and he were dating. A little off and on, but she knew him pretty well." He took a sip of his beer. "I talked to her briefly this morning when I left the police station. She's in complete shock. Said she didn't know of any threats or anything like that."

"He had to have been killed because he saw or knew something, right? Otherwise it doesn't make sense," I said.

"Right."

"Did you ask Melanie if Oscar saw anything the night Dan was killed?"

Gus shook his head. "She told me she didn't know anything. She's been interviewed by the police already, too. Apparently told them the same thing."

"Maybe I can talk to her. I mean, what if she's scared and just not saying anything?"

Gus nodded and pulled out his cell phone. "Here's her number. I had the same thought, but it seemed to me she was telling the truth."

I punched her number in my phone, and got her voice mail. I left her a message, then collapsed onto the couch next to Gus, feeling completely defeated.

Gus sat still, looking like he was falling into a depression.

Beepo sat at our feet, seemingly waiting for something exciting to happen.

"Gus, can I ask you something?"

He gave me a curious look. "You can ask me anything, Maggie."

"Did you and Dan fight all the time?"

A look of surprise crossed Gus's face. "Who told you that?" Gus's shoulders slumped. "Well, we were fighting a lot lately, but that doesn't mean I killed him. We were just going through a rough patch." He sulked in silence for a moment, then took a sip of his beer. "That's one of the hardest parts of his passing—that we were in a bad spot. I hate that I can't tell him how much he meant to me and . . ."

The look on Gus's face was full-on anguish, and I wished there was something I could say to soothe him. We sat for a moment and looked out at the ocean. Finally I asked, "Did Dan want out of the business?"

Gus's spine straightened and he looked insulted. "No! Absolutely not. You can ask his folks if you don't believe me. They came to see me yesterday—"

"Me, too."

Gus frowned. "Why did they come to see you?"

"I think they're looking for answers, too," I said simply.

Gus sighed, but said nothing.

"Did you want to buy him out of the business, have full control in the restaurant . . . ?"

"You know, one of the reasons I wanted to go into business with Dan is because he was savvy about the accounting side of things. I don't care so much about that. I just want to provide a nice experience at my restaurant, you know? People go out to eat to create a memory, get engaged, celebrate a birthday, a baptism. I wanted DelVecchio's to be part of that. Be part of the fabric of people's lives. I don't care about the money. When Dan told me we were losing our shirts . . ."

"DelVecchio's is in trouble?"

Gus buried his face in his hands. "Dan said we had about one month's operating expenses in the books. I don't know . . . what I'm going to do. . . ."

"Wait, have you seen the books?"

Gus looked up at me from his sunken position on the couch. He looked a bit like he had a fever, his face flushed and sweaty, his eyes wild. "What?"

"You said Dan told you DelVecchio's was in dire straits, but do you know that for certain? How often do you review the books?"

He scratched his head. "Maggie, I'm a chef. I don't look at the books. I mean, he'd show me spreadsheets and stuff, but what? The columns aren't any bigger than a gnat's eyelash and—"

"Can I see them?"

"Huh?"

I sat up straighter. "Will you show me the books? Maybe I can help."

"You want to help me save DelVecchio's?"

"Yes."

His face cleared a bit and the skin around eyes relaxed. "Why?"

I bumped his arm with my shoulder as I leaned into him. "So you can cook for me, silly."

He wrapped an arm around me. "Maggie," he said in a low voice that made my insides vibrate, "that's the nicest thing anyone's ever said to me."

He gently placed a hand under my chin and lifted my face toward his. Electricity fired between us.

Gus was definitely not gay!

His lips tilted toward mine, but before they reached me, Beepo sprang into my lap and growled at him. Gus burst out laughing.

◇◇◇

Later that day, Gus and I decided to try to catch Oscar's on-again, off-again girlfriend, Melanie, on the way to the farmers market to stock my fridge.

We walked on the cobblestone streets toward Magic Read. Gus said the guy that worked there with the Mohawk was Melanie's brother, and we took a gamble that he might know where to reach her.

When we got there, the Mohawk dude was sprawled on a multicolored carpet doing a trick for Coral. Coral watched him excitedly, her eyes fixed on the card the clerk held in his hands.

"But how did you know it was the queen of hearts?" Coral demanded.

The clerk laughed. "You always pick the same card. Anyone would be able to guess it. Even they would know which one it was." He gestured toward Gus and me, and the snake tattoo that covered his arm danced. "I'll do it again. This time pick another card."

Coral wiggled her fingers at me, and Beepo shot into her lap. She stroked his head affectionately and whispered into his triangle ear, "But the queen of hearts is my favorite!"

Gus pulled out a chair for me on the same carpet, then flicked a chair backward for himself to sit on, his arms resting on the back of the chair. We watched the clerk surprise Coral three more times, by picking her card out of the pack. He even indulged a small math tutorial from me when I started yelling out, "Now add three to the number. How about take away one?"

When he began shuffling the cards again, Gus asked, "Say, do you know how to reach Melanie?"

The clerk frowned. "Didn't she show up to work?"

Gus's eyes darted toward Coral, who was busy murmuring sweet nothings to Beepo. I figured he didn't want to talk about Oscar's demise in front of her. Instead, he said, "We're closed for the week. I just need to talk to her."

The clerk shrugged. "Did you try her cell?"

Gus and I nodded.

The clerk chewed on his lower lip. "She's probably at the caves."

Gus clapped him on the back. "Thank you. Next time, you'll have to show me a couple tricks."

The clerk nodded, then waved at me. "I'll see you Friday at the Tails and Tiaras fund-raiser."

"Oh, you're coming?" I asked.

"Not coming. Performing. Yolanda came by yesterday and asked me to do an opening number for The Howling Hounds. Right after the auction."

Oh my God: auction, magic, music. It was going to be one busy night.

"You're the opener? That'll be fun." I looked around at the area where we were seated and I couldn't imagine Evie playing in such a small space. "Where does she play when she comes here?" I asked.

The clerk frowned. "Here? Evie doesn't play here."

Hadn't she told me yesterday she had a gig here?

"Oh, maybe I misunderstood her. Well, I'll look forward to seeing you perform at The Wine and Bark." I leaned in closer to him, out of earshot of Gus and Coral. "Can you make people disappear? There's a few patrons I'd like to get rid of, and their dogs," I said. Beepo howled insanely at us.

The clerk smiled widely. "I'm perfecting that trick myself."

I waved at him and Coral as Gus and I left the shop. Beepo followed, albeit reluctantly.

"The caves are near the farmers market. We can stop by there first and see if we can find Melanie, what do you say?"

Beepo barked a response as if Gus had asked him.

"That sounds great," I said. "I haven't been out to the caves in so long. Not since I was a kid and we'd visit Grunkly. I'd love to see them."

◇◇◇

The sound of the Pacific can be soothing and frightening at the same time. As we looked over the ocean from the cliff above the caves, the relentless pounding of the water was downright deafening. It rattled my teeth and sent a shiver of fear up my legs.

Beepo pressed his nose into my ankle and I picked him up. He was shaking and attempted to bury himself inside my shirt. "Do you think she's down there?" I asked Gus, indicating a trail that meandered to the caves.

He shrugged. "We won't know until we hike down there." He looked at me speculatively. "Do you want me to go? And you and Beepo stay up here?"

Beepo yapped appreciatively, his tail wagging madly.

"No, no, no. I can hike down."

Beepo barked sharply at me in protest. As if in answer, the sea lions that sheltered in the caves began to bark, and Beepo's ears shot up. Suddenly, he was curious about whatever lived down below, and he raced out of my arms and darted toward the trailhead.

Gus followed Beepo and said to me, "Let me go first. It's steep. You can hold on to my shoulder if you want."

He led me down the trail, the sound of waves crashing against the rocks increasing as we descended toward the shore. The dirt trail was slippery and slick. I squeezed Gus's muscular shoulder to steady myself. If I hadn't been scared out of my mind about toppling into the ocean, I might have found the setting romantic. As it was, I wondered about my sanity, coming here with a man that just last night had been held by the police on suspicion of murder.

As if reading my thoughts, Gus turned around and said, "Don't worry, Maggie. You can trust me."

I smiled, hopefully in a reassuring manner.

"The farmers market is much less treacherous," he said. "We only have to navigate zucchinis and tomatoes."

My foot slipped out from under me and I slid up against his back. He swung an arm around my waist and kept me from falling into one of the blueberry shrubs that lined the Pacific Coast Trail. My heart unexpectedly leapt as I felt his arms around me. I giggled, relief flooding me. It was fine to trust Gus. At least with my life; I wasn't so sure about trusting him with my heart, but nonetheless I clung a little tighter to him.

All I wanted to do was stay snuggled up next to him. Beepo, however, had a mind of his own and barked up ahead of us, his tiny feet having already carried him to the first cave.

Gus cleared his throat and separated from me slowly. "Let's see if Melanie's here."

The cave was cold and dark, and Gus's voice echoed off the rocks as he called out, "Mel? Melanie?" The tide was low, thankfully, otherwise we would have been in ankle-deep water, calling her name over and over again as we searched the recesses of the cave.

"Gus?" a voice called out.

Outside of the cave was a small woman; she waved at us and motioned us out. She had a blanket laid out and a small knapsack open. Beepo shot out ahead of us and buried his nose into her bag.

"Your brother told us you might be here," Gus said, by way of explanation. "I was worried about you. Are you all right?"

Melanie lowered herself onto the blanket and pulled Beepo onto her lap. "Yeah, I just needed time to think. This is where I come . . ." She looked me up and down.

Gus said, "This is my friend, Maggie. She's taken over The Wine and Bark while Rachel's away."

"I'm sorry for your loss," I said. "We were so saddened to find Oscar."

Melanie nodded. "Thank you. I'm still in shock. I feel like he's going to text me at any minute and ask me out."

Gus settled himself next to her on the blanket; she buried her face into his chest and wept. He hugged her, letting her cry, and stroked her long black hair. She was young, probably only twenty, and the tears stopped just as abruptly as they'd started.

"We were supposed to go out last night, you know, since the restaurant was closed. He texted me and said he would meet me, but he never did. Then this morning the police showed up. I can't believe he was killed." She clutched at Gus's arm. "Just like Dan!"

Gus pressed his lips together, his face showing his distress.

"Someone shot him in the back," Melanie said. "The police said it looked like he was running away from someone. That he almost got away, because the gun they fired was so small, but the bullet lodged in the wrong place. . . ."

I suddenly felt weak, and I fell to my knees on the blanket. Beepo circled around me protectively.

Oh God, say it isn't so.

Clearing my throat, I found the strength to ask the question. "Did the police mention what type of gun?"

Melanie nodded. "Ruger P45, whatever that is."

I knew exactly what it was. It was a small-caliber handgun . . . the kind Rachel owned.

Chapter Twenty-five

Beepo and I followed Gus around the farmers market like two children following an all-star celebrity. Everything Gus did seemed important: If he picked up a tomato and sniffed it, I wanted to know why. If he passed on the broccoli and selected the zucchini instead, I questioned him. When he squeezed the eggplants, I asked him what he was looking for.

Beepo, of course, didn't ask any questions, he only begged for scraps.

Finally, after a fragrant trip spent taste-testing our way through the market, we headed back to my apartment, stopping briefly at DelVecchio's for Gus to dig out the financial reports.

I hadn't let on to either Gus or Melanie that the gun that killed Oscar was the same type of gun Rachel owned, but when we stopped at DelVecchio's for the reports, I told Gus I would pick out a bottle of wine for us for dinner from The Wine and Bark. It was an excuse, of course: I was dying to look for the Ruger P45. If I knew my sister, she'd likely kept it in the bar for protection. Somewhere close, where she could get to it quickly but also a place that was hidden.

I avoided looking down the alley where we'd found Oscar; nevertheless, I still saw that there was yellow crime scene tape cordoning it off. We'd stay closed for the night and maybe the following night, too, or until the tape was removed. Staying closed wasn't the worst thing; after the day I'd had, the last thing I wanted to do was tend bar.

I absently wondered if we'd be open for the Tails and Tiaras fund-raiser. It was good Yolanda was out of town; otherwise, she might just have had a stroke at the thought of canceling it.

The first place I looked was the small storage room that Yolanda wanted Evie to rent in exchange for the storefront side. Rachel had several boxes stacked there, mostly liquor but a few marketing boxes with leashes, bowls, and even doggie sweaters with the Wine and Bark logo on them.

When I finished searching the small storage room, I rummaged around behind the bar, opening and closing every conceivable drawer I could find. Beepo followed me around as I scoured the bar, yapping at me until I gave him a Bark Bite. Next, I searched the makeshift kitchen and came up emptyhanded.

I shuddered, thinking that I'd left Max alone in the bar the other night when I'd gone to DelVecchio's . . . could Max have taken the gun? Did he have a reason to frame Rachel?

Where else could the gun be? Was it at her apartment and I'd missed it? Of course, I'd had no reason to look for it when I'd been there last.

Through the window I could see Gus making his way across the courtyard. I grabbed a decent bottle of merlot and rushed out to meet him.

⋄⋄⋄

The smell of tagliatelle al sugo di funghi permeated my entire apartment. At the farmers market we'd picked up the key ingredients, like mushrooms, onions, and garlic. Gus sang in the kitchen while he cooked and I pored over his spreadsheets.

The restaurant brought in plenty of money, yet every month showed a loss. It seemed like money had been disappearing every which way. Poor cash handling, poor records, and worse, poor management on Dan's part.

And worse still, it was clear that someone was stealing from DelVecchio's.

A sickening thought kept pinballing around my head: either Dan had taken the money and Gus was innocent, or someone else was stealing it. . . . Could Dan have been killed to keep the truth from coming out?

I shifted on the couch to watch Gus cook. He was chopping garlic so expertly it looked like a dance.

He must have felt my gaze, because he looked up and asked, "You like garlic bread, Maggie?"

"Love it," I said.

A smile brightened his face, but I could see the toll the night at the police station had taken on him. He uncorked the bottle of merlot and poured me a healthy serving. "Did you know new studies show drinking wine is better for you than going to the gym?"

I took the glass he offered and smiled. "Somehow I've always known that."

"Me too," he said, sipping from his own glass.

"Anyway, I think I'm allergic to gyms."

He chuckled. "Well, they certainly don't smell like this." He sniffed the wine, which was slowly opening up and becoming fragrant, but it was no competition for the aroma wafting out from the cooking garlic bread.

He leaned back on one of the bar stools at my kitchen counter, crossing his long, jean-clad legs at the ankle. I couldn't help but notice how sexy and taut his entire body was.

Trying to navigate to a safe topic, I said, "Hmmm. I think it smells like heaven in here. Don't you?"

He said, "Only if heaven smells like garlic."

"Well, what else can it smell like?"

Gus smiled. "The ocean: salty, rich, and intense."

"Does intensity smell?"

"Yeah."

"It does? What does it smell like?" I asked.

He shrugged. "Energy. Metallic."

A chill came over me, goose bumps covered my arms, and I shuddered.

Gus frowned. "What is it?"

"Metallic. That's what blood smells like. The Wine and Bark, when I went in that night and found Dan dead—there was a metallic scent in the air."

Gus's face grew solemn, and he dragged a hand through his thick dark hair.

"I heard a rumor that Rachel wanted to buy Dan out. Was that true?" I asked.

He shook his head. "No."

We stared at each other.

He shrugged. "Did Yolanda tell you that, too?"

Beepo's ears perked up at his mistress's name, and he kept his eyes on Gus, waiting for an invitation to yowl at him.

I thought about what else Yolanda had said about Gus. Seemed like there was history there. . . .

Gus sipped his wine and eyed Beepo. "I won't say anything bad about her in front of her dog."

Beepo let out a deep growl followed by a sharp bark.

Gus nodded. "I know. I feel that way, too."

Laughing, I said, "You talk dog now?"

He shook his head. "I'm not a dog whisperer."

"Me either," I admitted.

"How'd you get stuck watching him?"

Beepo looked at me, his Yorkie ears perking up.

"Yolanda jetted out of here to Vegas. She was asked to be an exhibitor in some accessory show."

Gus let out a laugh that started like a locomotive: first a chuckle, then a sidesplitting guffaw. "Not for those God-awful chicken bags. Please tell me it's not a trend."

Laughter bubbled out of me until tears spilled out my eyes. We laughed so hard we ended up leaning against each other; suddenly, we were belly to belly, chest to chest, our faces inches away from each other.

My breath caught as he leaned into me, tilting his head so that our foreheads and noses touched. "Maggie," he whispered.

"Hmmm," I whispered back.

"You're driving me crazy," he said in low voice. His hand wrapped around my waist and he pulled me closer.

"Why's that?"

"Because all you want to do is talk about Dan and Rachel, and Yolanda and her stupid dog," he whispered. Beepo yowled up at us. "And all I want to do is kiss you," he said.

I looked into his dark eyes and his gaze was so intense it inflamed my blood. "I want to know what happened to Dan and Oscar," I murmured.

"Me too, but tonight I want to forget about them and think about us."

His mouth pressed against my lips, shutting down my mind and sending my body into overdrive.

Us?

Uh oh, I was in trouble.

◇◇◇

Miraculously, we didn't burn the garlic bread. We came up for air just as the oven chirped. Gus rushed over and pulled out the crispy warm bread.

He plated the tagliatelle al sugo di funghi and motioned for me to have a seat. "Signorina, please sit down and enjoy."

He was going to serve me, too? It seemed too good to be true.

I sat down and sipped my wine. My head was spinning. Was it possible something wonderful could happen between us during this awful time? And then, like a bad recurring dream, the thought came to me: What if Gus really was responsible for Dan's death . . . and Oscar's, too?

Gus had been alone all night at DelVecchio's. I'd seen him walk in with Oscar. . . .

No, Gus was too gentle to be a killer, and he was committed to getting to the bottom of these murders. But someone did it—and I knew it wasn't Rachel.

Of course, there was another sexy guy committed to finding the killers, too. . . .

Then, as if to play on my Catholic guilt, Brooks's face flashed before my eyes. I'd never dated two guys at the same time in my life. Not that I'd had that many boyfriends, but still. My first boyfriend had been in grade school and we'd dated until I'd graduated high school. After that, it had been a series of boyfriends, through college and living in New York, but never two at one time. Not that I was exactly dating either one of them. . . .

Who knew being unemployed and tripping over a body could spruce up a love life?

Gus watched me shovel the tagliatelle al sugo di funghi into my mouth. He broke off a piece of garlic bread and placed it on the side of my plate. "It was a good thing we got to the farmers market. There's nothing like fresh food. They have the market again tomorrow. I can get fresh asparagus, zucchini, tomatoes, eggplant. I can make you caponata alla Siciliana, and make it for your great-uncle, too, as soon as the hospital releases him."

"You can make me anything anytime, Gus," I said, savoring the next forkful.

He plated himself a dish and sat next to me at the counter, our thighs resting against each other. Heat surged through me and I suddenly felt happy. I had fears about Gus, sure. I mean, a guy this sexy, and one who could cook? He was certainly destined to be a heartbreaker. Why wasn't every woman in town after him?

I squinted at him, watching him swirl the food around on his plate while I inhaled mine. Finally he asked, "Did you find anything in the books, Maggie? How bad is it? Is DelVecchio's really in dire straits?"

"Cash flow's a problem. Looks like you're bringing in enough, but the expenses are so high. Rent, utilities, and discretionary spending. It seems like you guys are burning more money than you're bringing in."

He frowned. "Discretionary spending? What do you mean?"

"A partner draw every month for fifteen thousand."

Anger flashed across his face. "What?"

"You were paying yourselves, right?"

"Yes, but not fifteen thousand."

I pushed aside my plate and grabbed the books. We covered each line item until we got to the partner draw. "I don't take a draw. I've been living off my savings for the last year since we opened the restaurant."

I pressed my hand against his. "Gus, it looks like someone was stealing from the business."

Gus frowned, but before he could reply, the phone buzzed. It was a message from Grunkly. "Sprung from the hospital, can you come get me?"

Gus looked over my shoulder as I read the message, his hand on my lower back. "Looks like I'll be cooking for him sooner rather than later. Let's go!"

◇◇◇

"Will you tell them I don't need another nurse, Maggie?"

I stood between a male nurse in blue scrubs and Grunkly, who was relaxing in a wheelchair, ready to be loaded into Gus's BMW. The nurse had a scowl on his face, which led me to believe he wasn't going to listen to Grunkly's evasion techniques. "I'll be at your house tomorrow at noon."

"You gotta listen to them, Ernest," Benny said. "I can't lose another good client this week or I'll be out of business." He patted Gus's arm. "I'm sorry about your friend. He was a regular."

Gus bolted upright. "What do you mean?"

Gus and I exchanged looks. Suddenly we knew where the fifteen-thousand-dollar monthly draws had gone. Horse races!

Chapter Twenty-six

I was roused from a beautiful dream, where Gus was declaring his undying love for me over a bowl of steaming spaghetti marinara, by Beepo howling in my ear. His front paw was tapping at my eye socket while his wet nose jabbed against my mouth.

"Get off!" I said, rubbing at my eye as he barked in my ear.

He growled at me, and something else registered in my psyche: the insistent ringing of my cell phone. I reluctantly pried an eye open as the cogs in my brain started to turn.

I sighed, sitting halfway up in bed, and fumbled for the phone. "Hello?"

"I found her!" Yolanda shrieked.

Beepo let out a cacophony of doggie noise as he registered the voice of my caller. Yolanda heard him and let out her own matching symphony of noise: "Beep, Beep, Beep, Beepo, po, po, baby!"

"Found who?" I asked, trying to break through the racket.

"Rachel!" she said.

My knuckles turned white, gripping the phone. "Put her on!" I screamed.

"Oh, she's not here, here. I mean she's not with me. But I saw her in the lobby. I tried to get her attention, but then I ran into a sales rep for The Show; did you know that they're launching an all-new marketing plan that—"

"Wait! Stop! Where's Rachel now?"

"I don't know."

I resisted the urge to throw the phone across my bedroom. "What do you mean you don't know?"

"Well, by the time I got through talking to the rep, she wasn't in the lobby anymore. And anyway, once I finished talking to the belt accessory rep, I ran into the scarf rep. Did you know that handkerchiefs are back in? They're very green, you know, as in good for the environment, not the color. All that tissue, it can clog up our landfills, definitely not good for—"

"Stop blathering or I'm going to kill you!"

"Sorry. I'm excited. It's so, so incredible here!" she trilled.

"Can you find her again? Did you ask at the hotel for her room number?"

Silence greeted me. "Oh, good idea. I didn't think about that."

I sighed again.

"Let me go talk to the front desk."

◇◇◇

When Yolanda didn't call back right away, I dialed The Mirage on my own. I left a message at the front desk, although the clerk wasn't sure a Rachel Patterson or Hazelton had checked in.

Finally, I couldn't wait at my apartment any longer. I decided to have another look at Rachel's place. Maybe now that I had a few more pieces to the puzzle, I'd make a better detective. In fact, maybe I could snoop around for her gun or for the contract that said that Rachel was to buy out Dan's share of DelVecchio's that Yolanda was so certain existed.

Even though Gus thought Dan wasn't trying to sell, it did seem rather like he needed the money. Maybe Dan had been using the threats as a scare tactic to force the sale through—telling Rachel she had to buy him out or he would file that complaint letter with the health department.

I walked the short distance to Abigail's apartment house, figuring I could borrow the key to Rachel's from her. She lived close to me, but because Beepo stopped to sniff every crack of cement along the way, the walk took over fifteen minutes.

When I got to Abigail's, I was surprised to find Evie Xtreme there. She sat in Abigail's window looking over the street, her hair wrapped in aluminum. She wiggled her fingers by way of greeting, but immediately resumed her quiet surveillance of the street.

Abigail pressed Rachel's key into my hand. "I'm a hair stylist," she said by way of explanation.

"Oh, I didn't know."

Beepo found Missy under the couch and growled at her. Obviously, he wanted to play.

"Yeah, only the storefront space is so expensive in this town that I just work out of my house." She frowned at my hair. "Do you need a touch-up?"

I ran a hand through my hair, evaluating it. It had been a while since I'd had a trim. I agreed quickly.

"Come over Friday before the Tails and Tiaras fundraiser. I'll doll you up. Rumor has it you have quite a few admirers."

Evie turned her head away from the street and appraised me, smiling.

"Deal," I said. "Come on, Beepo. We gotta go." He darted behind the couch, out of sight.

Abigail glanced at her wristwatch. "Don't worry about him. I'm going to walk Missy before heading over to The Wine and Bark tonight. I can walk both dogs. You'll be open, right?"

"I guess it depends . . . was the . . ." I hesitated, feeling it was somehow indelicate to mention a crime scene.

"Oh, the crime scene's all cleaned up," Evie said, shuddering. "Thank God. So gruesome."

◇◇◇

Once inside Rachel's apartment house, the pull to visit Gus was undeniable. I even lingered outside his apartment for a moment with my hand on his door, as if I could feel or touch him right through the wood. I figured calling on him after last night might be construed as too needy and decided to pass on knocking.

Pulling out the key Abigail had given me, I shoved it into the keyhole in Rachel's door. I realized the door wasn't locked.

Had I left her apartment unlocked? A chill swept me from head to toe and my stomach turned sour. Twisting the knob, I pushed open the door a crack.

"Hello?" I called out.

A voice in my head warned, *Don't go in, don't go in, DON'T go in.*

What should I do? Call Officer Brooks? I bristled, thinking about our last conversation. Maybe I should just get Gus from down the hall?

My hand recoiled off the door. I should get help.

But then, before turning away, I called out again, "Heeeelloooo? Is someone there?" I was frozen at her doorway. I pushed the door open an inch further.

There was no sound from inside, but the air seemed charged with a strange energy. I sniffed and suddenly wished I'd brought Beepo with me.

I pressed the door open a bit further and could now see into the living room. I was being silly. Everything was fine.

"Hello?" I called out again, this time stepping into her apartment. My internal warning system went off, my muscles tensing. The couch was upturned, her books tossed off the shelves and onto the floor, the mail open and flung across the counter. The entire living room had been ransacked.

"Damn!" I ran to her bedroom. Her mattress was overturned and her computer gone.

Someone had come looking for something.

Had they found it?

Could it have been the gun?

I pulled my cell phone from my bag and dialed 9-1-1.

The 9-1-1 operator answered. "What is the nature of your emergency?"

"Oh, hi Jen. It's Maggie." Part of me couldn't believe I was already on a first-name basis with the 9-1-1 operator. "I need the police over at Rachel's apartment immediately."

"What's happened? Another uh . . ."

"Oh God, I hope not. Her place has been broken into. Ransacked."

"Okay, stay out of the apartment. They could still be inside."

I didn't have the heart to tell her I'd already poked my nose into the apartment. She was right, what if I'd interrupted the burglary? What if Dan's killer had been here? What if the killer had come barreling out of the apartment and taken me with him or her . . . ?

Chills spiraled down my spine.

"I'm putting out a call," the operator said. "Officer Brooks will be there in a minute."

I waited with mixed emotions to see my favorite officer.

◇◇◇

Officer Brooks had a one-of-a-kind gait; he stalked down the dark, narrow hallway with his broad shoulders practically bumping into the walls, and my heart lurched, hammering like crazy inside my chest.

I cleared my throat to calm my nervousness.

He smiled warmly at me, but there was a note of urgency in his voice. "Maggie, are you all right? What's happened?"

"Someone broke into Rachel's apartment," I said.

Officer Brooks leveled his gaze at me. My knees turned weak as I stared back into his clear bright blue eyes. "Is anything missing?" Brooks asked me.

"As far as I can tell, only her computer," I said.

And her gun! It's got to be missing, I wanted to scream, but I wasn't exactly supposed to know any of that, so I kept my mouth shut and let him do the detecting.

I regretted that Rachel hadn't had better security. Surely, the person who'd taken her computer would figure out her password as easily as I had. And as for the gun, she should have had a safe!

I brought Brooks up to speed with what Yolanda had said about Rachel being in Vegas.

"She spotted her at The Mirage," I said.

He nodded slowly at me.

"You're not surprised?" I asked.

He looked down, his eyes almost closing, and he took a moment too long to respond. "You knew?" I asked.

"Not exactly. I'd had a report . . ."

"I've been worried sick about her. You knew that. I didn't know where she was. Why didn't you tell me?"

"I'm sorry, Maggie. It wasn't confirmed. I—"

I turned away from him, feeling sick and confused. Why couldn't anything be easy? I felt betrayed by the guy I thought I could most likely trust, and the guy who probably wasn't trustworthy was working his way into my heart.

"Do you have any more information on Oscar's death? I talked to Melanie, Oscar's on-again, off-again girlfriend. Apparently, she was expecting him—"

"Why did you talk to her?"

"Hmm?"

"Why did you talk to Melanie?" Brooks pressed.

"Uh, I thought she might tell me something that could help us figure out—"

"Wait, wait, wait. Help us? Help us, who? You're not investigating these murders. I am."

My throat constricted and I blinked back the tears that threatened. He was right, of course, what was I thinking? I said, "If you don't want to help me, then—"

"Help with what? I think you might be deliberately obstructing justice, here." He glanced around the ransacked apartment. "Are you trying to mess up my investigation?"

"No! Of course not. I've told you everything I know."

The lie was caught in my throat—I hadn't told him about the letter or the photo of Dan used as target practice at the cabin, or my suspicions about Rachel's missing gun.

He stepped close to me. "All right, I'm sorry, I don't mean to upset you. But please, next time you think that you've come across a burglary, don't go inside. Just call me, okay?"

I nodded.

He reached out and grabbed my chin, pulling my face close to his. "Promise?"

"Yes." We were so close, I could smell mint on his breath, and even though I was upset with him, I had the crazy desire to mash my lips against his.

He dropped his hand. "I don't want anything to happen to you. Someone is desperate to cover their tracks, and it seems like you're desperate to catch them. . . ."

I watched his eyes, biting my tongue.

"Catching them is my job, Maggie."

"I know," I whispered.

"Do you trust me?"

Yes. No.

"You were trying to pin this on my sister."

He put the small notebook away in his breast pocket. "She wouldn't very well have ransacked her own place, right?"

Something hung in the air between us. What was he implying? That I'd ransacked her apartment in order to clear her from suspicion? Or did he think I might be setting up a fake crime, so I could steal her gun and get rid of the evidence? My throat went dry and I stepped away from him.

A look of regret flashed across his face. "I'm going to find whoever is responsible, Maggie."

A door opened and closed down the apartment corridor, and my intuition told me it was from Gus's apartment. Brooks's instincts must have played the same message, because he jolted forward. "Do any of the neighbors have keys to her apartment?"

Before I could answer, Brooks disappeared out the front door, and he called out sharply, "DelVecchio! DelVecchio! I'd like a word!"

I rushed out of the apartment behind him, nerves rattling my system and a headache threatening.

Gus stopped in front of Brooks, a look of concern on his face. He saw me running behind Brooks, and his face became unreadable.

"What is it, Officer Brooks?"

"Can you give me your whereabouts last night? I know your restaurant was closed—"

Gus's eyes darted over to Rachel's apartment door. "Is everything all right?"

I leapt forward. "Rachel's apartment has been—"

Brooks held up a hand to silence me. "Please, Maggie."

Gus looked from me to Brooks. "The restaurant was closed. Yes. My partner's been murdered and then one of my staff. . . . I didn't think it was appropriate to be open for business. I'm grieving. I'm keeping the restaurant closed for now."

Brooks feigned disinterest. "So, where were you?"

I chewed my lip.

Gus sighed. "Do you want to bring me in again for questioning? Should I bring an attorney with me this time?"

"A simple answer will do," Brooks said.

"I was with a friend," Gus said.

"Does your friend have a name?" Brooks asked.

"Me. He was with me," I said.

A look of disappointment crossed Brooks's face. He pinched the bridge of his nose between his thumb and forefinger. "Perfect. Okay. I see," he mumbled.

Chapter Twenty-seven

I rearranged the table and chairs in the lounge area while Max set up behind the bar. He fixed me a stiff cocktail and then one for himself. I watched him carefully as he worked side by side with me to get ready for Yappy Hour. Tomorrow was the big Tails and Tiaras fund-raiser, and I couldn't wait to find Rachel so I wouldn't have to be in charge of anything.

I daydreamed about getting the job on the cruise line and sailing away. Why hadn't they called me yet? Was it the watercooler fiasco?

Beepo and the beagle with the plush bunny in its mouth alternated between watching Max and I prep the bar and looking out the window, awaiting the crowd.

"I think you've got your hands full, Maggie."

"I know." I eyed him. "I keep having the awful premonition that I'm going to find another body tomorrow during Tails and Tiaras."

"Oh God. Don't say that, you'll jinx us."

"Are you superstitious?" I asked.

He shrugged and took a drag off his cocktail. "Sort of."

"Well, I won't talk about it then. I don't want to spook you. I wouldn't be able to do any of this without you. Thanks for your help."

He laughed. "Well, I had a meeting with an angel investor yesterday. It didn't go well. So I might have to ask you for a full-time job."

I wiped down the bar. "What happened with your angel?"

Max dumped a bucket of ice into the ice well. "Ack. The same thing they all say. There's a similar technology already available, blah, blah."

I thought about Dan, and then about the fight Norma had told me Max and Dan had had. I'd asked Max about it at his beach house, but I hadn't gotten a straight answer. I watched as he shifted the bottle around. He was strong. He could have easily killed another man with a blow to the head. I shifted away from him and asked, "Max, what exactly did you fight over with Dan?"

Max sighed. "Oh, it's not important now."

I took in a deep breath. "Since he was killed in my sister's bar . . . well, I think it's important," I said, suddenly scared of the answer.

"Brenda," Max said.

I laughed. "Really?"

He nodded. "Dan and Rachel had been broken up a few weeks, and he seemed to be sniffing around Brenda."

"Are you guys together?"

"I wish. But he was saying some pretty rude things around town about her and, well, I just couldn't stand it. I confronted him and it got a little vocal, but it didn't come to blows or anything. I have to say the guy was a class-A jerk."

"Did Brenda know he was talking about her?" That could be a motive, right? Kill someone to save your own reputation. Although it seemed far-fetched to me. Brenda was an attorney, and she seemed so small and delicate, I couldn't picture her whacking a man over the head with a wine bottle. Max, on the other hand . . . how far would he go to protect her reputation?

Max shook his head. "I don't think so."

"Are you going to ask her out?"

He reddened. "No way, she's out of my league."

"You think so? Why?"

Beepo, who'd taken to following me around, bolted toward the door and yowled like crazy.

Max laughed. "The crew must be approaching."

Through the window of the bar, we could see a crowd forming on the patio, two women I hadn't seen before alongside Brenda and Abigail. Every one of them had a small dog attached to the end of a Wine and Bark Day-Glo-green leash. They had just come from the Roundup Crew walk on the beach and all were decked out in walking shorts and sneakers, except for Brenda, who was dressed in her signature black clothes with a striking pair of three-inch-high Louboutin pumps in fire-engine red.

She must have walked barefoot on the beach, but judging by the way Max whistled when he saw her, I got the distinct impression she'd worn the shoes to the bar for his benefit.

The door flung open and they streamed into the bar, the energy instantly changing with their laughter and chitchat. One of the women I hadn't seen before approached the bar. Her hair was cut short and she had a tomboy appearance. On the end of her leash was a small poodle. Beepo went absolutely mad barking at the woman and her dog. The woman only laughed at him, which actually stoked my ire.

The woman smiled at me, flashing wide, even, square teeth. "How about a pitcher of Pomeranians?"

I glanced at Max, but he just nodded. "Sure thing, Geraldine. I'll bring it out to the table."

Geraldine?

This was the lady Yolanda had had a problem with. My curiosity was piqued.

Max poured white rum, a splash of triple sec, and some pomegranate juice into a shaker filled with ice, then added a dash of fresh lemon juice. He shook the concoction, then strained it into a pitcher for the table.

"Who are the new ladies?" I asked.

"Geraldine and Sarah. They're usuals, but they were in Carmel last weekend because of the dog show."

"What's Yolanda's issue with Geraldine?" I asked.

"Pfft—darned if I know," Max said.

Just like a man to stay out of women's squabbles.

"I bet there was a lot of gossip on that beach walk today," I said in a low voice.

Max chuckled. "Oh, you better believe it. Want to take the pitcher out and I'll get the arf d'oeuvres going?"

Brenda approached the bar. Her eyes seemed to twinkle as she turned her attention to Max. "We missed you and Bowser on our walk today." Max beamed at her. Brenda turned to me. "Maggie, can I have a word with you?"

I took the pitcher from Max. "Okay, let me serve this up and I'll be right with you." I dropped off the pitcher of Pomeranians at the table, receiving a queer up-and-down glance from Geraldine. Brenda waited for me by the front door and together we walked out to the patio. It was still early, but an ocean breeze had picked up and gently wafted across my face. I realized I'd been dying for an excuse to come outside.

DelVecchio's was still closed, and I felt a heaviness in my heart. Gus had decided to remain closed for a few more days to try and make sense of which direction he should take the business.

"Dan's folks are in town," Brenda said. "They came by the office to talk to me about your insurance."

A bead of perspiration trickled down my back. "You mean the building insurance?"

"Yeah. It seems like Dan's death was caused by trauma to the head."

"We know that, right? From the wine bottle."

Brenda shook her head. "Unfortunately, no. He was hit with the wine bottle on the temple, which caused an injury, but his death was caused by a fracture at the back of the head, from the fall. He cracked his head on the terracotta."

My mouth went dry and I felt dizzy. "What are you getting at, Brenda?"

"Basically, The Wine and Bark could be liable."

"But that's ridiculous. I mean, even if he fell and hit his head, he fell because somebody whacked him with a wine bottle. That was the *cause* of the fall. How could The Wine and Bark be liable?"

Brenda glanced over her shoulder, making sure we were still alone. "Well, the landlord is liable for injuries of visitors in cases where the landlord's negligence has caused the injury."

I blinked at her. "Rachel was negligent?"

"They're saying Dan could've fallen because of something else," Brenda said.

"Like what?"

She leaned into me and whispered, "Like he could've slipped on a wet floor."

I frowned. "Wet floor?"

"The forensic examiner found traces of dog urine on his trouser ankles and shoes."

Oh God, Dan had slipped in dog pee and now Rachel, Grunkly, and I would all be sued for manslaughter.

"His folks said Dan had been trying to get Rachel to stop allowing dogs on the premises. Said he'd written countless letters to her and then had threatened to go to the Environmental Health Committee to get an ordinance violation written up against The Wine and Bark."

They knew about the letter.

A stress headache began pounding behind my temples. "We have insurance, though, right? The insurance takes care of this type of stuff—"

Brenda grabbed my arms and steadied me. "Maggie, I'm so sorry to be the one to tell you, but your insurance may have expired."

An image of Grunkly handing me his mail flashed through my mind, the insurance bill unpaid.

"The payment is late," Brenda continued, "but I'm trying to get them on a technicality. We may have been in a grace-period window."

My blood pressure skyrocketed and I felt faint.

Grunkly was going to lose everything.

◇◇◇

Back inside The Wine and Bark, cocktails and laughter were flowing. The volume in the room had increased significantly, and I suddenly felt like I wasn't going to make it through the night. A lawsuit would ruin Grunkly. It would wipe him out completely, breaking his heart and probably killing him.

Even though Brenda had assured me she'd fight Dan's folks and press our insurance carrier, there was still a possibility that we wouldn't be covered. She wouldn't know until the next business day or possibly even Monday. It was gearing up to be the longest weekend of my life.

Beepo let out a howl and bolted toward the door. Through the window I could make out the now-familiar figure of Yolanda sashaying up the cobblestone path. I ran to the door and together Beepo and I pounced on her.

"Beep-Beep," she squealed, picking him up and rubbing his tummy. "Beep, Beep, Beepo!"

"Where's Rachel? Did she come back with you?" I asked, looking past Yolanda down the cobblestone path.

The wind picked up and Yolanda's blond hair flew into her face. She flicked it back with a whisk of her hand. She looked very Vegas, in a low-cut clingy white dress with ruffles placed in strategic locations around her hips and chest, which made her figure look like an hourglass on steroids.

"I couldn't find her after we talked. But I did lock in my exhibitor show! Isn't that fabulous?"

Disappointment hollowed out my insides. I needed my sister now more than ever and she was nowhere to be found.

Yolanda linked an arm through mine. "Come on, honey, you look like you're about to cry." She steered me toward the front door of the bar. "Let's join the party and forget your troubles—"

I disentangled myself from her. "Yolanda, I don't have the heart." I filled her in on Brenda's update about Dan's fall and our insurance predicament.

Her eyes flashed and darted about when I mentioned the trace of dog urine on Dan's shoes. Suddenly she clutched Beepo possessively. "Can they tell what dog?"

"What?"

She bit her lip. "You know, like on CSI when they match the bullet to the gun, the blood to the victim, the print to the killer. Can they match the, you know, pee to the dog?"

The evening air stilled and we were silent a moment. Beepo looked from Yolanda to me and let out a little whimper.

Well, of all the dogs I'd met recently, Beepo was quite a marker. . . .

And there was no question Yolanda had been in the bar before me the night I'd found Dan dead. . . .

"I don't know." I stared at Yolanda; she stared back at me. We both looked at Beepo. He looked away from us, guilt written all over his doggie face.

"Maybe I can talk to Sergeant Gottlieb," Yolanda said.

"Maybe I can talk to Officer Brooks," I countered.

We stared at each other again in a game of chicken. Beepo let out a little cry.

"That's probably a good idea," she said.

"I agree," I said.

The door to the bar flung open and Abigail rushed out. "Yo! You're here. How was Vegas? Did you land your booth?"

Yolanda sprang toward Abigail, desperate to get away from me. She linked her free arm through Abigail's and hustled her back into the bar. "I'll tell you all about it over a salty dog!"

When the door had closed and I was alone on the patio, I crumpled into one of the patio chairs and contemplated my dilemma. The sun was just setting, the sky orange and pink and purple. It looked peaceful, and I wished that my mood could match those soothing colors.

If I could figure out who killed Dan, would it nullify the lawsuit?

What if they could match the urine to the dog? Would that lead to the killer? Did it prove the killer was the owner of the dog? Uneasiness churned my insides. Yolanda and Beepo were fast becoming my friends.

There was also the matter of Rachel's missing gun and Oscar's death. Could Yolanda possibly be responsible? She'd had access to the bar when no one else had been there. Could she have taken Rachel's gun?

The thoughts swirled around my head, making me feel dizzy. Perhaps Officer Brooks had been right. I should leave the investigation to the professionals.

Chapter Twenty-eight

A tall, imposing uniform-clad figure approached. A nervous energy coursed through me as I watched him. He stepped in front of me.

"Speak of the devil," I said.

"What? Were you talking about me?" Officer Brooks asked, glancing at the empty chair next to me. "With who?"

"She's gone now. I scared her away."

Brooks laughed. "Is this seat taken?"

"No." I patted the chair. "Please, take a load off and tell me you've come for a pleasant social call. Maybe even a drink."

"I can't drink, I'm on duty, but yes, just making my rounds and making sure you were safe."

"No more dead bodies," I joked. But seeing his serious expression I regretted my levity. "That was a joke. Sorry, a very bad joke."

He nodded. "I just didn't want you to feel like you had to call 9-1-1 to see me."

Smiling, I said, "Right. Well, Yolanda and I were just

talking about you, wondering about your toxicology friends."

He frowned. "Toxicology?"

"Pathology? Forensics? I don't know what they're called. The CSI guys."

He quirked an eyebrow at me. "What exactly are you getting at?"

"Dan's parents are in town and it looks like they might want to sue The Wine and Bark because your forensic guy, whoever that is, or the medical examiner—"

He waved a hand at me to continue. "Don't get caught up in the administrative details, just tell me what you're thinking."

"Well, whoever the powers that be are ruled that Dan was killed by hitting his head on our floor and not from the impact of the wine bottle."

Brad's eyes shifted. "So that makes you liable?"

"Well, I would argue that the fall was caused by whoever hit him with the magnum bottle."

"Right," Brad agreed.

"Only, I guess they found dog urine on his shoe and think he might have slipped."

Brad frowned. "Wow, people read a lot into our reports. How exactly did that get out?" He studied me a moment. "Because I haven't shared any of that information."

I shrugged. "Well, that I don't know. Brenda told me, and she said Dan's parents told her."

Brad's lips pressed together as he processed the information. Obviously there was a leak in his department. How else had the information gotten out?

"So," I asked, "is it true then? There was a trace of urine?"

"Yeah, but we don't know how old the urine was. It could have been on his shoes from earlier. It doesn't mean he slipped on it. Anyway, don't worry about it too much.

Brenda's a pretty talented lawyer, she should be able to get you out of a lawsuit."

"Can you match up urine to the dog?" I asked.

He squinted at me. "Do you have a dog in mind?"

"Yolanda's."

"Yolanda? I thought she was your new BFF?"

I chuckled. "Right. The yap monster."

It was his turn to chuckle. "She grows on you, though, and what with the drive to the country and all . . ." He paused and waited for my reaction.

My head turned toward him so fast, I nearly gave myself whiplash.

He smirked, clearly enjoying himself. "You didn't think I knew about that, huh?"

What else did he know?

A shiver danced on my spine, which I chose to ignore. "I'm sure stuff gets around town fast," I bluffed.

He cocked his head to the side and studied me for a moment. "What were you doing sitting out here alone when I came up?" he asked.

"Taking a break," I said. "I wish I could take a break from this doggie bar indefinitely," I confessed.

He snickered. "Are you wishing you were back in New York?"

"No." I laughed. "I won't go that far. I just wish things would be a little simpler here. Like, I wish I could take tomorrow off and not have to deal with the crowd for the fund-raiser and all the details . . . and . . ." I leaned in close to him and whispered, "Dogs."

He chuckled. "So, why don't you take tomorrow off, then?"

I grimaced. "I think the town would lynch me if The Wine and Bark didn't host the Tails and Tiaras fund-raiser."

"You're probably right about that, at least the Roundup Crew would. I don't know about the town."

"Do you have any new suspects for Dan's death besides my sister?" I asked.

"I have a couple," Brooks said, "but I have to tell you, my sergeant is pretty convinced Rachel's guilty."

Sergeant Gottlieb. He was tough.

"Is he interested in Yolanda?" I asked.

A look of surprise crossed Brooks' face. "Yolanda?"

"Yes, she's sweet on him," I said.

"I didn't know that. I'll have to keep an eye out." He slid his chair closer to me and added, "Well, I guess it's not against the law to have a crush on someone."

My heart beat a little faster as I looked into his eyes.

"Will you come by tomorrow to the fund-raiser?" I asked.

He chuckled. "If I don't come I might be lynched. Besides, I have a dog," he added.

"You do? I didn't know." This surprised me, as I hadn't pegged him as a man with a dog. I wondered if he'd heard about my "not being a doggie person" confession.

"Well, I'm not part of the Roundup Crew or anything."

We both giggled at the thought of him walking alongside the ladies of the Roundup Crew. Max, with his boy-next-door charm, seemed to fit in with them, but Brooks was so stoic it was comical to imagine.

After a moment, he said, "I have a big dog."

It seemed that his having a large dog made more sense. I studied him, trying to see if I could guess what kind of dog: a German shepherd, maybe, or a Labrador?

"It's a dog that I adopted from the shelter." He scratched at his chin and I averted my eyes. "Sort of at Yolanda's prodding. You know how big she is on pet adoption. It's the whole reason behind the Tails and Tiaras fund-raiser.

"Anyway, I'll only have Sizzle for little while, until Yolanda can find a home for him."

I chuckled. "She's not going to find another home for him, she already found you."

"No no no," he said. "I'm not keeping him for good. I'm really not supposed to have any dog at all. Not according to my lease."

I pressed a hand to my heart and feigned surprise. "You mean you're breaking a contract? Isn't that the same as breaking the law?"

"No," he said. "I can't go to jail for having a dog! That's not against the law. Worst thing is I could get evicted."

I wondered about it. He was right, of course. It wasn't against the law to own a dog. And yet, my family was in a strange predicament, possibly up against a lawsuit, for having dogs on their premises.

"How about the break-in? Do you have any leads on who broke into Rachel's apartment?" I asked.

He shook his head, but something unspoken was in his eyes.

"Do you suspect Gus?" I asked.

Brook glanced across to the patio at DelVecchio's, then back at me. "I hope you're not getting too close to him," he said slowly.

"He's been very kind to me," I replied.

Brooks shifted and I could tell he was uncomfortable with the topic; for that matter, so was I. I didn't really want to be discussing my feelings about Gus. What were they anyway? I wasn't even sure I knew.

A look crossed Brooks's face that was hard to read, a cross between disappointment and something else. "I don't think Gus broke into Rachel's apartment," he said. It looked like it pained him to admit it. Likely he wanted to keep me from being interested in Gus.

He drummed his fingers on the table. "Maggie, sometimes . . . and please don't be offended . . . but sometimes when people are trying to be well meaning . . . and by people I mean *family* members . . . they can unduly influence an investigation."

I sat a little straighter and leaned in. A message was coming to me loud and clear. "Are you implying that you think I ransacked my sister's apartment?"

He cringed but said nothing.

"What about my great-uncle? Someone spooked his horse. You think I was behind that as well?"

The door to the bar creaked open and some patrons floated out to the patio for a cigarette break. "I better get back in there and relieve Max," I said.

Brooks rose and grabbed my hand. "Don't be mad, Maggie. I'm just doing my job."

I leaned in close to him, so the patrons smoking wouldn't hear me. "You never answered me. Can you match urine to a dog?"

His eyes locked in on mine. "Yes, I believe so. What do you have in mind?"

I placed my finger over my lips, indicating silence. "Come by tomorrow for the fund-raiser and find out."

I winked at him and turned on a heel to return to The Wine and Bark, a plan brewing in my head.

Chapter Twenty-nine

It was the big Tails and Tiaras fund-raiser day. Max had promised to help me bartend, Evie and the Howling Hounds were set to play, and I'd received a new shipment of Bark Bites. Everything seemed in order for the big day, except my sister was still AWOL and I needed a new hairdo.

I walked the short distance to Abigail's apartment, wondering how far I should go with the hairstyle. Did I really only need a trim? Maybe it would be fun to lighten up the color? I glanced at my watch. I probably didn't have time for a dye job with all the errands I needed to run today.

Abigail opened the door, but I was soon accosted by Yolanda and Beepo. Yolanda's hair was in curlers and Beepo was sniffing around my feet, presumably looking for a treat.

"Thank God you're here, Maggie!" Yolanda shrieked.

"What's wrong?"

"Camilla's gone into labor!" Yolanda trilled.

"Who's Camilla?" I feared she was going to tell me it was someone's dog and that maybe I needed to assist with the labor and delivery.

"The lady that runs Piece of Cake," Yolanda said.

"Oh! She's so nice! I'm so happy for her." Yolanda only stared at me. "It is a good thing, right?" I asked.

"Well, sure, it's good for her, but bad for us. I was counting on her to provide the catering tonight for the Tails and Tiaras fund-raiser! We can't just serve those awful frozen dogs in a blanket, you know."

Abigail silently watched us debate as she swept hair trimmings from the floor into a dustpan.

"I think they're pretty bad, too, honestly," I said.

Abigail patted the floral-patterned beauty chair that dominated her living room and said, "Hop on up."

Taking a seat, I said, "Not too much off, just a trim."

Abigail got started by spritzing my hair. "Do you want to finish with an updo for tonight?"

"Well, nothing too fancy," I said, "I'll be working tonight—"

"I can't believe you two! Only concerned with yourselves and your hair!" Yolanda sputtered. "What about the catering service?"

"Oh, well, I guess I can ask Gus. DelVecchio's is closed—"

Yolanda's eyes grew wide and she thumped her hand over her chest as if she were experiencing a cardiac arrest. "Gus DelVecchio! Never!" she spat. Beepo immediately ran over to Yolanda and whined in sympathy with her.

I glanced at Abigail, who pressed her lips together and suddenly took great interest in my split ends. Her dog, Missy, took refuge under the couch, her bejeweled collar jangling as she darted out of sight. There was some serious history here that I was missing.

"What's wrong with him catering? I mean, if he's available and agrees and all. He's the best chef in town."

Yolanda shrugged off my question and turned to the

giant mirror on the wall. "How long do we need to leave these in, Abby?" She was referring to the curlers, but Abigail didn't seem eager to have her leave.

"A little longer, honey. If you want it to set properly. Why don't you have a seat?"

Yolanda examined her profile in the mirror but said nothing.

"Well," I demanded. "What's wrong with Gus catering?"

"You know what's wrong!" Yolanda said. "He's killed two people!"

I sprang out of the chair. "He didn't kill them!"

Abigail put a hand on my shoulder and reseated me in the beauty chair. "She's right, Yo. He probably didn't kill them."

"Thank you!" I said to Abigail.

Yolanda took a seat on the couch, then picked an imaginary speck of dust off her red leggings. "What makes you so sure?"

Abigail shrugged her shoulders. "Well, I don't know. Maybe I just miss his cooking. Remember last week, before all this happened, you and I went to DelVecchio's and devoured that fettuccini Alfredo?"

Yolanda licked her lips as if suddenly tasting the fettuccini again. She hesitated. "Okay, if you think he'll agree, Maggie, you can ask him to cater."

<><><>

After I left Abigail's, my hair a good two inches shorter and definitely with added volume, my first stop was Designer Duds. I'd thought about the jacket with the anchors on it long enough; it was time to buy it, along with the chicken purse. It seemed crazy, but I figured it would be the easiest way to get the sample I needed.

The salesgirl tried to talk me into a jaunty red scarf for dramatic effect, but I assured her that the chicken purse would be dramatic enough, especially with what I had planned.

I dialed Gus and got his voice mail. I left a brief message asking him if he was willing to help us cater the event that evening.

My next stop was to Magic Read for a latte; however, as soon as I stepped inside the doorway my cell phone buzzed. I hurried to answer it, expecting Gus. Instead, it was Jan from Soleado Cruise Line.

Oh my gosh! The jacket had brought me luck.

"Maggie, this is Jan. I'd like to make you an offer. Are you still interested in the purser position? I have a cruise leaving next week. Ten-day Mexican Riviera, but after that there's a two-week Bahamian Cruise, and the Keys. . . . Well, I can probably keep you busy until October. Feel like traveling a little bit?"

I nearly dropped the phone.

I got the job!

The Mexican Riviera, the Bahamas, the Florida Keys! It was happening. I was going to be traveling. Away from the dogs! Away from the bar! Away from Pacific Cove.

I almost screamed into the phone, but instead I composed myself and accepted the job gracefully.

The young clerk with the green Mohawk, whom I'd come to know as Melanie's brother, quirked an eyebrow at me. "Good news?" he asked.

"Yes. Excellent news. Wonderful news. I'm taking a trip far, far away. And for quite a while. It's a much-needed vacation and, better yet, I'll get paid for it!"

As soon as I'd said it, guilt engulfed me. I'd come to Pacific Cove to be close to Grunkly and Rachel. And now with Rachel absent and Grunkly's arm in a sling, I couldn't very well leave him. He'd refuse a nurse, I knew. And then there was the matter of the impending lawsuit, which I hadn't had the heart to tell him about.

What was I going to do?

As I ordered a latte and pondered my options, the clerk said, "Nice handbag, by the way."

Glancing down at the chicken purse, I realized that I was still on a mission. I couldn't leave Pacific Cove until I proved who the killer was.

Time for action!

◇◇◇

"I don't need a nurse, Maggie!"

I ignored him as I continued to vacuum. It'd taken an almost Herculean effort, but fueled by my latte and job offer I'd picked up everything off the floor well enough to vacuum. "I'm not a nurse," I told him, shutting off the machine. "I'm your niece. You have to let me help you."

The idea of getting sued and losing Grunkly's property sickened me, and it drove me to clean.

Grunkly may have put up more of a fuss as I shuffled the stacks of papers, straightened the table, and dusted his mantel, but since there was another horse race just minutes to post, he settled for clutching his remote with his good arm.

"Are you doing the exercises the physical therapists gave you for your arm?" I asked.

Grunkly squirmed in his leather easy chair and averted his eyes. "Sure, I am."

The announcer called two minutes to post; the horses took the field.

"Grunkly, I've been given a job offer," I said.

"That's nice, honey," Grunkly said, his eyes glued to the TV.

I stared at the graveyard of old electronics that I'd pushed aside in order to vacuum, and something inside me hollowed out. I wanted to travel so badly, see the world, and yet Grunkly needed me. He wouldn't discard an old broken-down TV or VCR, and yet I was ready to push him to the curb, let him hire a nurse and fend for himself. . . .

I collapsed onto the couch, sitting haphazardly between a semi-filled cardboard box and a wool blanket. "It's a traveling job, Grunkly. I'd be gone for months on end. Mazatlán, Florida Keys . . . Bahamas . . ."

His eyes were still on the TV. "Sounds great Maggie. Good opportunity to see the world."

I picked at the clutter on the sofa. "But I don't feel right about it. Leaving you—"

Grunkly waved the remote control at me. "Shhh. I have two hundred dollars on Flying Barb to place. Hand me my hat," he said, indicating a blue ball cap on the mantel.

I reached for his lucky ball cap and passed it to him. With his arm in a sling, he had to release the remote control in order to grab the hat. He flashed me a look as if he didn't trust me not to grab the remote and toss it out the window. And had his windows not been painted shut years ago, I would have been tempted. As it was, I settled down to watch the race with him.

"Two minutes to post, Magpie."

"Grunkly, I don't feel right about leaving you without someone around to care for you. If Rachel was here, it would be different, but as it is, with your arm in a sling and Lord knows when she'll reappear, well, I think—"

My thoughts were drowned out by the gunshot on the screen and Grunkly's war whoops. "Go, Flying Barb! Go, baby, go!"

Grunkly's pick started out strong, but soon fell back and finally finished next to last.

"Aw, that's a shame!" Grunkly said, turning off the TV with a disgusted look on his face.

When I knew I had his attention again, I asked, "Grunkly, do you know anything about Rachel's gun?"

"Like what?"

"Like where it is?" I asked.

He frowned. "Why?"

I hadn't wanted to tell him about Oscar. It seemed unnecessary to worry him, but now I didn't really see a way around it. "Someone was shot and killed the other night, and I heard it was by a gun similar to the one Rachel had."

Grunkly paled. "Doesn't she keep it in a safe?"

"I don't know. Her apartment was broken into and I can't find it. It's not at the bar . . . I'm afraid someone might be out to frame her."

"No, it's gotta be a misunderstanding. Maybe it's at the cabin? I think she liked doing target practice out there."

I cringed inwardly, thinking about the target practice someone had taken on the blow-up image of Dan's face.

"Set up a few aluminum cans . . . line them all up. Do you remember?" Grunkly asked. "You used to like that, too."

A nervous energy coursed through me. I'd assumed Rachel had been up to Stag's Leap recently, what with the cigarette smoke that lingered and the overall tidiness of the place. Not that Rachel either smoked or was tidy. But someone had been to the cabin recently, that was for certain.

Yolanda had been so eager to take me, even after we'd become friends, I had to wonder. Had she had an ulterior motive?

"There's something else I need to talk to you about."

He looked at me expectantly. I'd wanted to talk with him about the possible pending lawsuit, but suddenly I lost my nerve. He looked so fragile with his arm in a sling, and worse was the expression on his face—it was one of complete adoration and trust. He trusted me.

I knew then that I had to live up to his trust.

I had to see us, all of us, out of this mess.

Chapter Thirty

The evening was warm, and I happily clicked along the cobblestones in my new strappy sandals. They weren't the three-inch-high chartreuse sandals by Manolo Blahnik that Brenda had tried to thrust upon me. Instead, these had a sensible heel while still being sexy. They were a beautiful mulberry color that matched my dress exactly, and more importantly, I knew I'd be able to run around The Wine and Bark with them on and not have to change into sneakers.

I considered myself lucky to have found the perfect match and tried to ignore the fact that the heel was a bit, well, okay, a full inch higher than I normally wore, but Brenda had assured me that beauty was a petulant mistress and I'd better start making some sacrifices to the goddess of fashion if I wanted Gus or Brooks to be impressed.

Fortunately, the walk was short, and I got to the bar plenty early to set the trap.

The chairs were still on the tables, so I mopped and then placed the stools on the floor. It was strange how much solace I was taking in cleaning these days. Perhaps it was because there was something so cathartic about it. The evening was going to be out of control. I'd called Gus several times to ask him to cater and hadn't been successful in reaching him.

Where was he? Was he still depressed? Was he at the farmers market, strolling by himself, or worse, with another girl?

I scolded myself. I had some nerve being jealous when only last night I'd been flirting with Officer Brooks.

Maybe Gus was at the coves, thinking.

I longed to be there myself, seeking solace in the repetitive waves. No matter what happened, another wave rolled over the last and then another and another.

I put away my mop bucket and glanced around for the next thing on my to-do list. I grabbed my chicken purse and prominently displayed it on the bar. There, that should do the trick. Soon everyone would arrive and my plan would go into action.

Max had promised to meet me early, and true to form, at thirty minutes to opening he showed up and began to load the ice buckets and decorate.

"Any news on your investor?" I asked.

"Unfortunately no. It doesn't look good, Mags."

He caught sight of my chicken bag and laughed. "What in the world is that?"

"That's Yolanda's designer bag," I said.

A look of horror crossed his face. "Seriously? I've never seen anything so ridiculous."

"Or hideous," I chimed in. "You should see the frog one."

He snorted.

"Apparently Beepo has a problem with them," I said. "And so do I."

"Why are you carrying one around then? Just to be supportive?"

I blushed inwardly.

Should I let Max in on my plan?

I hated the thought of deceiving him, but I couldn't risk it.

He shrugged as if answering his own question. "I know, she's a hard person to say no to. You're a good friend, Maggie."

I sloughed off his comment and came around the bar to fuss with the box of decorations Yolanda had left. I pawed through it: tablecloths, candles, party hats, and New Orleans–style beads, only everything was in black to support the black dog syndrome Yolanda was working to raise awareness about.

Max whistled when he got the full view of my scoop-neck dress. "You're all dolled up tonight, Mags. New dress, new shoes, new chicken purse."

I laughed, pulling out the shiny black tablecloths. "Come help me."

He took some tablecloths from me and we divided the room, covering various tables each with the dark elegant covers. "Who are you trying to impress? The cop?"

I squirmed under Max's interrogation. I'd forgotten just how much of an open book a small town was.

"You mean Officer Brooks? We've gone on *one* date."

"What about Gus?"

"What about him?" I asked, suddenly defensive.

Was I that transparent?

I pulled out the candles and retraced my steps to put one on each table.

Max followed me around with the lighter, lighting each candle as I placed it. "I've seen the way you look at him."

"How's that?"

"Probably the way I look at Brenda."

"Are you going to ask her out?" I asked, hoping to derail his observations about my complicated love life.

Max fixed his gaze on me and leaned in close with a challenge. "I'll ask Brenda out if you ask Gus."

Anxiety squirmed around my center. "I can't."

He laughed. "Oh well, Brenda wouldn't go out with me, anyway."

"Why do you say that?"

He looked over his shoulder at the empty bar. His expression had changed; it'd gone from playful to something else entirely. In fact, he suddenly looked pale and panic-stricken. "Can I trust you?"

A nervous energy bolted through me. My mouth went dry.

Oh my God, what was he about to confess? . . .

Max took a deep breath. "Bowser, the beagle that I walk on Fridays . . . at the Roundup Crew . . . it's . . ." He gave a final glance over his shoulder. "He's not my dog," he whispered.

I clapped a hand over my mouth stifling a giggle. "What? You're an imposter!"

He covered his face with his hands in shame. "I know! I know. I'm a total fraud."

Laughter spilled out of me.

"It's not funny!" he insisted. "I'm totally not a doggie person, just like you said the first day I met you. But I moved into my parents' beach house last spring. And then every Friday, the Roundup Crew would stroll past my back deck . . . I'm not excusing it. I know it's wrong to lie. But every Friday they'd walk past with all their little doggies and The Wine and Bark leashes and . . . I found out about Yappy Hour . . . and before I knew it, I'd met Brenda and . . . she asked me about my dog and I totally lied."

I laughed until my side hurt.

"I've been borrowing Bowser from Mrs. Murphy ever since." Max paled and looked sick.

I clapped him on the back. "Do you think Brenda wouldn't be interested in you if she knew—"

"She's not interested in me now! How's she going to feel if she knows I've been pretending to have a dog?"

"Which, by the way, you were sloppy about. Do you know how many times I found poor Bowser's bunny?"

Max hung his head in disgrace.

Grabbing his shoulder, I said, "Don't do this to yourself, Max. You're a man among men. You're the only one who stepped up to help me, because you knew I was in over my head here."

He waved a hand around. "Oh, that was nothing, Mags. I'd help you out anytime."

"I know. That's why—and please believe me when I say this—Brenda would be lucky to have a man like you in her life."

He perked up a bit, the color returning to his face. "Really?"

"Absolutely." I resumed straightening the tablecloth. "Besides, I can't have you moping around. I need the help," I joked.

He snapped a bar towel at my arm. "Right. We have a lot of work to do. We can't get all sentimental."

We divided up the party hats and beads and spread the swag across each table. Before my very eyes the trendy little Wine and Bark was being converted into something elegant, even dreamlike.

"Where is Bowser tonight, by the way?" I asked.

"Mrs. Murphy will be bringing him." He nervously glanced out the window again. "I couldn't talk her out of it."

"Did anyone know?"

He shrugged. "The little girl, Coral, who paints. She knew."

I remembered talking to her at the Dreamery Creamery; she'd been very clear that Max walked Bowser, but I hadn't made the distinction between walking him and owning him. Obviously, I was not a very clever detective. "You're going to have to talk to Brenda before Mrs. Murphy shows up," I said.

He nodded. "Yeah. The only person in the Roundup Crew who sort of got a whiff of it was Yolanda. You know, contrary to what you might think, she's a pretty good secret keeper."

Right. She could be hiding a pretty big secret.

I'd find out later, if my setup was successful.

Through the window of the bar, I saw Gus walk up. A nervous energy coursed through me, and it surprised me how excited I was to see him. His step seemed more brisk than it had been in the previous days, and hopefully he was feeling better. He came up to the door of the bar and peeked in.

"Hey, Maggie, good to see you."

I rushed over to him, aware of Max watching us curiously. "I'm so happy to see you, Gus. I've been trying to reach you all day."

He frowned. "You have? What about?"

"The woman who was supposed to cater the event, the lady from Piece of Cake, went into labor."

Gus's fingers suddenly found my hand, and then laced through mine, sending a pleasant warm jolt throughout my body. "A baby. That's so nice. It's good to have news of a new life instead of . . . instead of all the bad news we've gotten lately."

"Yes, yes," I agreed.

His dark eyes filled with concern. "Is everything all right?"

"Oh, yes, I mean, I think so. It's just that we've been left without a caterer for the event and . . . I'm under strict orders to not serve the frozen hot dogs in buns, the awful arf d'oeuvres."

Gus laughed. "Thank God for small mercies."

Max, who was hanging up a string of multicolored lantern lights, said, "Well, not to be a complete food noob, but I happen to like those arf d'oeuvres."

Gus and I shared a smile. He said, "I came over today because I knew it was your big party, and I thought you might need a little help."

Before I could say anything, Max dropped the lantern lights and rushed to grab Gus's arm. "Yes, we need your help! Of course we need your help!" Max let go of Gus and headed for the kitchen, saying over his shoulder, "You can work in here. Simple pub grub stuff."

Gus's face lit up. "I'll get to work! You have an oven here, right?"

"Yeah, but the kitchen is bare minimum, really. Just the fridge, an oven. We don't have any supplies, like garlic . . . or . . ."

He stepped closer to me, watching my lips as I spoke. The air between us seemed charged. He lifted his hand, stroking my cheek. "I'll take care of it. Don't worry, okay?" He was so close to me I could smell his musky aftershave, his scent warming me from the inside out. All I wanted to do was bury my face in his neck.

Max returned and cleared his throat; Gus and I separated. Gus flashed me a lopsided smile, then disappeared into the kitchen.

Down the cobblestone path, I could see Evie, Bishop, and Smasher approaching. They seemed to be in a fight,

Evie walking quickly ahead of the men, who were lingering behind. She flung open the door and stormed inside. "Those two are no help," she said, exasperated.

The others followed her in and began to push around the tables Max and I had just decorated in order to create space for the makeshift bandstand. For the next few minutes they stormed around between the main bar and the storage space they rented, setting up an amplifier, drum kit, and microphone.

Gus appeared in the doorway from the kitchen. "How about cheese platters with the cheese cut in the shape of dog paws and the crackers in the shape of bones?"

"Yes!" Max shouted before I could reply.

Gus nodded. "And pizzettas in the shape of dog bowls? I can make a variety. Some with a pesto and cream base, some tomato and sausage?"

My mouth watered. "I can't argue. Sounds infinitely better than bar peanuts and pretzels."

"I think the best thing will be for me to use my own kitchen," Gus said. "I have all the necessary ingredients and it's close enough that I can still deliver and serve everything while it's hot."

"Agreed!" I said. As Gus moved toward the door, I followed him. "Gus." He stopped suddenly and looked at me. "Thank you," I said.

He cupped a hand around my neck and pulled me in for a kiss, taking my breath away. "You don't have to thank me, Maggie. Haven't you figured out by now that I'd do anything for you?"

My heart hammered inside my chest as I watched him walk out the bar door, cross the patio, and disappear into DelVecchio's. I turned to Max. "He's amazing, right?"

Max poured himself a cocktail. "I'm glad the caterer Yolanda hired couldn't make it. She's an incredible baker, but I think Yolanda talked her into a stupid vegetarian menu. Grass-fed grass."

I snorted.

"With DelVecchio cooking we'll actually be able to eat. He's the best chef in town."

"I know."

Max gave me a strange sidelong glance. "Has he cooked for you?"

"Yes," I admitted. "It was divine." *Not to mention he's a good kisser, too.*

Max thumped a palm onto the bar. "Oh my God, forget the cop." He waved his hands around dramatically in chopping motions as if suggesting I give Brooks the ax. "He's nothing! He can't cook. You have to dump him immediately and stay with Gus."

"Oh, shut up. I'm not even really dating either one of them."

"Well, start dating Gus." He took a sip of his cocktail. "And be sure to save me some leftovers. I can't really cook, either. There, now you know all my secrets. Not a dog guy and not a cook—there's no reason for Brenda to go out with me."

"Oh, stop! You're a nice guy and a computer genius. There're plenty of reasons for Brenda to go out with you."

The door opened and the videographer entered, followed by the social media maven. The pair made an unlikely couple: the videographer was stocky and bald, while the maven towered over him with mane of wild red hair. The pair seemed madly in love.

The maven made a huge fuss over my chicken purse. She thought it was wild and hip and would be the latest rage. She immediately went to work tweeting and posting to all the major social sites, while her boyfriend filmed her strutting about with it.

"I need another drink," Max confessed.

I giggled. "Me, too. I honestly never thought anyone could like the chicken purse."

"There's no accounting for taste," Max said, pouring a long shot of vodka into a tumbler for me.

I took the drink from him and toasted. "If it's all the rage on the Mexican Riviera, I'll let you know."

He frowned. "What do you mean?"

"Oh, I got the job I was interviewing for with Soleado Cruise Lines. I start next week, at least if I can figure out how to hire a nurse my great-uncle will keep."

"What? What job?"

"Purser on the ship. First stop is Mazatlán."

"So, you're leaving?"

I shrugged. "Well, I haven't exactly figured things out. Like my uncle—"

"You can't leave," he said. "Who's going to run Yappy Hour?"

"Rachel is! She'll be back." At least, that's what I'd convinced myself. She couldn't stay away forever. "She'll be back with Chuck, right? They'll be back soon and—"

The door to the bar flew open and Yolanda made her entrance. The conversations stopped short as all eyes turned toward Yolanda and Beepo.

Ignoring Max, I watched as Yolanda scurried toward the bar, Beepo happily trailing alongside her. She was wearing the most outrageous outfit I'd seen her in yet. It was a black lace dress that fit her like a second skin. It was practically see-through, and so short I feared if she stooped to pick anything up, she'd flash everyone.

Max made a strange wounded animal noise, then breathed. "Wow."

"Hello lovelies. I'm here to help!" Yolanda said.

"What are you wearing?" I asked.

She gave us a full fashion-model spin. "Like it? I got it in Vegas. I had to wear black . . ." She stopped suddenly and stared at me. "Why aren't you in black? Didn't I explicitly tell you to wear black?"

I shrugged. "I liked the way this dress fit," I said, looking down at my conservative-by-comparison mulberry number.

Yolanda glanced at her bracelet wristwatch and made a disapproving face. "I don't think there's time for you to change."

Well, that's good, because I didn't have any plan to.

"Look what I picked up." I popped my chicken purse on the counter.

Yolanda shrieked and then let out a childish giggle. Beepo growled.

"Hush now!" she said to Beepo, then dashed around the bar toward me, taking small clickety-clackety strides because her tight dress wouldn't allow her to take a normal stride. "Oh Maggie! I want to hug your neck! You're such a good friend."

"And it's posted all over Twitter now," the maven said. "We're trending *#chicken*!" She picked up the bag excitedly and swung it around in celebration.

Max snorted out his drink, and I threw a towel at him.

Yolanda squealed and danced about. "Trending chicken!"

"I'll start another thread with *#bokbok*!" the maven said.

Beepo growled at the chicken bag, launching for its hideous beak. Yolanda snatched it out of the maven's hand and passed the bag back to me.

Darn!

For a moment, I'd thought my mission would have been accomplished. But no, I'd have to wait a little longer, bide my time.

A man in a brown uniform appeared on the cobblestone path, rolling a black cart behind him. Next to him was a man dressed in a suit, whom he was talking to in an animated fashion. The man in the suit had over-the-collar wavy hair and a flamboyant tie. Despite the soft wave to his hair, his face had a decidedly chiseled appearance, complete with Roman nose and dimpled chin.

Yolanda's eyes went wide and she stood at attention. "Our auctioneer! I must get a closer look at him."

"I can see how he might be worthy of closer inspection," I joked.

The two men peeked into the bar. "Is this where the fund-raiser's going to be tonight?" the man in the uniform asked. "Where do you want the auction set up?"

Yolanda quirked an eyebrow at me. "Just give me a moment." She pranced over to the man in the uniform and gesticulated widely for him to unpack his rolling cart by our bandstand. Then she struck up a conversation with Mr. Roman Nose. Both seemed to evaluate each other as if secretly judging a beauty competition.

I looked across at the stage. Evie was texting on her phone, distracted. When she noticed the man in the uniform unpacking his cart before her, she shrieked, "I wasn't told that I'd have to share the stage with doggie shampoo and sweaters."

"Not just sweaters," Yolanda squealed. "These are hand knitted and imported from Scotland!"

"I don't give a rat's patootie!" Evie screamed.

"Well, you don't have to, because it's not your call! It's Maggie's."

I groaned. I knew Yolanda had it out for Evie. They'd been battling over the storage space for months now.

"Evie, can't we have the auction and then music?" I asked. "Think of the auction as your opening act."

Then I remembered there was an opening act. The magician. Oh well, better to address one thing at a time.

"People are paying good money to come to the auction!" Yolanda wailed.

"The auction? They're paying money to see me and the band," Evie countered.

Smasher scoffed at this, and Bishop said, "I need a smoke."

They disappeared out the front door, and Evie trailed, her cigarette case in hand.

"That woman is a pill," Yolanda said under her breath, while flashing a wide toothy smile at Mr. Roman Nose.

Max resumed stringing up the multicolored lantern lights. Yolanda distracted herself by chatting it up with the auctioneer, and I suddenly found myself alone with Beepo. He circled the counter where my chicken purse was and growled.

Oh! An opportunity!

Could I lower it just a tad and let him get to it?

I grabbed it off the counter and pretended to look inside it for something. When I was sure no one was watching me, I relaxed my arm, bringing the bag down to Beepo's level.

He sniffed at it, then bit at the fake chicken's wing.

Come on, Beepo, mark it.

He growled a low rumble and bared his teeth again. He seemed puzzled as to why the chicken wasn't fighting back. So I shook the bag a bit and he tore off running toward Yolanda.

Oh, good God! What a coward!

I tried to summon all my patience and left the chicken bag on the floor. I proceeded to uncork a few of the wine bottles I knew would be served first once the crowd started arriving. I could feel a set of watery doggie eyes watching my every move. As soon as he was convinced I was thoroughly disinterested in him, he returned to sniff the bag.

He lifted his leg, but instead of spraying the chicken, he put his leg down and then looked at me. He barked several times, and Yolanda broke away from Mr. Roman Nose and came around the bar.

"Beepo! Hush little doggie, what are you up to?" She scooped him in her arms and said to me, "Oh, Maggie, you better take the purse and put it away. Otherwise Beepo . . ." She made a gesture with her hand that could only be interpreted one way. She wanted me to safeguard the purse or risk Beepo spraying it.

"Right," I said.

The man in the uniform finished setting up the makeshift stage with dog paraphernalia and called out to Yolanda to come and examine it. She released Beepo and together with the auctioneer, aka Mr. Roman Nose, they headed in the direction of the stage.

Beepo shot out toward the chicken, raised his leg, and whizzed.

I covered my mouth with my hand.

Oh my God! I had my evidence.

Chapter Thirty-one

Victory!

I had the evidence that could possibly solve the crime.

I could barely contain my excitement. Like a child, I looked around frantically for someone to share my joy, but realized probably none of these people would be happy if Yolanda and Beepo were convicted of a crime.

Evie, Bishop, and Smasher were still on the patio smoking and yukking it up. Possibly the only person in the near vicinity that would be happy was Evie, but she had such a strange volatile energy I hesitated to share anything with her. Instead, I pulled the chicken bag away from Beepo and placed it into a plastic sack.

Beepo snarled at me, as if he was aware of my intentions. Nevertheless, I grabbed the purse and my cell phone and ran toward the bathroom. Leaning against the foyer door of the restroom, I dialed Officer Brooks.

He picked up on the third ring.

"Hi, it's me, Maggie," I whispered urgently. "I have it! I have the evidence!"

"Maggie? Are you all right?"

"Yes, yes. I called because I have it!"

"Have what?" His voice was low and deep, sending an involuntary rumble through my bones.

"I have the DNA evidence," I said.

"I don't follow you."

"Beepo peed on my purse."

"I'm sorry," Brooks said.

"No, you don't understand. Dan had dog urine on his shoes and trousers, right? Beepo marks everything. I'm sure it was him. If you get the bag tested, you'll get a match."

"And what will that prove?" Brooks asked.

"That Yolanda is the killer," I said.

"Yolanda?" he asked, with a note of incredulity in his voice.

"Yes, she had a grudge against Dan."

"She did?"

"Well, I don't know that for certain, but let's say she did. They met up here at The Wine and Bark, and they fought. Say Dan threatens Yolanda; Beepo protects her furiously. He pees on Dan's foot in order to get him away from her. Then, say Dan gets mad at Beepo and Yolanda whacks him with the magnum bottle!"

There was an uncomfortable moment of silence. Apprehension inched its way across my skin. Why wasn't Brooks saying anything? I crinkled the pink plastic bag in my hand.

Finally, Brooks cleared his throat and broke the silence. "It sounds a bit far-fetched."

"She's far-fetched," I countered.

He chuckled. "Well, that's true."

"Can you come collect it?" I asked awkwardly, suddenly feeling like I'd done the wrong thing.

What kind of person tricks their friend's dog into peeing on a purse?

I reminded myself that this just might be the evidence to keep The Wine and Bark out of a lawsuit, although some part of my brain must have disagreed, because I was overcome with remorse.

Here was the woman who had stood by me during this torturous week, and now I was suspecting her of murder? A wave of nausea swam through me, and I rushed into one of the stalls in time to be violently sick.

When I finished, I went to the sink to splash water on my face; it wasn't enough to feel any relief, but I hesitated to stick my head under the faucet as I would ruin Abigail's work on my hairdo.

I ran the water on my wrists and panicked.

Breathe, Maggie. Everything is going to be fine.

There was a brief knock on the restroom outer door and Yolanda popped her head into the bathroom. "Oh my God!" she trilled. "Look at you. You're a hot mess. What happened? Are you ill?"

I grabbed a paper towel and rubbed it across my face. "I'm fine, I'm fine."

Yolanda plucked a paper towel of her own and soaked it, making a quick compress for the back of my neck. "You look like a chicken with its head ripped off!"

I shuddered at the mention of a chicken and kicked the pink plastic bag back under the sink, hoping it was out of her line of sight.

She fussed over me. "What is it? You look like you did the night we found Dan. Are you having another panic attack?"

Ugh. I did feel hot and claustrophobic, but mostly I felt guilty. Hot with guilt—was that a side effect?

"Can you open a window?" I asked.

"Sure, sure, of course." She pranced over to the side wall and tugged on the window, while I scanned the room for a better hiding place to stash the offending pink bag.

When she turned around, she said, "I came to tell you Officer Hottie McHottie is here to see you. But maybe you should just take a minute."

I glanced into the mirror. The hairdo I'd been hoping to salvage was a wreck; one side was plastered flat against my face, while the other side was frizzy to the extreme. My lipstick was smeared and there were giant wet splotches on my beautiful scoop-neck dress.

Tears threatened.

Oh God!

All I needed was streaks of mascara down my face. I was a disaster.

"You should have told me you weren't feeling well," Yolanda said. "I would have held your hair—"

"Stop!" I couldn't bear to listen to her be kind to me.

She closed the distance between us and rubbed my back. "What is it, honey?"

I couldn't find a way out. I had to go through with it.

A sharp rap came to the door. "Everything all right?" Officer Brooks asked from the hallway.

Yolanda gasped. "I'll cover for you." She poked her head out the door and said, "Maggie's indisposed at the moment. Is Abigail out there yet?"

There was a brief silence, and then I heard Brooks's baritone voice: "Uh, I'll check."

Before Yolanda could close the door, Beepo shot through like a bullet. He immediately found the pink bag I'd stashed under the sink and barked his little Yorkie head off.

"Hush, Beepo!" Yolanda said, ignoring the bag.

Beepo pulled open the bag with his teeth, exposing the chicken face, which returned his glare.

Suddenly Yolanda took interest. "Oh! What's that?" She looked at me. "Why's your chicken purse inside a plastic bag? Is that to protect it from . . ." She stopped talking abruptly and looked at me. The moment stretched between us, and when I said nothing, Yolanda's expression changed, as if she now understood my intention. She pressed her lips together and waited for my reply.

I sighed. "It turns out they can match a dog's urine to a particular dog through a DNA analysis, just like human blood or hair—"

Beepo chewed on the chicken's rubber wing and growled.

Another rap came to the door, and Brooks called out, "Abigail's not here, yet. How's Maggie doing? Can I talk to her?"

Yolanda's face flushed red and she flung open the door, seeming to not care anymore about protecting Officer Brooks's opinion of my disheveled appearance. "She's right here! The traitor!"

Brooks glanced from Yolanda, to me, to Beepo and the chicken purse, quickly assessing the situation. "Oh, all right, let's all calm down."

Brooks was out of uniform, wearing a black tux for the event. The dark suit set off his blond hair and looked so handsome and smart that my legs quivered in response.

"I'm here! Did you need me?" a voice singsonged from down the corridor, and suddenly Abigail appeared behind Officer Brooks's shoulder, looking into the foyer of the ladies restroom. She wore a flouncy black dress that swayed when she walked. Missy, her white Shih Tzu, was fluffy to perfection, the bow on the top of her head black. "Rumor has it Maggie needs a touch-up."

Missy leapt out of her hands and tramped over to Beepo and the chicken bag.

I snatched it away from them. "No, no. This is my evidence!" I thrust it at Brooks. "Here, see if it matches."

Suddenly Brenda appeared in the door. She was dressed to the nines in a black floor-length strapless number, complete with a slit up the side. She held Pee Wee in her arms; he was dressed in a black doggie-tux. Pressing past Abigail and Brooks, she said, "What's going on? Maggie, are you okay? What evidence?"

I turned to Yolanda, but before I said anything, I gave her my best stare-down. Soon, it seemed all eyes were on her, and the hush in the foyer was deafening.

"All right! All right!" Yolanda screamed. "I admit it. Beepo peed on Dan's shoes when we got here and found him dead. He couldn't stand him. I didn't know what was going on. It was dark and I hadn't even had a chance to put the lights on. You know that, Maggie. The bar was dark when you got here, right? I only put down the box of flyers and saw a lump on the floor. Beepo knew much faster than me that it was Dan." She scooped him into her arms and stroked his triangle ears. "Didn't you, boy? You knew it was Dan and you got your revenge for all the times he was mean to you." She looked at Brooks, Brenda, and Abigail. "But I didn't kill Dan, that's ridiculous."

"Of course, you didn't!" Abigail clucked defensively.

"It's absurd," Brenda chimed in.

Pee Wee and Missy barked in agreement.

Brooks looked as if he had indigestion.

"But we're going to be sued!" I screamed over the cacophony of animal and human protestation.

Another voice, so familiar it made my heart soar, repeated, "Sued?"

My long-lost sister suddenly poked her head into the rest-room foyer. "Who's suing us?" Rachel asked.

The group erupted into cries of "Rachel!" and "Have you heard about Dan?" and "Good to see you!" Missy and Beepo lunged at her feet, yipping and yapping with their tails shaking their entire bodies. The piercing voices echoed and bounced off the tile walls. I thought that, be-tween the noise and the claustrophobia I was fighting, I was finished.

I grabbed the sink for support and demanded, "Where have you been?"

"It's a good thing you're here. Your sister's just accused Yolanda of being a murderer!" Abigail said.

"And Beepo, too, really," Yolanda said.

"Well, yes," Abigail agreed. "There's that, too!"

"What?" Rachel said.

A collective hush came from the group. Although the silence was welcome, the angry looks on their faces were enough to scare me into glancing around the restroom foyer, praying for an escape.

Brooks must have realized that I was about to succumb to a claustrophobia attack, because he said, "Let's give her some air. We can settle this outside."

As he ushered the group out of the restroom, relief flooded me, and I let out a huge exhalation.

Brooks waited for the gang to leave, then stayed back a moment with me. "Are you all right? I was afraid for a mo-ment they were going to lynch you."

I laughed. "Me too."

He grabbed my elbow and looked into my eyes. "It wouldn't prove she killed him, you know. Even if there's a match. There're just too many possibilities of how it could have happened, like exactly the way she said. They came in after the fact and the dog—"

"I know. I'm sorry." I hung my head onto his chest and leaned against him "I'm just so desperate for a solution. And I'm afraid of losing the bar . . . my great-uncle's property . . . everything."

He stroked my hair. "Oh, Maggie, what am I going to do with you?" His breath caressed my ear.

Pulling away from his chest, I looked into his blue eyes and said nothing.

"I told you I'll get to the bottom of it," he whispered. "You have to let me do my job. Do you think you can do that?"

I nodded, even though I was entirely unconvinced. The way my stomach fluttered when he was around, I would have agreed with anything he said.

He opened the door and held it for me, waiting for me to walk out of the restroom in front of him, but I didn't have the heart. I wanted to hide for the rest of the night. He wrapped an arm around my waist and gently ushered me out to the corridor with a reassuring smile.

There was a general hubbub coming from the main room, and I suddenly realized that with Rachel back, I might not have to work behind the bar, but I would certainly have to face Yolanda.

Brooks held the pink plastic bag in one hand, but held out his free arm for me. "Come on, honey."

Honey? He'd called me honey?

"I won't let 'em bite," he joked.

I took his hand and let him guide me along the corridor. After all, I needed to get to my sister and wring her neck. When we entered the main room, it seemed transformed in the short time I'd been having my breakdown.

Yolanda had resumed her flirting with Mr. Roman Nose and giggled at something he said. When she spotted me, she deliberately turned her back. Brooks's cell phone vibrated, and he checked the display.

"It's my sergeant," he said. "I have to take this. Will you excuse me a minute?"

I nodded and watched him leave the bar to take the phone call on the patio. There was a big black Labrador, lounging, that bounded toward him as soon as he exited the bar. Ah, that must be Sizzle.

Inside the bar, Rachel was having a powwow with Brenda and Max, and I beelined over to her.

"Where the hell have you been? Do you care to explain yourself?" I demanded.

She wrapped her arms around my neck. "Oh Maggie! I can't believe all the awful things that have happened this week. Two people dead! I'm so sorry I didn't call you!"

"No, you're not! You told Grunkly you were afraid to call me. Do you know he had an accident and someone broke into your apartment and we're going to lose our shirts over this ridiculous doggie bar?"

"Whoa!" Rachel held up her hand at me. "You don't have to go that far."

"We are going to lose our shirts," I insisted. "Unless we can prove—"

"I meant the part about my bar being ridiculous," Rachel interrupted.

"This is stupid. You know what? You can figure it all out. I've got a job and I'm on my way to Mazatlán. In fact, I think I'll go home and pack right now." I flung open the front door in time for Melanie, the hostess from DelVecchio's, to appear in front of me with a tray of fragrant pizzettas.

Gus was right behind her with another tray. The aroma of garlic and olive oil assaulted me and made my empty tummy howl.

Gus smiled broadly when he saw me. "Hi, Maggie, what do you think? Voilà! Dog bowl pizzettas. Would you like to try the pesto or tomato?"

"What do you mean, you're going to Mazatlán?" Rachel demanded.

"Mazatlán?" Gus asked.

"You can't leave me now!" Rachel said. Her eyes glassed over and she looked ready to burst into tears.

"Leave? You can't leave," Gus said.

"What?" Brenda said, leaning in. "Where are you going? You can't leave."

A man with long hair and a scraggly beard appeared at Rachel's side. "What's the matter, babe?"

Ah, he had to be the infamous Chuck.

The door flung open and a swarm of patrons began to descend. Melanie started serving the pizzettas around, and I realized I'd probably be needed to tend the bar. In a huff, I spun on my heel and took refuge behind the bar, mixing salty dogs and mutt-tinis.

Gus glanced nervously at me, and I felt I owed him an explanation. I mouthed to him, "We'll talk later."

He winked at me. "Sure thing. Glad your sister is back," he said.

And I realized, so was I. She was a pain in the neck, but she was my sister, and if anything had happened to her, like I'd feared all week, I would have been devastated. Together we could figure things out.

She sauntered up to the bar with Chuck in tow. "I didn't get a chance to properly introduce you," Rachel said. "Maggie, this is my fiancé, Chuck. Chuck, my sister, Maggie."

Fiancé? So she hadn't had the nerve to elope after all.

What had gone wrong?

I came out from behind the bar and hugged Chuck, then

my sister. She clung to me. "I'm so happy to see you, you have no idea. You can't leave . . ."

"Did you have a bad week, too?" I asked.

"The worst," she whispered. "I don't know what I was thinking. I wanted to go on the cruise and get hitched, but then Chuck talked me into Vegas. When we got there all he did was work and gamble. He ignored me the whole time. I was bored to tears."

I stifled a laugh. "We were anything but bored here in Pacific Cove."

"I told him I needed more time," Rachel whispered. "But I don't think we're going to last."

Chuck struck up a conversation with Max. "Looks like I might have found an angel investor in Vegas."

Max perked up as he mixed a pitcher of muttgaritas.

Rachel came back behind the bar with us and began to mix cocktails like a pro. I brought her up to speed on the murders and the impending lawsuit as Brenda made her way toward us.

"So, I think I have relatively good news," she said. "I was able to reach your building insurance broker and I think I have grounds to argue that even though your payment is late, you're still in the grace period, and if you pay the insurance premium within the next fifteen days—"

"The check's in the mail," I said.

Rachel blew a long rush of air out and thumped me on the back. "My sister, the accountant! We can count on her!" Then she glanced nervously around the room. "Now, if only we can figure out who among us killed Dan and Oscar."

Chapter Thirty-two

Melanie's brother, the magician, took the stage. He began by doing some simple card tricks. The patrons inside quieted down and watched him as they sipped their greyhounds.

Meanwhile, outside, a crowd was forming on the patio: Mrs. Clemens, several of the ladies that I recognized from the Roundup Crew, and several other people that I didn't recognize. Inside the bar, Yolanda separated herself from Mr. Roman Nose and sprang over to me.

"Geraldine is here!" she hissed.

Max looked up from his bar prep work. "Don't worry, I'll protect you," he said, tongue firmly planted in his cheek.

Yolanda squeezed my arm. "You don't understand. The woman is pure evil! We can't have her in here. I'm sure she didn't buy a ticket to the fund-raiser, because I wouldn't have sold it to her for all the tea in China! Can you go and block her from coming in here?"

I found myself ridiculously happy that Yolanda was speaking to me again. Even though it had only been a few minutes since I'd accused her of murder, it seemed like the Geraldine feud was worse. "Are we monitoring the door?" I asked.

"Yes!" Yolanda shrieked. "She's not allowed in here!"

The bar door flung open, and before they could stream inside, I leapt toward them. "Tickets, tickets, everyone, I need to see the tickets."

As much as I hated playing enforcer, I was guilt-ridden over suspecting Yolanda and Beepo and wanted a chance to make it up to them.

Mrs. Clemens patted my arm. "My dear! Certainly I don't need a ticket. I'm the entertainment."

Evie overheard this, to which she loudly hollered, "No, I'm the entertainment. You're a sideshow. Like in a circus. People gawk at you."

Mrs. Clemens raised a perfect pencil-thin eyebrow at me. "Oh dear!"

"Don't mind her," I said. "Come on in, Mrs. Clemens."

Mrs. Clemens looked flustered. "I have to set up outside. I only came in for a glass of wine."

"Sure, sure. Of course." I hailed a finger at Max, who smiled and took Mrs. Clemens's arm.

Abigail approached Mrs. Clemens. "Can I help you set up?"

Brenda powered over to them. "Oh, no you don't. You only want to help set up so Missy can be first with the pawcasso, but Mrs. Clemens already promised me Pee Wee is supposed to be the opener."

For the first time that evening, I noticed Brenda's feet. Instead of flashy designer high heels, her feet were clad in suede Dog-Face shoes.

I giggled. "Love your shoes."

Brenda twirled for me. "Aren't they a hoot? They're Shorty Suede Dog-Face Smoking Slippers, by Marc

Jacobs. They're so comfy, too. I can order you a pair, but don't distract me now, I have to fight for Pee Wee's rights!"

Abigail feigned innocence. "No, no, no. That's fine. Pee Wee can be first. I have to set up the baby pool." They all streamed back out onto the patio landing in front of the bar. Rachel rushed out after them to supervise, and I was left to enforce the door policy against Geraldine.

Geraldine was dressed in a stunning sweeping black gown. The top was beaded and it had a full pleated skirt, making her look regal as she clutched the leash of her perfectly coiffed black show poodle. She pushed her way past the crowd and up to the door.

I gave her my best smile. "May I please see your ticket?"

She frowned. "Ticket? Oh my, I don't have one. Can I buy one here?"

"I spoke with the lady in charge. I'm sorry, we're all sold out."

"That's nonsense," Geraldine insisted. She waved frantically at Yolanda, who turned her back on us.

"I'm sorry," I said. "Fire marshal and all . . ."

"Tell Yolanda, I'm not going to be turned away!" Geraldine said.

I glanced over my shoulder to where Yolanda stood at the bar. She was whispering something to Max, who came around from behind the bar and approached us.

We waited for him expectantly.

He cleared his throat. "Last minute ticket purchases are five hundred dollars."

Geraldine stomped her foot, alarming the poodle, who howled. "That's highway robbery!"

"It is for a good cause," I said.

Gus appeared by my side and waved a platter of the salivation-inducing pizzettas under Geraldine's nose. The poodle barked ravenously at the tray of food and Gus smiled.

More guests arrived behind Geraldine, and Mr. Roman Nose began to hand out the bidding paddles.

"Oh all right!" Geraldine said. She reluctantly opened her black beaded pocket purse and wrote me a check.

Max gripped my wrist. "It's her," he said suddenly.

I looked out at the crowd streaming in now in time for the auction. There was a woman, with a helmet of gray hair, dressed in an explosion of black sequins. Resting on her chubby wrist was a leash attached to one very familiar beagle with a pink plush bunny in his mouth.

Uh oh. Mrs. Murphy!

The auctioneer's booming voice silenced the crowd just as Brenda was about to intercept Mrs. Murphy. "Get out there!" I said to Max. "Now, before . . ."

Max rushed out to the patio and distracted Brenda as Mrs. Murphy came inside and handed me her ticket. I sat her in front for the auction, hoping that would buy Max the necessary time with Brenda.

Mrs. Murphy stroked the dog's head. She looked up at me and said, "Max has told me so much about you! I'm Patty Murphy."

"Yes, of course," I said. Bowser dropped his bunny at my feet and I picked it up for him. "And this is Bowser." I rubbed his ears. "I know him well."

Various dogs began to swirl around, barking and sniffing each other. The auctioneer's voice bellowed, announcing the next item. Mrs. Murphy leaned in and said to me, "I hope you don't think me too cruel for showing up with Bowser. I know what the girl means to Max, and I figured the only way for them to start up a real relationship was to end the charade."

I watched my sister come back in through the bar doors

and figured now was as good a time as any to end another charade. I smiled at Mrs. Murphy and patted her on the back before I left. "You may be right."

Yolanda and Abigail flanked the bar.

"Two greyhounds! One for me and the other for Mrs. Clemens," Yolanda said.

"How about a pitcher of salties?" Rachel asked. "You can take it to the patio. If we keep the drinks up, the auction might be more profitable."

Rachel whipped up a quick pitcher and I hovered next to her. I was dying to ask her some questions, but there were so many ears around it hardly seemed possible. I closed my eyes and thought, *Rachel? Where did you keep your gun?*

Any hope or faith I'd had in our sibling ESP evaporated as Rachel said, "I just had one of the pizzettas; can that guy cook or what? I heard you two are having a fling."

I made a gun out of my pointer finger and my thumb.

"Oh, would you stop it," Rachel said. "I'm sure he's not a killer, just like I'm sure Yolanda isn't, either."

I shook my head and pointed at Rachel.

Rachel thumped a hand across her heart. "Are you accusing me now? For God's sake, Maggie, what's wrong with you?"

Patrons crowded around the bar, and Rachel thrust the pitcher into Yolanda's hands. "Will you take this out to the patio for me?"

I leaned in close to her ear and hissed, "Where did you keep your gun?"

She frowned. "My gun?"

"The waiter, Oscar, was killed with a Ruger P45," I said.

"Someone broke into your apartment, did you keep it there?"

"I don't remember the last time I even used it. Probably some silly target practice at Stag's Leap, but I haven't been there in ages."

"Did you use Dan's picture for target practice?" I asked.

Rachel's face registered confusion. "What? What are you talking about?" Before I could answer, some patrons pressed up against the bar and ordered wine. Rachel uncorked a bottle and asked me out of the side of her mouth, "Are your sure it was my gun?"

"No," I admitted. "I just heard it was the same type of gun."

Someone called out an order for a mutt-tini, and Rachel shooed me, with a worried look on her face. "Let's talk more," she said.

◇◇◇

The auction was well under way: doggie jewelry, sweaters, beds, and bowls were being sold at scandalous prices. The bidding paddles flew around the room as fast as the drinks. I retreated to the relative safety behind the bar.

Bishop was stationed there, consuming a worrisome amount of alcohol. "Are you still going to be able to play?" Max asked as he topped off another drink for him. "I know Evie doesn't like you to—"

Bishop waved a hand around, annoyed. "I don't care what she says."

"How long have you two been dating?" Max asked.

Bishop looked surprised. "We aren't dating."

"Really? I thought you were," Max said.

"We always fight."

"That's why I thought you were dating," Max said.

I poked Max in the ribs.

Bishop laughed. "You're probably right. I'd like to get with her. But she's still hung up on the guy who died."

"Is that right?" I asked.

She hadn't seemed all that interested in Dan when she'd spoken to me.

Bishop finished up his cocktail and wiped his mouth with the back of his hand. "She's been hung up on that guy for ages. Ever since they took that trip together to the hunting lodge. I don't think he was all that interested in her, though. He was more into your sister. Broke his heart when she showed up with that Chuck guy." Bishop looked around as if he was suddenly worried about being overheard. "No offense, man," he said.

Max laughed. "It's okay. Chuck's an odd duck. We're business partners, but even I don't know how long that will last. We're running out of money fast."

"Anyway," Bishop said, "I'd been hoping that after the guy died and all, you'd think she'd be ready to move on."

"It's only been a week," Max said.

"Yeah, well, I think they only dated a short time, so it should be easy enough to get over him, right? I mean, you can't date a dead guy." He ordered another round of salty dogs, which I noticed Max watered down significantly.

"What happened with Brenda? What did she say when you told her Bowser wasn't your dog?" I asked.

Max smiled widely. "Oh, she knew!"

I laughed. "All this time, hiding and sneaking around, and she knew?" I asked, incredulous.

Max grinned. "Yeah, we're going to the movies to-morrow night." He winked at me and said, "Don't wait up, Mom."

The bar was getting overheated, and I felt the need for fresh air. I glanced out at the patio; it seemed hectic out there. "I'll take a pitcher outside, keep the refreshment flowing," I said.

Max handed me a pitcher of muttgaritas and sent me on my way. I emerged out on the patio with the pitcher in hand and felt like downing it myself. Dogs were lollygagging poolside with chew toys and floaties, while others were busy getting their paws dipped in colorful paint.

I looked around for Officer Brooks, but he and Sizzle were gone. Disappointment dragged me down. Had I completely alienated him?

Evie was sitting alone at a patio table that had been pushed to the side to make room for the pool. She was smoking, and I envied the peace she seemed to be enjoying.

Ah heck, with Rachel back, I supposed I was allowed a break. I took the pitcher over to Evie and poured her a glass. "Can you have a drink before you take the stage?"

She blew out a smoke ring and studied me. Her eyes were ringed in heavy black eyeliner that gave her a wolfish appearance. "Maybe just one," she said, glancing back toward the bar. "Is Bishop drunk?"

"Not really," I said.

She shook her head. "Smasher went off to get stoned and Bishop is drunk. Tonight is going to be a disaster, not that it matters. What with all the hoopla going on around here, who cares what we sound like?"

As she spoke, I tried to piece together an image of her with Dan. I'd already formed an opinion about him over the last few days. He was complicated. A gambler, a playboy. And Evie was such a brooder.

I swirled my muttgarita in my glass, wondering how Evie and Dan could have ever gotten together.

Evie suddenly realized that I was watching her in a very intense way.

"What?" she asked.

"I was just thinking about what an unlikely couple you and Dan must have made."

She swirled her drink around and took a sip. "Huh?"

I leaned closer to her. "Do you like to travel?"

She shrugged. "Travel? Yeah. I'd like to do that. I haven't gone away in ages."

"But with Dan you got away, right?"

Evie sat straight up as if I'd just electrocuted her. "What?" she demanded.

"Oh, nothing. I didn't mean anything by it. It's just that, well, Bishop mentioned you guys dated and you went to a hunting lodge."

She relaxed back into her chair and lit another cigarette. "Oh that. Well, Rachel told me I could use the cabin whenever I wanted. Fringe bennies from renting out the storage space. Anyway, about Dan, I wouldn't say we dated, exactly. It was nothing serious. Just a little fun." She took a drag on her cigarette and blew out a smoke ring. "It was never going to last, between us. I mean, even if he had lived, poor guy. He was too uptight for me."

Uptight? The gambler and playboy?

The door to the bar flew open and Bishop stumbled out. "They're wrapping up the auction now, Evie. If you want that fancy collar you better get in there."

Evie made a rude hand gesture at him and he laughed.

"Seriously, we're up in a few minutes," he said. "Where's Smasher?"

Evie motioned toward the garbage alley and mimicked smoking a pot cigarette. I watched Bishop stalk toward the alley, goose bumps raising on my arms as I thought of poor Oscar shot dead there.

When would there be justice for Oscar and Dan?

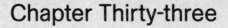

Chapter Thirty-three

As I thought over what Evie said, nausea threatened to overtake me again. I'd made a mistake. Yolanda hadn't killed Dan, and neither had Max. It had to have been Evie. The hunting lodge Bishop mentioned must have been Stag's Leap, not a hunting lodge at all, but those were easy to confuse. If Evie was dating Dan and had visited Stag's Leap, then that explained both the cigarette smell in the cabin and the corkboard with Dan's image.

The corkboard hadn't really struck me as something Rachel would have done. Rachel was so go-with-the-flow it was hard to imagine her getting so caught up with some guy that she'd take the time to have target practice with his image. And the cigarette smell in the cabin had never added up for me. Rachel didn't smoke.

Also, Evie had access to The Wine and Bark. It explained why the doors to the bar were unlocked that night.

A chill zipped across my back. I'd just given Brooks evidence against Yolanda and yet . . . I'd been wrong.

How could I prove it'd been Evie all along?

I watched her skulk around, getting the stage ready for the show. Now she seemed so obviously a murderer to me, but could I be wrong again?

Gus found me and offered me some cheese and crackers. I grabbed his hand and pulled him out of earshot from the crowd.

"It's her!" I said. "Evie Xtreme. Did you know she dated Dan?"

Gus frowned. "What?"

"I think Evie killed Dan. I found out earlier that they'd dated." I explained my theory to him, but before I could finish, Yolanda sauntered up to us.

"Darlings! This is such a fabulous success," she trilled. "I can't thank you enough for helping me. Without you—"

"Yolanda!" I interrupted. "I think I know who killed Dan."

She giggled, obviously drunk by now. "I know you think I did it but, darling"—she wiggled a finger playfully at me—"just because the pee-pee matches, does not a murderer make."

She swooned dangerously and Gus caught her. "Yolanda, I think you should have a seat. Can I get you a glass of water? Or food? Have you eaten anything tonight?"

Yolanda waved him off, as Evie took the stage and screamed into the microphone like a madwoman, "Who's ready to howl!"

The dogs all picked up on her pitch and joined in an ear-shattering yowl.

"Yeah, let me hear ya!" Evie screamed.

Smasher banged on the drums and Bishop joined in with the guitar. They sounded hideously out of sync, but based on the crowd's reaction, I suspected I was probably the only one who noticed.

I glanced nervously outside. Brooks was nowhere to be found. "I have to call Brad," I said to Gus. Gus's face registered something that was difficult for me to make out. Disappointment?

"If you think it's her, let's just call her on it. Here in front of God and everyone." He motioned with his hands in true Italian fashion to take in the room.

"How can we do that?" I asked.

"Easy," he said, storming over to the sound system.

My eyes grew wide as I realized what Gus was about to. He was ready to pull the plug on the entire operation. Oh my God!

How sure was I of my suspicion? Before I could stop him, Gus yanked the cord of the amplifier. The band's volume decreased drastically, but the dogs and the crowd picked up the slack, so the overall effect was stunted.

Rachel ran over to us. "What are you doing?"

"Evie killed Dan," I said.

"How do you know?" she asked, a look of horror overwhelming her fine facial features.

"Instinct," I said, ignoring the fact that my instincts had been absolutely abysmal lately.

But Rachel was my sister. She'd trusted me all her life, and if I said something with conviction, she'd get in front of a freight train for me. "Murderer!" she screamed out, pointing toward Evie. "Murderer!"

Yolanda, who just now seemed to rouse from her inebriated state, screamed out, too, only she didn't know exactly who to point toward, so it took a minute for her to focus and get her finger to point in Evie's direction.

Brenda and Abigail soon joined in, followed by Gus, Chuck, and Max. Soon the entire crowd was chanting "Mur-der-er! Mur-der-er! Mur-der-er!"

Smasher was the first to stop playing. A dumbfounded

expression on his face, Bishop toned down the guitar to a strum, and soon Evie finished her last note and looked out toward the crowd.

"Wha . . . Wha. . . . ?" She looked around desperately for an escape hatch, her eyes darting back and forth like a caged rabbit. "What's going on?" She turned to Smasher and Bishop and screamed, "Play! You idiots!"

"You killed them!" I shouted out. "You murdered Dan because he didn't love you, and then you shot Oscar because he knew it was you."

Evie's eyes bulged out of her head. "You're crazy," she said into the microphone.

The crowd hushed up, waiting for my response. All eyes were on me. "You took Dan up to Stag's Leap, professed your love for him. But he wasn't interested in you. He'd been in love with Rachel. You were just a pastime to him. Like the horse races." I was winging it now, but figured she'd be forced to defend herself against my allegations, so I might as well get it all out on the table. "You couldn't stand the fact that he didn't love you; you even took target practice on an enlarged image of his face."

Several men in the crowd gasped, as if that was their worst fear: a scorned woman taking revenge on their likeness.

"You ran into Dan in the bar; he was delivering a letter to my sister. You took advantage of the fact that he was alone and there were no witnesses, or so you thought. You hit him over the head with a magnum bottle of wine. He died when his head hit the terra-cotta, but make no mistake . . ." And then for dramatic effect I extended my arm its full length and pointed at Evie. "*You* killed Dan Walters, not the terra-cotta floor of The Wine and Bark!"

"Hear, hear!" someone in the crowd shouted out.

"You were here the night Oscar was killed. We sat at this very table." I thumped my palm onto a table by the window. "And we watched him enter DelVecchio's. I saw it then, but I didn't realize it. You remembered he was a possible witness."

"No!" Evie screamed out. "It's a lie! You're crazy!"

A strange vibe was circulating through the crowd, almost as if they were about to turn into a mob.

"It's not true!" Evie yelled.

The doors to The Wine and Bark flew open and Officer Brooks and Sergeant Gottlieb stormed in. Sizzle was next to Brooks and he beelined for the stage, a big black giant mass.

"You stole Rachel's gun while you were at Stag's Leap!" I yelled.

Sizzle stopped short of the stage, but it was enough to scare Evie. Suddenly, she whipped something out of her waistband, a slim black object.

Beepo leapt toward her, becoming a small fury of brown and white fur as he lunged toward her leg.

Officer Brooks and Sergeant Gottlieb screamed, "Freeze!" in unison, reaching for their weapons. A sharp noise rang out into the crowd, followed by a flash of light and the smoldering smell of a firecracker.

Gus jumped in front of me, pushing me to the ground. Something burned in my shoulder, but I figured it was the fall. A rush sounded in my ear, like the sound of the mighty Pacific. I realized later it was the rush of my own blood, but it sounded distant at the time, like when you put a seashell up to your ear.

Then it seemed like the lights dimmed, and I found solace in silence.

Wet noses rubbed my legs, and yapping and yipping

both human and canine came to me as if through a tunnel, growing increasingly louder, and blotted out any peace I'd momentarily found.

"What's going on?" I asked Gus, suddenly feeling woozy.

"You've been shot, Maggie. I think you passed out for a moment. Hold still, someone's calling 9-1-1." His hand was on my forehead, warm and soothing.

I was vaguely aware of my sister wrapping her arms around my wrist and sobbing. "You're going to be okay, you're going to be okay," she repeated. "Please don't die, Maggie."

"Was I right?" I asked, dumbfounded, the words coming out of my mouth before I could figure out what they even were.

"Yes," Gus whispered. "You were right. Evie was the one."

I nuzzled my head into his chest. "My shoulder hurts," I said.

"That's where she shot you. We're lucky it was a small gun, otherwise . . . it could have been—"

He stopped short, not needing to say anymore.

A hand rubbed at my back and a slurred voice said, "She missed a main artery because Beepo got to her."

I looked up to see Yolanda's face close to mine.

"Oh yeah?" I asked.

She nodded and flashed me a self-satisfied smile. "He peed on her and ruined her aim." We both giggled.

I looked around the room, disoriented. The crowd had diminished considerably. On stage, Evie was being handcuffed by Officer Brooks and Sergeant Gottlieb.

"I told Gottlieb to check out Evie. I never did like her much," Yolanda said. She looked around the room. "Do you think I can rent the storage space now?"

Before I could answer, Max leaned in toward Yolanda and me. "I heard they found evidence at Evie's apartment. They were coming to arrest her."

"What evidence?" I asked.

"Rachel's computer, and some other stuff I didn't catch." He looked around and Brenda appeared. She was suddenly his second half, and that gave me a warm fuzzy feeling.

"She was blackmailing Dan. That's where the money was going," Brenda said.

"I thought it was horse races," Gus said.

"That was only part of it," Brenda said. "Evie wanted to buy Dan out of DV's but he didn't want to sell to her. She was in love with him, true enough, but she was also out to steal his piece of the business."

Officer Brooks and Sergeant Gottlieb escorted Evie off the stage. She let out a frightening howl as she passed by me. Brooks flashed me an apologetic look. Sizzle followed behind him.

"An ambulance is on the way," Brooks said over his shoulder. "I'll come in the morning to check up on you, Maggie."

Was I going to be in the hospital overnight?

I looked up at Gus and asked, "Am I that bad off?

He smiled. "Your shoulder looks pretty bad, but I think you'll be wielding that mutt-tini shaker in no time."

Chapter Thirty-four

The sun was only just rising in the east when I decided to walk to the beach. At the hospital, they'd stitched me up quickly and sent me on my way with some strong painkillers. Gus had driven me to Grunkly's to sleep and so Grunkly and I could take care of each other. His arm was healing fast, and now I was happy that I'd cleaned up his house.

In the morning, I'd called Jan to ask her to delay my start date. She was happy to, giving me a fifteen-day reprieve. I'd miss the cruise to the Mexican Riviera but would be able to catch the one out to the Florida Keys.

Right now, relaxing on the beach was just what the doctor ordered. I walked the length of the beach, enjoying the solace of the lapping water and cawing seagulls. In the distance, a figure approached. The man was walking a big black lab, who was frolicking in and out of the water catching a red rubber ball.

The man had a gait I recognized. A warm sensation spread across my chest as he neared.

He tossed the ball toward my feet and the Labrador

raced toward me, ignoring the ball and almost knocking me over to lick my face.

"Sizzle! Down," Brooks said. He smiled widely when he saw me. "How are you feeling?"

My shoulder was bandaged, but I had full mobility. "It was just a graze. I was lucky," I said.

Brooks closed the distance between us until his face was close to mine. "Yes, you were very lucky. I thought I asked you to stay out of the investigation."

"I did," I said, surprised by the accusation.

He squinted at me. "Did you think chanting *mur-der-er, mur-der-er* was going to help things?" he asked.

"I didn't really think about it," I admitted.

"I can tell." He laughed.

"Anyway, how did you know about that? You weren't even there for that part."

"Believe me, I heard about it," he said. "This is a small town, things get around. Besides, Evie confessed. Looks like having the crowd chanting at her sent her over the edge."

"Did she say why she killed him?"

Brooks looked out toward the water and tossed the ball for Sizzle, who jumped out toward the waves. "Dan had gotten wind of Rachel dating Chuck and that they were planning to elope. He'd come over to talk to her and ran into Evie instead. They argued." Brooks shrugged. "I guess he said some nasty things to her and she got pissed. She hit him on the head, didn't think it would kill him . . . but . . ." Sizzle returned the ball and dropped it at his feet. He absently stroked the dog's head.

"What about Oscar?" I asked.

"He saw her leave the bar that night. She thought he was a threat. You were lucky, she thought you were a threat,

too. That's why she spooked your great-uncle's horse."
He stopped talking, his eyes resting on mine. "Life is
fragile, you know. You never know what can do someone
in." He took my chin in his hand. "When I saw you drop
to the floor . . . and all that blood, I thought . . ."

"I'm fine. It was a just a graze. . . ."

"If we're going to date, we have to have an agreement
that you stay out of my cases."

Date? If we were going to date?

He wanted to go out with me again!

My heart leapt. I had two men that I liked interested in
dating me . . . and bonus, now neither was a suspected
killer! But before I could get too excited, an image of the
Soleado Cruise Line sailing to the Florida Keys crossed
my mind. Oh well, I had fifteen days before the next
cruise—certainly a lot could happen.

As Brooks lowered his face to mine, Sizzle jumped between us, barking and howling. In the distance, his barks
were returned by a crew of yappy little dogs.

"Seems like your friends are out early today," Brooks
said.

"Yes."

He glanced at his watch. "How's your uncle?"

"Recovering, and still betting like crazy. I'm on my way
over there later to watch a race."

He laughed. "Be careful, it's addicting. Are you free for
dinner? I hear a knuckle burger is the thing for a bullet
graze. Lots of protein, you know?"

"I'd love a burger," I said.

The Roundup Crew approached, led by Yolanda, who
was decked out to the nines in hot-pink capri pants, a
clingy off-the-shoulder white blouse, and sky-high gold
sandals. Brenda followed, in her classic all-black ensem-
ble, and I couldn't help but notice that she gripped Max

by the hand. Abigail chatted with my sister, Rachel, while the dogs jumped in and out of the water and chased each other.

The ocean lapped gently at my toes; the water was frigid, but even so, there on the beach, surrounded by Chihuahuas, beagles, Shih Tzus, and their lovely owners, I decided that Pacific Cove was a great place to be. Even bartending at The Wine and Bark was fun now that I had friends. I'd found a home with these crazy people, and if they'd have me, then I'd be happy to call them family now.

The water around my toes warmed up and I glanced down to see that Beepo was marking me.

Yolanda laughed and clapped me on the back. "He likes you!"

Cocktail Recipes

• • • The Salty Dog • • •

1 shot glass of gin
Mix with grapefruit juice
Salt

Rim your favorite glass with salt and fill with ice.
Add cocktail. Garnish with a lime.

• • • Greyhound • • •

1 shot glass vodka
Mix with grapefruit juice

Fill your glass with ice. Add cocktail.
Garnish with a lemon.

••• Pomeranian •••

1 shot glass white rum
1 oz pomegranate juice
Splash of triple sec
Splash of fresh lemon juice
Splash of grapefruit juice

Put it all in a shaker filled with ice.
Strain and pour into glass.

••• Mutt-tini •••

Cracked ice
2½ ounces Bulldog gin
½ ounce dry vermouth
Green olive for garnish

Put it all in a shaker filled with ice.
Strain and pour into glass.

••• Muttgarita •••

2 ounces tequila (preferably 100 percent agave)
1 ounce Cointreau
Freshly squeezed lime juice
Salt

Put it all in a shaker filled with ice.
Salt the rim of your glass. Shake, strain, and enjoy!

Acknowledgments

Thanks to my wonderful agent, Jill Marsal; this book would not have been possible without your enthusiasm and support. Thanks to my editor, Anne Brewer, for loving my Yappy Crew! Special thanks to my dear friend, Marina Adair, for all the brainstorming, chats, and most importantly laughs!

Thanks to my early readers for your notes and support, specifically: Camille Minichino, Mariella Krause, and Laura-Kate Rurka.

Shout-out and hugs to my Carmen, Tommy, Bobby, and Tom Sr.: you all are simply the best personal cheering crew anyone could ever want.

Finally, thank you to all you dear readers who have written to me. Your kind words keep me motivated to write the next story.